GOLDILOCKS

GOLDILOCKS

LAURA LAM

www.orbitbooks.net

Cover design by Yeti Lambregts
Cover images by Shutterstock

Orbit
Hachette Book Group
1290 Avenue of the Americas
New York, NY 10104
orbitbooks.net

First Edition: May 2020
Simultaneously published in Great Britain by Wildfire, an imprint of Headline Publishing Group

Orbit is an imprint of Hachette Book Group.
The Orbit name and logo are trademarks of Little, Brown Book Group Limited.

Library of Congress Control Number: 2019954817

ISBNs: 978-0-316-46286-0 (hardcover), 978-0-316-46289-1 (ebook)

Printed in the United States of America

LSC-C

10 9 8 7 6 5 4 3 2 1

To the Mercury 13
and all the female astronauts since,
and those still to come.

GOLDILOCKS

"Men could not part us with their worldly jars,
Nor the seas change us, nor the tempests bend;
Our hands would touch for all the mountain-bars:
And, heaven being rolled between us at the end,
We should but vow the faster for the stars."

—Elizabeth Barrett Browning

30 Years After

In thirty years, Dr. Naomi Lovelace has never given an interview.

Whenever I asked her to tell me what happened up there, Naomi would say no one who has been to space could ever describe it to someone who hasn't.

They could use all the pretty language they liked. You might be able to come close, she told me once—she was always complimentary about my writing—but you'd never really know what it was like. Others will judge the choices she made, what she risked, how close she came to utter destruction. Let them, she always said. I'm used to their hatred by now.

Over the years, I've often imagined Naomi up there, floating alone, curled up like a white comma against a black sheet of paper. Her bulky spacesuit, the tethering cable an umbilical cord back to the ship. The silence but for her own breathing and the crackle of the comms. Twisting out to gaze at the stars, their reflections shimmering across the gold-lined visor of her helmet.

I don't know what she thought about the expanse before her, if it changed her understanding of humanity and our place within it. If that led to the decisions she made.

I've watched the recording of the court testimony. Even there, she'd said as little as possible. The whole world had been desperate to hear her statement, to put her on trial as much as the others.

Naomi had stood surrounded by the polished wood of the courtroom, all warm browns compared to the white metal of the *Atalanta*. It must have all seemed so loud, so messy, after so long breathing recycled air, drinking recycled water, seeing nothing organic except for the plants she had grown in her greenhouse.

Naomi had lifted her chin, her posture ramrod-straight in her pressed, stiff suit, her short hair only beginning to grow out again. The scratches on her cheek were still fresh. Thirty years later, they were the barest seams, hidden among the faint wrinkles. Her face was drawn, not only from what she saw among the stars, but what she'd faced when she'd returned.

Dr. Naomi Lovelace has been many things over the years. Scientist. Criminal. Villain. Hero. Famous. Infamous.

Who would she have been, if she'd never gone? In the home clips I watched of her before she left Earth, Naomi was still quiet, but a smile often hovered at the edges of her lips, as if she held a secret she wished she could share. In one clip, taken the year before she left Earth, she'd opened her Christmas presents with the careful, considered way she did everything. A scientist through and through. Lifting the tape with a plum-purple nail, peeling back the shining paper to fold it up and set it aside. Opening the cardboard top, peeking in, the dark wave of her hair covering her face. The slight laugh as she took out the snow globe Valerie had given her, her mentor looking on with her own crooked half-smile. Valerie had bought one years ago at the Kennedy Space Center, and growing up, Naomi had always played with it. They had likely been out of production for years, but Valerie had found another just the same. Naomi shook it, the blue glitter murky and opaque before it settled to reveal the little space shuttle on its little launch pad.

She brought it with her when she left Earth. It still sits on her nightstand, even though the glass is cracked and the glimmer within leaked out long ago.

I never knew the first, early incarnation of Naomi. Sometimes, I'm not sure I've ever seen her beneath that meteorite mask. Not really.

Every anniversary, journalists try again, begging for just one feature. Or a publisher will contact me on her behalf and offer me an eye-watering deal for her memoir as one of the Atalanta 5. No one understood why she kept saying no.

I do. Naomi has never craved fame or money.

Over the years, people have tried to fill in the blanks, or simply made up lies that further poisoned her legacy. She always claimed that her past was better left forgotten—what really mattered was what happened after. What we built from the remnants and rubble.

You'll be wondering who I am to her, but I'm not the important part of this story. I never have been.

I'd only meant to stay with her for a week. One of my infrequent visits—always so difficult to get away and see her, and it's so far to travel. It was easy to let too many months pass. At least I visited her, though. The rest of the family never does. She spends so much of her time alone.

I was meant to leave tomorrow, yet just half an hour ago, at two-thirty in the morning, she shook me awake. She leaned over me, greying brown hair tickling my face, her hands like claws on my shoulders.

Dark eyes wide, she said she'd tell me everything. Her face was red, splotchy with tears, her voice nothing more than a whisper, her sour breath hot on my cheek.

I've checked the news long enough to understand what's set her off. Naomi will have turned off all incoming comms—the journalists are going to be circling and buzzing like flies.

They'll dredge up all the old pain anyway, so perhaps that's why she's finally telling me what I want to know. Better than finding out via the news drones. She owes me that much.

I've gone to fetch a pen and paper—an anachronistic affectation, but writing longhand helps me think better, even if decoding my handwriting is a struggle. I'm scribbling my thoughts, trying to untangle them before I go back through.

Naomi had offered me the same silence as everyone else over the years. Given me answers so slantwise to the truth they might as well be lies. I might hear it all, tonight, but will it be worse than what I've imagined or managed to piece together over the years?

The night sky is so clear—spilled ink speckled with stars. Naomi always said no matter how dark the night is, you can never mistake a planetside sky for the true black of space.

I'll start at the beginning, like she wants.

CHAPTER ONE

Launch

Michigan, USA, Earth

If it had been a normal launch, they would have made a spectacle of it all.

There would be picnic blankets laid out on the parched dirt, legs oily beneath smears of sunblock, faces shadowed by hats and hidden behind sunglasses. They'd lift their filter masks long enough to nibble at packed treats. Kids would suck down juice in silver pouches, pretending it was what the astronauts had in space. Adults would sip something stronger, enough to take the edge off and help the time pass on by.

Ten. Nine. Eight.

If this was a normal launch, the masses would be lined up along the flight path. Excited, fairground chatter would twine around the tinny music blasting from speakers. People would imagine what it must be like for the spacefarers clustered in the cockpit, their hearts in their throats as they waited. Family and friends would group four kilometres from the launch pad—as close as allowed—waving farewell even though their loved ones couldn't see. Tears would weave salted tracks down their cheeks, and they'd be trying very hard not to remember the footage they'd seen of the *Challenger* shuttle, fine one moment and a fireball the next.

Seven. Six.

But this was not a normal launch.

Naomi clenched her hands into fists, then released, tension flowing out of her. She was strapped down to her chair in the depths of the shuttle, her body cocooned in a bulky spacesuit and fishbowl helmet. All her senses were dulled. Nothing touched her skin but the cotton undergarments beneath the fabric of the suit. No smell, her hearing muffled, her vision hedged in. Everything was distant, as if she were viewing herself from the outside and this was happening to someone else.

Five. Four.

There was no one waiting around the launch pad hidden on the edge of the Keweenaw Peninsula. It had been the site of secret Cold War rocket launches, and those few who had ever heard of it thought it long since decommissioned.

So there were no picnics. What had once been popular cottage country was now largely bare, acidic bedrock hostile to both vegetation and tourists. No line of cars threaded through the cracked highway that bisected the patches of dead and dying forests. No hopeful faces tilted up towards the clouds, ready to trace the arc of the rocket as it made its way up, up, and away.

That was the point.

They were all alone, the five women in the capsule strapped to this rocket. The launch pad was much larger than the tiny site where NASA had sent up rockets in the late sixties. No one knew what they had planned. The work had been done by robots and AI, the launch sequence fully automated.

If the secret leaked, they would be finished before they started. It also meant if something went wrong, they were on their own.

The five of them locked eyes through the visors of their helmets. The others tried to hide the fear that must have been rattling their bones as surely as the engines. Naomi's muscles were rigid as steel. They had come to this corner of the world in the dead of night two weeks ago. Locked themselves in a makeshift quarantine, done each and every step to ready themselves for launch. Startling at every sound, as the robots crawled along the surface of a rocket. They had to put their entire trust in machines, for humans could too easily betray them.

Right up until the end, she was afraid someone would come. Turn off the robots, disrupt the launch sequence. Pull open the hatch and drag them from the craft just as they were about to finally escape. Naomi held her breath.

The five women chanted along with the robotic voice blaring through the capsule.

"Three. Two. One."

They'd willingly strapped themselves to a bomb and lit the fuse. Engines roared. Naomi's teeth shook in her skull, the skin of her cheeks pressed flat against her cheekbones. The rocket rose, shuddering, hovering over the launch pad, frantically burning fuel, battling against gravity. Victory screams came from the four other women Naomi trusted with her life as the capsule veered and accelerated towards orbital velocity. Once they hit it, each second would take them eight kilometres further away from the Earth's crust. Naomi was crushed against her seat, as if a demon crouched on her chest.

There had been so many close calls, so many setbacks.

A year ago, she thought that her life's work would never culminate in that moment. Never mind her two degrees, the cap tassels and framed certificates at the bottom of a box left behind in storage. Never mind the months of gruelling, invasive physical and psychological tests. The missed parties, dinners, dates. The relationships she'd left in the dust. She was never meant to make it to space. None of them were.

So much had been stolen from them. From all women. Naomi and her conspirators were stealing something back. Conservative politicians and their sock puppets in the media would accuse Dr. Valerie Black, CEO of Hawthorne, and her crew of stealing a spaceship. But the people on the surface were wrong.

The women were stealing a planet.

They were stealing a future.

Far below them, further every second, people would be peeking out from their windows, faces turned towards the capsule as they held their filter masks over their noses and mouths. There wouldn't be many, in this dry pocket of the world—most had long since moved closer to slivers of green and cleaner water. The journalists would be frantically typing up their clickbait headlines, well behind the news spidering its way across social media. Fuzzy photos uploaded. A video taken with shaking hands, the plume of smoke like a comet's tail.

The spent boosters separated, the capsule shaking. The shuttle left the last of the atmosphere behind, pushing through the vestiges of the stratosphere. Naomi went from being crushed by acceleration to abrupt weightlessness. The straps of the chair harness *whooshed* the air from her lungs. The troll doll Hixon had tied to her station as a good luck charm floated, twisting, plastic face frozen in a grotesque rictus.

For an hour, Naomi clutched her chair as they hurtled through space. There were no windows—all they could stare at were the readouts on the screens.

Hixon's hands were steady on the controls even though their path was automated, her pale skin grey-blue beneath her freckles in the dim light. Valerie emanated calm and satisfaction. Hart and Lebedeva were stiff in their seats, and Naomi was unable to see anything through the reflections off their visors.

Valerie was so many things to Naomi—her boss at Hawthorne, her captain. Long before that, she'd taken Naomi in when she was nine, her father dead and her mother unable to care for her. Once the world found out what they had done, Naomi would never escape the nepotism whispers that had followed every step of her career. Naomi had once moved away from Hawthorne to prove herself but was lured back to Project Atalanta as though by a siren's song.

Valerie had handpicked the first all-female crew into interstellar space.

Just not the first *authorised* crew.

The government had dangled the project before Valerie, let her spend her money, her expertise, before snatching it away and replacing the crew with last-minute substitutions from NASA. It was physically impossible for the five men to do as much training, to run through the simulations, to know the ship from the inside out. President Cochran was so determined to keep those five women off the *Atalanta* and their destination of Cavendish, he was willing to risk everything.

Oksana Lebedeva, lead engineer, the cosmonaut who left the Roscosmos to work for Valerie under suspicious circumstances. Jerrie Hixon, their lead pilot and mathematician, who quit NASA when President Cochran was sworn into office. Her wife, Irene Hart, who followed suit when NASA edged out most of its women a few months later as Cochran's policies began coming into effect.

It hadn't happened in a moment, but a series of moments, as slow and insidious as the melting of the ice caps. Women had been ushered out of the workplace, so subtly that few noticed until it was too late. There had been no grand lowering of an iron curtain, with passports voided and bank accounts emptied. There had been a few men in sharp suits quoting scripture with silver tongues, but it was cursory, just enough to wrangle part of the Christian vote. Really, they were afraid of women. Or hated them. Wasn't that much the same thing? The country saw those angry men as a fringe movement right up until one was elected president.

"ETA to the *Atalanta* ten minutes," Hixon said at one point, voice clipped. Naomi could almost feel their brains ticking, their thoughts swirling through the cramped cabin.

Finally, their true ship came into view on the cameras: the *Atalanta*. Valerie smiled. Hixon allowed herself a triumphant clap, muffled by her gloves. Naomi, Hart, and Lebedeva stayed silent and awed.

It was a beautiful craft, all smooth and white metal. A sleek, bird-like body formed the ship's central axis, the bow showing the disk of the bridge, quadruple-reinforced windows dark, and the ion and plasma thrusters strapped to the side.

Jutting up from the ship were three spokes that led to the

large, round ring—the labs, quarters, and communal spaces—that circled the ship like a halo. If they managed to pull this off and leave Earth's orbit, the ring would turn, generating gravity. The ring perfectly matched the one built just outside Mars' orbit and provided a set location via atomic clocks. When they'd figured out how to harvest exotic matter to create negative energy, it meant the Alcubierre theory for warp drive was no longer the realm of science fiction. A spaceship could contract space in front of it and expand behind, travelling faster than the speed of light without breaking the laws of physics.

Though they had sent various probes through the rings and back again, Earth's sundry countries were too afraid to build the warp ring directly in lower orbit or around the moon. It wasn't essential for the warp drive, but it helped ensure the craft was in the proper location and their calculations were exact. The *Atalanta* would make its slower, sublight journey to Mars with the ion engines. Once it slotted neatly into the ring, they could go anywhere.

Their destination was ten and a half light years away.

Cavendish.

The *Atalanta* was still bolted to its construction hub. It was an ungainly host, filled with scrap and the latest model of drone robots originally designed by Naomi's mother, not dissimilar to the ones that had just helped launch the shuttle. Last week, these ones had still been skittering along the shining hull, tightening every screw, bringing it to life. The *Atalanta* had been assembled far enough from the Lunar Orbital Platform Gateway and the International Space Station that the astronauts on board those vessels would not be able to easily stop the five women.

In two weeks, the new crew was meant to board the *Atalanta* to head out to Cavendish to determine whether or not it was a viable new home for humanity. Naomi had worked under the new proposed commander, Shane Legge, during her time at NASA. She'd also seen him outside of work more than she'd cared to—he'd been her ex-husband's close friend. He was brilliant, but a terrible leader. One who deliberately made others feel inferior, who nursed resentments and stoked petty competition. Even if they all managed to keep the *Atalanta* going from a science point of view, they'd be at each other's throats by Mars.

The capsule drifted closer to the *Atalanta*'s docking port. Valerie knew this ship—Lockwood's veneer over the security systems couldn't keep her out. NASA and Lockwood hadn't thought to stop access from orbit, had never anticipated Valerie would be able to take off from the surface without their knowledge. Earth couldn't stop them, not without huge costs. Even if they tried to interfere with the warp ring at Mars, Valerie could turn off the Hawthorne robots on the surface remotely. Worst-case scenario, they could still use the Alcubierre drive in another location, though it would require a lot of extra calculations on Hixon's part. And a lot more risk.

The crew held their breath as their craft slid into place. The probe connected, drawing the two vehicles together. A hiss as the seals tightened. Naomi exhaled.

Valerie gave them all a wordless signal and the astronauts unbuckled their seat belts, floating up in the capsule. Naomi moved her weightless arms in wonder.

Lebedeva twisted the latch on the craft, hauling the steel door open. The astronauts glided into the ship. Their ship.

Naomi still felt cramped—the airlock wasn't much bigger than the capsule. All was pitch-dark until the motion detection lights flickered on, too bright after the dimness.

They'd connected to the main body of the ship, the centre holding the loading bay to the back, the bridge to the front, and excess storage along the right side of the connecting hallway.

As they moved into the corridor, Naomi drank in every detail. She had seen this spaceship countless times on the simulators, either on two-dimensional screens or through virtual reality that was almost like the real thing. Almost.

"All clear?" Valerie asked, her voice tinny through the speakers around Naomi's ears.

Hixon gave a thumbs up.

Valerie's hands rose, twisting off her helmet. Curly brown hair that normally fell to her chin haloed her face. Her normally stern features opened with a wide, toothy grin.

Naomi followed suit, her helmet hissing. She breathed in sterile, scentless air. She was here, her body untethered by gravity. The closest she'd come was either underwater in the Neutral Buoyancy Lab during NASA training or brief thirty-second bursts at the tip of parabolic flights on zero-G planes. She took off a glove. Touched the cool white wall of the hallway. Solid. This was not a recreation. This was reality.

The others took off their helmets. These were the women Naomi would see every day for the foreseeable future. Soon their features would be as familiar as her own.

Valerie pushed off the wall of the corridor, making her way to the bridge. The others followed, silent as ghosts. It was a small ship, all things considered, just large enough to comfortably fit up to seven crew and all the supplies they'd need to make it to Mars, the ring, and Cavendish. Naomi wanted to swim through the air and explore every corner of the vessel. It was novel, but soon it would hold no secrets.

In the bridge, they paused, hovering above the seats and the consoles.

"Well, goddamn," Valerie breathed.

Below them lay Earth.

It didn't look like a marble; it was too clearly alive. The clouds crawled slowly, the planet bisected by the line of day and night. On the night side, the lights of cities glimmered. There was Europe, a gleam of brightness over Paris, Berlin, Kiev, strung together by smaller cities like linked synapses. Southern Europe was largely dark in summer as people who could fled north to places like Finland or Estonia. Lightning flashed over Morocco. Far to the north was the green glow of the *aurora borealis*. Charged particles from solar wind burning up in the atmosphere. It was Naomi's first time seeing the Northern Lights. She'd seen the Southern Lights, and thought them beautiful on the expedition to Antarctica during her undergraduate degree, smothered in a parka as she gazed out at the horizon. From up here, it looked like magic.

The day side illuminated what the night could not—there was no ice in the Arctic Sea. The Antarctic wasn't visible from here—this time of year was constant darkness for the southern pole. In summer, it'd show expanses of black land dotted by large, turquoise lakes, some the size of small European countries, the glaciers melting. She wondered if the lights from the oil rigs recently put up in the Ross Sea would be visible from space. The Antarctic treaties had been broken long before they were meant to run out in 2048.

The land on the other continents was too brown and golden, the green too sparse. There were swathes of land where humans could no longer survive, and the habitable areas were growing crowded. There was even some gold-green in the oceans from dust storms blowing off the continents and fertilising phytoplankton blooms. They'd managed to fish out most of the Great Pacific garbage patch, at least, though even if they hadn't, it might not have been visible from orbit.

Earth was such a little, vulnerable thing in the grand scope of the universe.

Down on the surface, those mountains were larger than life, but from the ship they were only a ripple. The world she'd known was nothing but a suspended, lonely rock. It'd keep itself alive, in the end, but that didn't mean large animal life would do the same. Humans were finally confronted with their fragility. Within a generation, they could all be gone. They'd outgrown this world, drained it dry. They needed a new one.

The women held their helmets, gathering around the window. The exhilaration and adrenaline of launch was fading, everyone sobering as what they had just done set in. They knew what they risked, yet that was different from being confronted, so baldly, with what they stood to lose. With what they were so desperate to save, they'd steal a ship.

"We spent so long thinking about getting off the planet, it's easy to forget this is only the beginning," Hart whispered, the blue light making her brown skin glow.

How well did Naomi know these women? She'd trained and worked with them, but they were also the only humans she'd interact with for years. Valerie's chosen aegis.

Tears clung to Hixon's face, clustering by her nose in a

bubble. Hart reached out, wiping them away. Naomi drifted closer, pressing her hands against the window. To her right, Lebedeva was inscrutable as always, her cheekbones standing out in stark relief against her white skin. Both of them had shaved off their hair when they were in quarantine. Hart had taken out her braids and cut her hair short months ago, and Hixon had a pixie cut since she was twelve. The Russian had buzzed her own blond hair into a bristle before snipping Naomi's dark locks. Naomi had watched them fall to the ground, realising she wouldn't be able to take gravity for granted much longer.

Valerie gave a whisper of a sigh before hardening. "Hixon."

The pilot nodded, coming to attention, her military background embedded deep. She pulled herself down to the console and started the sequence to disengage the *Atalanta* from the construction hub.

An error message blared, harsh and jarring in the quiet. A red flash against the blue-white.

Hixon tried again. Another burst of red.

"They've locked the ship to the hub from the ground. That's a recent spec change." Valerie pointed to the world with her chin. "Oh, they're so spitting mad. I love it."

As if her voice conjured it, a different beep sounded—an incoming message from Houston.

"Do we answer?" Hart asked, chewing at the edge of a fingernail.

"Of course not," Valerie said. "Lebedeva. Lovelace. Dig out the EMUs."

Naomi worked through her words. "You can't mean—"

"Manual override. Worked it into the design. Figured they'd

pull this kind of shit. They're going to send up a Dragon or send people from the Gateway to come arrest us. You want to be here when they do? Now's your chance to speak up."

Silence save for the insistent beep from the men trapped on the crust of the Earth.

"Suit up," Valerie said, giving them another wide, white smile. "Spacewalk."

CHAPTER TWO

3 Years Before Launch

Sutherland, Scotland

Valerie appeared out of the mist like a spectre.

Naomi recognised her former guardian as soon as she left the doors of the Sutherland Spaceport, tucking her employee badge back into her purse. There was no mistaking the tilt of those shoulders, the confidence emanating off the silhouette in waves.

Naomi halted by her car, waiting, hands deep in her pockets. Valerie wore a floor-length, dark green coat, a large umbrella shielding her from the worst of the Scottish wind and rain. Only tourists used them. Those who lived in Scotland long enough simply acknowledged that any umbrella was bound to be blown inside out, and it was better to resign yourself to getting a little wet.

"Valerie." Naomi didn't reach out for a hug. Valerie Black didn't do hugs.

"Hello, Naomi," Valerie said, as if she'd run into Naomi by chance around the corner from her mansion in the Santa Ana mountains rather than flown five thousand miles and travelled up to the remote north of Scotland. As if the last time they'd seen each other in person hadn't resulted in a fight that meant they hadn't spoken in a year. "Happy birthday. I thought I'd treat you to dinner."

Valerie stood before her, but so many other versions of her floated in Naomi's memory, like overexposed photos. The first birthday after she'd come to live with Valerie, a silent nine year old with smoke-scorched lungs who saw soot drifting down like snow every time she closed her eyes. There had been no candles on the cake. Her twelfth birthday at a theme park, Valerie buying the most expensive ticket so they never had to stand in line. Valerie had waited for Naomi at the exit of each ride, saying she saved her thrills for things that were more dangerous. Valerie had always loved birthdays and Christmases. A chance to watch others light up with joy and then grow bashful at her extravagance no one else could meet.

Naomi glanced behind her at the glass dome of the spaceport, still skirted with scaffolding. Naomi worked for Lockwood on a contract for the UK Space Agency. People already whispered at her being raised by the CEO of their prime competitor. If they saw Valerie here...

Valerie opened the door to Naomi's car, as if reading her thoughts. "Come on," she said. "Let's get out of the rain."

Naomi settled inside, pulling the door shut.

The ESA and the UKSA were slowly following in NASA's footsteps in terms of restricting women's presence in the workforce. Until they caught up, Naomi still had a chance at going to space on this side of the pond.

They were silent as the self-driving car cut through the mist, the grey shifting to violet in the growing dusk. Naomi remembered how cold Valerie had been, when she told her mentor she was leaving NASA, moving somewhere so much further from Houston and her problems there. The barest trace of that ice remained frozen into the lines of Valerie's profile, lit up in the soft purple of the gloaming. She caught Naomi's eye, gave a flicker of a smile.

"Your mind is whirring away, I can almost hear it," Valerie said.

"We can do the small talk if you want. Or should I wait until you get settled and you decide to tell me why you're really here?"

Valerie laughed, exposing the column of her throat. "Fair enough, my girl. Fair enough."

They twined through the winding Highland roads. When the car pulled into the village of Tongue, darkness lay thick on the stone buildings.

Having largely grown up in America, even though her father had been Scottish, Naomi was always struck by the sense of time and history in these old crofting villages and towns. Picts, Gaels, and Vikings had passed through Tongue over the centuries, and generations of farmers had lived in the same cottages as their ancestors. This section of Scotland was, so far, less ravaged by the rising temperatures, though it wasn't unscathed.

Valerie chose one of the two hotel pubs, Naomi trailing behind. The conversation stalled when they walked in. With their nice coats and fine shoes, everyone assumed they were from the SSP. Valerie had taken them both into the heart of the local community, many of whom had protested the construction of the spaceport. Some because the rockets would be launching several hundred metres from the borders of their land, startling the sheep. Others because the peat bog of the A'Mhoine peninsula was meant to be a wildlife sanctuary for Highland birds. That delayed things for a few years, until the wild bird population dipped so precariously it didn't matter any longer.

Naomi had researched the birds when she first arrived here, rolling the names along her tongue. In winter there should have been cormorants, little grebes, redshanks. Summer should have sandpipers, black-headed gulls, skylarks, and meadow pipit. There should have been birds of prey, like peregrines, merlins, and golden eagles. On weekends when she'd first arrived, she'd stomped through the squelching bogs in her best wellies, oversized binoculars around her neck, trying in vain to find them. She'd spend the whole day outside and return, cold and soaking, perhaps having spotted one or two scrawny birds all day. The occasional roar of engines couldn't drown out the absence of the bird calls.

Naomi blinked, back in the warm interior of the pub. Valerie strode through the tables as if she didn't have a care, their occupants' wariness rolling off her like water off an otter's back. She chose a table near the central hearth. All smelled of woodsmoke, stale beer, stewing meat, and the dust from past memories. Stag heads with cobwebs between their antlers lined the walls, glass eyes blank. Framed black-and-white photos hung under them, showing the village looking much the same. It was such a contrast to the sterile smoothness of the spaceport, or the employee apartments five kilometres from her work that still smelled of new paint and plasterboard.

"All right, out with it," Naomi said after they'd settled and the bartender had brought them two glasses of whisky—top shelf, Valerie's treat. "It's nice to see you, but it's not exactly round the corner. I was expecting a card in the mail."

"Oh, yes!" Valerie plucked a white envelope from her purse and passed it over. Naomi felt the stiffness of the card inside. She didn't open it.

Valerie took a sip from her bell-shaped glass before setting it down. She leaned forward, her elbows on her knees, spread out, taking up room.

"If you could do anything just now, anything—what would it be?" Valerie had that intensity about her that had never failed to draw Naomi in.

"You know what it'd be. Get up there." A glance at the window. The moon, the stars.

Valerie tilted her head, lips quirking at the corners. "I have a job for you that might help with that."

Naomi took a taste of her own whisky. She felt that flicker of excitement, deep in her chest, tingling at her fingertips.

"I already have a job." Naomi strove for lightness. If Valerie realised someone was too keen, she couldn't help but tease whatever it was out, dangle it like a cat toy until the other person cracked.

"Not the one you really want. Come on, open your card."

The smell of the smoke in the grate was distracting Naomi, sticking in her throat. She needed to stay sharp. Naomi's mouth went dry. She drank more whisky to wet it, but it tasted of fire, too. She wished for water instead.

Naomi tore open the white envelope. Slid out a card with a cartoony illustration of the Earth on the front, curling white clouds, the sea an even blue. She looked closer. No. Instead of larger continents, the world had smaller islands.

It wasn't Earth.

She opened the card.

Happy birthday.
Let's go.
V

Naomi glanced up at Valerie sharply. "Is this a joke?"

Since moving to Scotland, Naomi had often wondered what Valerie's latest project was. More than once, she'd picked up the phone, their fight be damned, just to find out. She followed Valerie in the news, sifting through the sneering, patronising articles for clues of what she was truly up to.

"I'd never joke about that." Valerie shifted closer, the firelight flickering along skin smoothed by good gene therapy, expensive creams and injections. No one would peg her for forty-nine. Her mouth curved. "I can promise you a world, Naomi."

"Cavendish." Her whole body felt alive, struck by an electric bolt.

The exosolar planet had been discovered the year Naomi turned sixteen. As soon as she'd seen it on the screen in Valerie's living room, she'd blurted out how much she wanted to go. Valerie had laughed, said she'd come along too. Turned out she'd been dead serious. Hawthorne came upon harder times just after that and Valerie had to shut down some of her medical subcompanies, such as Haven, the one that beat the government to developing viable cloned organs. Growing embryos had already taken off with celebrities who could afford to pay the premium—Naomi remembered the selfies of smiling, glamorous celebrities in front of the tanks showing their growing child suspended in liquid, a hand on their flat and toned tummies. The next level of surrogate. Valerie planned to grow the foetuses in orbit in microgravity, where they wouldn't need growing supports that could damage the tissue once removed.

It was all snuffed right before it could become relatively affordable. Couldn't very well make it easier for women to stay in the workplace, could they? Valerie had to fire the head of Haven and throw him under the bus. She redoubled her investments in the robots and AI that had put Hawthorne on the map and focused on interstellar space enterprise instead.

Yet now Naomi was nearing thirty, her teen years long behind her, and they were no closer to that planet just over ten light years away. Probes had been there, and brought back samples, but even if they sent humans, Naomi would never have a chance. Not with how the world was changing.

Naomi still hoped for the moon, or Mars. Maybe even as far as Titan. But no further. She'd long since come to terms with the fact that the little biome of Cavendish she'd made with seeds from the probe was the closest she'd ever get.

"Don't taunt me, V. They'd never let the likes of us go. Even if you could figure out how." The news had reported NASA's latest failure—a probe full of rats, returned in one piece, every rodent frozen solid.

Valerie waved a hand. "We have Jerrie Hixon with the team now."

Naomi raised her eyebrows, impressed. She remembered her. Sharp pilot. Sharp mind.

"She's on the case with the calculations. We'll be able to get within one AU of Cavendish using the drive, I'm certain of it. Let me worry about the government. I need you to keep us fed all the way to that planet. I need you, Naomi. No one else will do."

Naomi felt something bright and white and hot as a young sun deep in her chest. The shock and depth of her want winded her. Cavendish. A chance at Cavendish.

Valerie motioned to the barkeep—a dour man with a face like a walnut—to bring water. Naomi buried her head in the glass, gathering her thoughts. She prided herself on never showing too much. She was the calm one, the collected one. The one that others turned to when they were losing it.

The conversation flowed around them, people in the pub unwinding after a long day at work.

"I can't break my contract," Naomi said, hoping she still sounded cool.

Valerie scoffed, deep in her throat. She knew she had Naomi on the hook. "If Lockwood goes after you, I have plenty to threaten them with. Honestly, Nomi—" Naomi noted Valerie's use of her childhood nickname; clever—"do you even realise who you're working for? They've done some messed-up shit."

As if you haven't, Naomi wanted to say. All corporations were the same. As long as they paid the bills to let her continue her research, Naomi tried not to think about the darker edges. A privilege, she knew, and one that still made her culpable, even if she pleaded ignorance.

"Let me show you the data and where we are," Valerie said. "Take some leave, come to California with me. You have to at least see the *Atalanta*. We'll start ferrying the pieces constructed on the ground to space in the next three months. The assembly hub is already being built." Her eyes rose, as if she could see through the smoke-stained timber to the sky.

An actual spaceship. Not a shuttle, not a satellite, not a rocket. Something built to fold space and time to bring humans to another solar system. To the planet that had been hidden from humans' radar, hidden among the data of Hubble until the James Webb telescope was able to reveal it in more detail.

Naomi thought of her lab in Sutherland. It was good, well stocked. Not as state of the art as her old ones at NASA or Hawthorne. She was involved in two projects: perfecting the hydroponics for the ISS and the Gateway as well as experimenting on crops that could grow on Mars. Not so different from what she had done at NASA.

On the space stations, the European astronauts currently grew forty per cent of their food and she was hoping to bump it to fifty next year. Growing plants was harder in microgravity. There was talk of building a new space station with a gravity ring, if the partnership countries could stop squabbling about the funds. It was a good job. A worthy job.

A job that would leave her tied to a desk, if she were honest with herself. NASA had reluctantly bowed to growing governmental pressure—women had been forced out of active space flight, and they were leaving most management, engineering, and science jobs in droves. The UKSA hadn't followed suit, but deep down, she'd known for months they'd never let her on one of those rockets she saw every day. For her own safety, so the men in power claimed, as piece by piece they eroded women's abilities to feel safe.

There were others Valerie could have asked. Maybe even better qualified. *No one else will do.*

Despite their fight, their silence over the last year, Valerie still wanted *her*. Naomi went to the window, taking her whisky with her. Valerie let her go, crossing her legs, making a pretence of surveying the sticky, laminated menu.

The clouds were too thick to see the stars, but Naomi let herself imagine being up there, the whole world spread below. She'd wanted a shot at this since she was a child, and even the odd space shuttle blowing up as she watched the live broadcasts hadn't dissuaded her. She'd tackled botany and astrobotany, mechanical engineering, astrophysics. Learned Russian and a smattering of Chinese. All for a chance of something that each day faded further into grey.

Naomi came back to the table, setting down her empty glass.

"I want to be second in command."

Valerie's face split into a grin and she gave a whoop that startled the people in the pub. "I would, you know I would, but that role's already Hixon's, I'm afraid. She has the military and the Ares experience."

Naomi's shoulders folded.

"But," Valerie said, sensing Naomi's disappointment, "you know that you'll always have my ear. Compromise?"

Naomi sucked her lower lip. Held out her hand.

Valerie laughed but shook it in that firm, CEO grip. Then she whooped again, professional veneer dropped. "This calls for more whisky."

"You knew what answer I'd give before you even arrived," Naomi said.

"Still thought it'd be polite to ask. I taught you manners, didn't I?"

No mention of their fight. Valerie seemed to want to pretend it'd never happened, and that worked well enough for Naomi.

There were a thousand ways the project could go wrong. A million obstacles before them. That night, as the moon blurred the clouds silver, and the whisky made them both warm, Naomi vowed she wouldn't let anything stand in their way.

When the car dropped them off at the plasterboard spaceport employee apartments, Valerie walked Naomi to the door. She'd be heading down to London for meetings before heading back home to Los Angeles.

Valerie leaned her forehead against Naomi's. "Happy birthday, Nomi," she said, the closest she'd come to an apology, and then she was gone.

CHAPTER THREE

3 Hours After Launch

126 Days to Mars

249 Days to Cavendish

They should have had weeks to prepare for a spacewalk, not hours. They'd prepped, of course, through simulations and in EMUs underwater, but that was not the same. Every second they lingered in orbit, their window of escape grew smaller. The U.S. would be preparing to capture them like butterflies in a net, dragging them back down to Earth.

Valerie had lowered the atmospheric pressure in the *Atalanta* by thirty per cent so coming in and out of the airlock meant less chance of the bends. It was still risky, and everyone on board knew it.

Naomi adjusted the mask over her face, breathing in pure oxygen rather than the usual mix of oxygen and nitrogen. Lebedeva was across from her, her face likewise covered, tubes snaking into the spare canisters. Head and neck covered with absorbent cloth, the mic tracing the curve of her cheekbone. Her blue eyes were serious, blond brows drawn down as she stared, unblinking, at the hatch leading to space. Nine minutes.

They were both lost in the spacesuits, so puffy that Naomi's arms fell to her sides like a ballerina about to pirouette.

Naomi always thought calling it an Extravehicular Mobile Unit sounded too technical and uninspired. But scientists veered from naming things poetically—drawing from myth and legend—to incredibly factual, with letters and numbers or baldly stating the obvious. Naomi had burst out laughing when as a child she'd learned they were naming the new telescope in the Atacama Desert in Chile the Very Large Telescope. It was, at that.

In truth, Naomi was in a tiny spacecraft in the shape of a human. Layers of high-tech fabric, the hard fibreglass torso, the life support system in the back like she was a mountaineer climbing Everest. It still seemed so flimsy compared to the vastness of space. If their ship was named the *Atalanta*, she'd call her small spacecraft the *Argo*, even if it was just in her mind.

Hixon floated between them. Double-, triple-checking their suits, despite the inbuilt integrity sensors. She ran a hand over every join, every seam, in wordless superstition. Hixon had been the one to help them climb into the suits, adjusting everything except for the helmets.

Naomi found her calmness again, waiting for the hatch to open. She did not think about what could go wrong. She did not let herself clasp on to dizzying excitement that could make her reckless.

"You ready?" Hixon asked, the helmet in her hands.

"Yes." On went the helmet, shutting out most sound. Hixon fastened it, double-checked it, and went to do the same to Lebedeva. Inside the helmet was a tube to suck down water, and another to breathe into on the off-chance her helmet filled with liquid. It had happened to other astronauts before, though they had survived.

The spacesuit was heavy, but microgravity kept her limbs light. Naomi held her hands out in front of her. Thick fingers, like white bananas. Soon they'd be holding the tools, grappling with the reduced motor skills, having to work as quickly as they could without being unsafe. Ten main bolts to loosen, and the *Atalanta* would be free.

"Can you hear me?" came Valerie's gravelly voice through the comms of the helmet.

"Loud and clear," Naomi replied.

"Affirmative," said Lebedeva.

Hixon gave them a last pat on the shoulders. "Good luck."

Hixon left, the metal door clanging shut behind her. Lebedeva and Naomi faced each other, legs treading the air like water. Naomi allowed herself a slow somersault. Lebedeva gave a rare laugh and did the same. They locked eyes, gave a little nod before clinging to the handholds.

"Open the hatch," Valerie commanded.

Lebedeva grunted, twisting the wheel of the hatch and opening it into darkness.

Lebedeva went first, sticking her head out of the craft. The spacewalk had mentally started at different points for them. In Russia, a spacewalk began when the hatch opened. In the U.S., it was when at least the head was out of the airlock. Lebedeva snapped her tether on to the nearest handrail. One moment she was there, outlined against the black, and then she was gone. Naomi straightened her shoulders and guided herself out of the airlock.

It was like she'd expected and yet like nothing she could

have prepared for. A chasm of darkness with no pressure, no sound. Black above, below. The *Atalanta* sheltered her from the worst of the sun, so she was cold, despite the high-tech gear under the EMU. It was 250 degrees Celsius below zero. Once she and Lebedeva clambered over the spacecraft to the assembly hub, they'd be in direct sun and the pendulum would swing up to 250 degrees the other way.

Naomi gripped the tether, even though it was connected at both the waist and the handrail. She had a local one she could move herself and a long one that led back to the ship at all times. If there was one thing they'd told her in training, it was always be aware of the tethers. If you floated away, that was it. There was no getting you back. An astronaut had lost his tether a few years ago, off the ISS. By the time they gathered a rescue mission, it was too late. He was gone. His corpse had eventually burned up in the atmosphere. The tiniest meteor.

Floating out there was a little like standing at the shore, looking out to the sea, beautiful but cruel. The currents would pull you under and would not care. In that moment, Naomi fully understood the meaning of the word "awestruck." The word "sublime."

"Naomi," came Valerie's voice. Commanding and comforting.

Naomi's attention snapped back to the task at hand. "Following Lebedeva."

Naomi drew herself along the tether and clasped the handrail with her gloves. Her legs kicked out behind her. It was like ballet. Like swimming. Like neither of those things. She drew herself along, her breath echoing in the helmet along with Lebedeva's on the comms.

The cosmonaut reached the front of the ship, leaving Naomi's field of vision. The helmet was static, and she was hemmed in.

Sun glimmered along the white hull of the ship. Only a few dings from space debris marred its veneer. She drew a hand along the metal. The golden light of the sun glimmered through the Earth's atmosphere below her before striking her suit. She was already warm from pulling herself along the handrails. Sweat pooled along the small of her back, beneath her arms, wicked by the cotton under-layer. She flipped down her helmet shade to protect her eyes.

Lebedeva had paused, legs streaming out horizontally, taking in the dying world below. Naomi drifted beside her.

Lebedeva whispered something in Russian Naomi couldn't quite catch. An exclamation of wonder. A prayer. They were nearly the same thing.

They allowed themselves half a minute of drinking in the swirling clouds—including the spiral of a hurricane above the blue of the ocean. It was a little too early for wildfires, at least. Naomi was grateful not to see the grey plumes visible from all the way up here. It had been night when they took off, and from their position, the *Atalanta* had already seen two sunrises and sunsets. In orbit, they were travelling more than 17,000 miles per hour over the Earth's surface. Five miles a second.

"Lebedeva. Lovelace." An edge in Valerie's voice.

The astronauts continued their journey. They passed the bridge. Hart and Hixon waved, and Valerie made a shooing motion. The ground must be closer to launching than she was letting on.

The construction hub was ugly compared to the ship. All

dark, gunmetal grey, inelegant modules clamped together. Minimal life support. It wasn't meant for humans.

Valerie had chosen their launch date carefully. Construction was finished, the robots on the hub either shut down or shipped back to Earth. Those were still Hawthorne property, and Valerie had made damn sure they couldn't be turned on remotely.

Ten giant bolts connecting the starboard side to the hub. Ten bolts keeping the *Atalanta* from flight.

Lebedeva and Naomi took their tools from the transparent kit at their belts, clipping more tethers to their waists. They'd be using long, large ratchet wrenches, not much different from what they'd use on Earth except for a larger wheel so they could twist easier with their gloves. Lebedeva took the closest connection and Naomi moved along to the far end.

Earth spread below them, sunset deepening back to night. They were over Asia—there was the little finger of Japan and Korea, the sprawl of China. Shocks of light from Tokyo, Beijing, Seoul. The cities were bigger, buildings for accommodation and business, but also vertical farms. Sea walls protected the changed coastline as best they could, and more walls bisected landmasses in a futile attempt to stop the next wave of climate change refugees who had nowhere else to go. So many millions of people far below them. If the *Atalanta* didn't make it, all those lights would darken.

Naomi braced herself, using a rail as a foothold so the torque wouldn't twist her around with the wrench. Each connection had a dozen smaller bolts in turn, and each took at least a hundred turns to loosen. They pocketed each bolt in an empty container so they wouldn't be floating within the vicinity of the craft when they left. Before long, her hands hurt despite the padding of the gloves. Sunset brought back the night and she cooled again despite the EMU's protection. She adjusted the temperature of her suit, using the mirrors at her wrists to read the backward-printed controls. Her elbow joints grew stiff.

She and Lebedeva finished their first connection at the same time. Four each to go.

Naomi pulled herself to the next one, grunting. The second one seemed to take even longer. Were people down there even now prepping a rocket to launch? Was the Gateway a hub of activity, as they calculated how long it'd take them to travel to the other side of Earth's orbit? Another capsule could attach to the hub or the spare dock on the *Atalanta*. Helmeted men arriving to let them know their time was up.

They moved on to their third.

Naomi and Lebedeva gave regular updates of their actions. Valerie or Hixon responded with further instructions. Naomi's awareness zoomed in on those little bolts, focusing on nothing else but vanquishing yet another one.

"Mission finish ETA twenty minutes," Lebedeva said.

"Good," came Valerie's curt reply.

Naomi kept twisting, willing her fingers to move faster. Four out of five of her main connections. Everything hurt. She swivelled her head towards Lebedeva, who was already on her fifth connection. Naomi grimaced and braced herself against the handrail, turning the torque again. And again.

"Your readings are blipping a little, Lovelace. Glove check," Valerie said.

Naomi finished the fourth bolt. She released the wrench,

letting it float near her chest. She wriggled her fingers, willing sensation back to the tips.

Space debris was sharp, and even though the craft was new, it'd be easy for a small meteorite's impact to leave a rough patch, despite shielding. A snag could cause a tear, not deep enough to cut a finger, but enough to compromise the suit. The back of her gloves looked fine. She twisted her palms and felt a stab of adrenaline.

"You see it?" Naomi asked, staying steady. "Small tear on the left ring finger."

"Check it's patching," came Valerie's reply.

Panicking about the fact there was a hole in her suit while in space would do nothing except make her use her oxygen faster. Work the problem. Find the solution.

She stared hard at the tear, at the readout displays on the small screen on her right wrist. Slight wobbles.

Naomi's spacesuit was brand new. No one else had worn it aside from testing. The outer layer was fitted with a new material that would theoretically heal itself. It was meant to detect the oxygen in the event of a minor puncture and release a resin to seal it.

It wasn't the first time Naomi had thought she would die.

—She wakes up to flames. Calls out for her mother and breathes in smoke. Falls to her hands and knees. Can't see. Feels her way across the room, hoping she crawls further from the flames instead of right to them. The heat has cracked the tiles of the kitchen. Blisters form on her hands and knees. She staggers out into the warm, dark night, furred with fire, rolling on the remnants of her front lawn to put out the searing heat licking up her legs, her arms—

The pressure dipped again, the readout doing another scan. Was that a glimmer of blue around the tear of her glove?

—Most of her hair has burned away, the scent acrid and chemical. The silver blanket the paramedics gave her crinkles. Burn gel is smeared over her face, her hands, her legs, her feet. Firefighters are like ants staring up at burning logs. Droplets of water from the hoses catch the light as they fight the flickering yellow and orange. The roof caves in, sending sparks into the sky. She feels the burst of heat on her raw, exposed skin. Her throat is a pulsing coal, red and hot. Her mother stumbles across the singed grass a few minutes later, almost untouched by fire.

Her father never came out—

Naomi wriggled her glove. The scan completed.

"It's sealed," Naomi said, even as Hixon gave a shout from the bridge as she spied the readouts.

"Finish the job, Lovelace," Valerie said, as if she were any other member of the crew.

Lebedeva drifted over to her and the last connection to the hub. Wordlessly, the cosmonaut put her wrench to one of the bolts, and Naomi took a deep breath and tried to do the same. She twisted slower, keeping the ring and pinkie fingers of her left glove out of commission. Lebedeva did most of the work of the last bolts, but then finally—finally—the ship was free.

"Return to ship," Valerie said.

Naomi secured the wrench in the toolbelt at her waist and pulled on the tether, gripping the handrails as hard as she dared with her damaged glove.

"You take the lead," the cosmonaut instructed.

Naomi turned her back on the hub, kept her eyes on the

white hull, focusing on where each hand should go. The Earth still swirled beneath them, night fully fallen. She could see the moon, a grey-white orb, waning gibbous, hovering over the curvature of the Earth. Still so far away, even from up here.

They took the same route back, and at the bridge, Hart floated to the window and pressed her palms to the quadruple-paned glass, a grin splitting her face. Naomi gave a salute, and Lebedeva touched her gloved hand to Hart's bared one, separated by the tempered acrylic planes, in a high five before moving on.

Naomi pushed herself into the airlock first. Her suit pressure had dipped again, just a little. Naomi was light-headed—was it damage or simply the pure oxygen and adrenaline? Lebedeva followed, shutting the latch and checking the seals.

The airlock filled with the usual levels of oxygen and nitrogen. Naomi kept her breathing slow and even. When it was safe, the airlock opened. Hart and Valerie entered. Hart worked on Lebedeva's suit and Valerie came to Naomi. She grasped Naomi's injured glove, inspected it critically. Pressed the blue-patched hole, which held.

"You live to fight another day," Valerie said. Did her voice give the tiniest catch?

"Let's get out of here," Naomi said.

She shed her armoured *Argo*.

Valerie connected the life support to the wall stand, keeping Naomi steadier. The gloves came off first, and Valerie gathered them into their storage bag. Naomi wore her cotton gloves underneath, and she tore them off, breathing a sigh of relief when she could clasp her bare palms together. She felt so cut off from her body while in a spacesuit. It was easy to imagine she'd find blackened fingertips from the rent in the suit once the skin was unveiled, even though the HUD showed no damage.

Valerie undid the helmet and Naomi twisted her head from side to side, revelling in the return of something as simple as peripheral vision. Of breathing normal air. Naomi was freed from the trousers. Awkwardly, she pulled her arms through and then shimmied out of the hard upper torso.

Next came the cooling garment, the head cap. And finally, she was free, in little more than cotton long johns threaded through with the plastic cooling and heating tubes, soaked through with sweat.

As Valerie finished storing the suit, Naomi floated to her quarters, thankful they'd already claimed cabins when down on the ground. It was as small and cramped as she expected, but she barely took it in before shucking her clothes. She ran a hand along the faint scars on her legs from long ago burns. The rest of her skin was smooth save for the skin on her forearms where she'd crawled across the tiles. She changed into her new uniform of dark blue, fitted coveralls. Men's sizes—she had to roll up the sleeves and ankles. She'd hem them later. There, alone, she let herself curl into a ball in mid-air, clasping her hands to her chest, squeezing her eyes shut. The adrenaline ebbed. Her limbs shook, the sweat on her skin cooling, leaving her clammy. She thought of fire and a smoke-scorched throat.

She let go, slapped her cheeks lightly, and met the others on the bridge. Hixon had been busy. The *Atalanta* was nearly ready for launch.

Valerie entered scant seconds later, heading to the console and loading the comms down to Earth.

"Evan?" she asked. "You reading us?"

A pause. A crackle. "Hello from Earth, *Atalanta*." Evan's voice was faint. Naomi had first met Evan Kan when he was eleven, two years older than her, not long after she'd come to live with Valerie. He lived in Singapore with his father, usually ignoring Naomi when visiting his mother, sending messages to his friends back home in a blend of English, Chinese, and Malay.

Naomi imagined Evan there in the underground comms hub Valerie had built on one of her many pieces of land in southern California, hidden in a room of machines beneath satellite dishes and radio waves. By day, he'd still work as a postdoc research fellow at an immunology lab in La Jolla, but each night, he'd come back and sleep there.

He wouldn't be much help in an emergency. In a pinch, messages could be routed to his tablet, but they'd be more easily discovered. At least until Mars, he was Valerie's main contact on Earth, someone who could ferry through additional information if required and give them updates on how the world was reacting to what Valerie and her team had done.

"Status update?"

"Lockwood's rocket is taking off in half an hour, tops. Gateway will send another craft just after if there are any issues from the ground. You better split." Naomi had slowed them down with her minor suit malfunction.

"Readying engines as we speak. They're pissed off down there, I take it?" Valerie leaned towards the window again, twisting her head in the direction of Washington DC. She bared her teeth in triumph.

"They'd skin you alive if they could. Get going. I'll send you a report later."

"On it. Over and out," Valerie said, cutting the call. "Strap in," she said to her crew. "Let's keep our skin."

Naomi made her way to her seat at the right hand of Valerie's captain chair. She buckled herself in tight.

Down on the surface there would be an emergency meeting of men in dark suits, red or blue ties, American-flag lapel pins. The chief of the Federal Aviation and Space Administration would be wishing he could shoot them down. The Army generals present would wish the same. Space wasn't quite militarised, though it was on the way. Any missiles were automated, designed for incoming threats, not retaking a stolen, parked spaceship. Theoretically, they could shoot the *Atalanta* down, but the five women were betting that they'd baulk at wasting the amount of money that had been invested in the craft. Higher-ups in NASA would be grim-faced and nervous, wondering if anyone's job was on the line. President Cochran himself might even be there. All of them realising a group of women had screwed them over.

The sun angle shifted, painting the cockpit golden, shadowing the women's faces. As the engines blared to life, Valerie started ticking tasks off on her fingers. "Take a little jaunt to Mars and its shiny new warp ring. Fold space and time. Travel ten and a half light years. Establish a hardy colony on an alien planet. Wait for Earth to build the ships to start ferrying people across. Save humanity. Sounds doable enough, right?"

Her laugh echoed through the bridge as the ship coiled in on itself. The orbit gave them a 17,000 mile head start and they slungshot out into the stars.

They didn't scream this time. It was different to leaving the Earth in the capsule. Quieter, smoother, and so much more final. Soon the planet beneath them would be nothing more than a memory.

Naomi locked eyes with Valerie, who held her head up. Beatific as a saint, she smiled.

"It's time to find our world."

CHAPTER FOUR

4 Days After Launch

122 Days to Mars

245 Days to Cavendish

No amount of training or simulation could have prepared Naomi for the *Atalanta*.

The engines were so quiet. She hadn't anticipated how odd it would be to walk along the corridor of the centrifugal ring of the ship and its artificial gravity. It felt flat enough as she walked past the closed, white doors—here were the sleeping quarters, there the med bay. She patted the door of the greenhouse as she passed it. The canteen, the rec room—fully outfitted with virtual reality for much needed variety and stimulation in downtime—the gym, and the observation room, which served as a second rec room, office, or meeting room.

The floor curved up at the end of the hallway. A perfect circle that would align with the warp ring, forever turning above the static, gravity-less main body of the ship. Once they arrived at the ring, it'd be a push of the engines, a pulse of negative energy, and they'd bend space and time. The Alcubierre drive made possible and concrete. They'd either slow down on the other side of Mars after the test jump, or they'd die horribly.

"It'd be painless," Hixon assured them, sipping her third cup of lukewarm tea. No boiling water allowed. As second in command, she got up before the rest of them, going through and assigning them their daily tasks. That left Valerie more time to strategise and design the base on Cavendish.

"Liar," Naomi pointed out mildly, sprinkling some of their precious stock of brown sugar over her instant oatmeal. If they sped past their destination, they'd be stranded until their food ran out. Not quick or painless unless they chose to help things along.

"To be determined in one hundred and twenty-two days," Hixon said, far too cheerily. If they survived the test jaunt, it'd be another five days' travel back to the ring for the proper jump to Cavendish.

Naomi's new quarters had all the personality of a hospital room. A tiny bunk, only big enough for one. Hart and Hixon had two adjoining cabins and turned one into a bedroom, both the mattresses side by side on the floor. Each cabin had a few cupboards for storage. A miniature sink. A teeny desk and chair. Everything white, pale blue or grey. Naomi had lived in some bare studios in her time, but this was like living on a boat.

She kept the snow globe Valerie had given her next to her bed, stuck down with some magnets just in case gravity ceased. Valerie had taken hers too and given Naomi a conspiratorial smile about it.

Naomi had brought a small art kit with her, and in her scant downtime used too much of the precious spacecraft-approved paints brushing leaves, berries, and twisted tangles of green vines on to the fronts of cupboards, around handles, on the corner of her desk, the pocket near the bed where she stored her tablet. It was a way to let her mind drift after a long day at the lab. Valerie would think it a waste of time when she saw it, or wryly tell her she was defacing government property. But Naomi wasn't the one who had concocted a plan to steal it.

Once they landed on Cavendish, provided they survived, the outer ring of the ship would be broken down to form the base of the new colony as they sent back word to Earth and waited for them to finish building the ships that would ferry humanity across. Naomi would grow food both in the original greenhouse and—with luck—outside in Cavendish soil and underneath the Cavendish sun. She may as well get used to her cabin. She'd be sleeping in it for years.

Valerie had given the team the same spiel as everyone on Earth—Cavendish was an unpopulated planet. No sign of animals larger than microfauna. Naomi didn't expect little green or grey men with bulbous eyes and misshapen heads, of course. But Cavendish was not barren or dead; it was full of tiny photosynthetic organisms creating oxygen. Water. Sun. Bacteria. All the ingredients for life.

Even if there were no signs of animal life larger than a few cells—and who's to say they weren't just better at hiding from probes and scans than they'd thought?—life was stubborn. The panspermia theory postulated that interstellar dust, meteors, and comets throughout the universe could pepper organic matter on other planets. Perhaps the same dust that helped Earth on its way had scattered across the surface of Cavendish.

Naomi's first job would be working with Hart to ensure the planet didn't harbour unknown pathogens and parasites that could wipe humanity (and their food supply) out as soon as they arrived. That the crops they planned to grow wouldn't become invasive and unbalance the ecosystem. Or that the bacteria lurking within humans' own guts, their skin, their breath, wouldn't do the same to the planet around them. The complex feedback loops that make up a planet could easily be knocked into a configuration that could threaten human life rather than support it. If the last hundred years should have taught humanity anything, it was that planets were more delicate than most people thought.

Even if life wasn't skittering away from the probes and the planet was nothing but sea, sand, rocks, and benign microorganisms just beginning their own evolutionary experiments with multicellularity, that didn't mean life, intelligent or otherwise, couldn't one day evolve over the next million years. Humanity's arrival would at best nudge it in a particular direction, and at worst disrupt it entirely.

But humanity's arrival meant their survival.

Cavendish was like the Earth long before the dinosaurs. Plants developed first in the water then moved to land. Cavendish had algae and fern-like or moss-like plants, but few early trees like gymnosperms. Naomi planned to start cultivating crops as soon as she arrived. Earth plants would therefore come in to fill the niche that Cavendish plants could one day fill. Naomi would essentially help the planet jump many evolutionary steps. None of them truly knew the long-term ramifications of that.

Naomi twisted open one of the hatches in the corridor. There were passages in the spokes connecting the centre of the ship with the corridor ring. As soon as she entered the shaft and began to descend the ladder—although who knew which way was truly up or down on a rotating ring in space? Her feet grew lighter, until near the bottom (top?) she could float towards the heart of the ship. She had to move slowly, to let her blood pressure and ear canals adjust to the shift.

Down in the main body of the ship was the bridge, the storage, and the bodies.

Naomi pushed off the ground, swimming through the air and making her way to the storage bay. She needed a few supplies for the lab, but mostly she wanted an excuse to float again, even if it meant entering what everyone on board save Valerie had started dubbing the Crypt.

They had discovered their surprise guests almost immediately after launch. Five cryogenically frozen members from NASA, installed by Lockwood when they took over the contract.

Their second dinner on board the *Atalanta*, the five women had gathered at the round table of the canteen to properly discuss the backup crew, all a little green around the gills. Seasickness was one thing—space sickness quite another. It'd taken most of the first day for gravity on the corridor ring to activate, and longer for the crew to acclimatise. Hart had been the worst affected, followed by Naomi, who had thrown up into waste bags, hoping the plastic held. Hixon and Lebedeva had stomachs of steel, evidently, and Naomi suspected Valerie had felt queasy but would never show it.

"I'm just as surprised as you are," Valerie had said about the appearance of their unexpected stowaways. "Though I shouldn't be. It makes sense logistically. I had it in an earlier version of the plans myself, but it was nixed for being too expensive and too heavy. Guess they gave Lockwood a last boost." She'd made a sour face.

Hixon had twirled a strand of limp pasta on her fork.

"Can we send them back? Or drop them off on Mars?" Hart had asked.

Valerie had shaken her head. "We're stuck with them until Cavendish, sadly. Can't send cryopods on the launch shuttle—and we need that for ferrying parts down to the surface once we arrive. We don't have enough spare food to send 'em back defrosted anyway." A pointed look at Naomi.

"I'm on it." Naomi had put her fork down, despite her plate being half full. The chemical aftertaste turned her stomach. They had limited astronaut rations, but they wouldn't last long.

"So looks like they're with us until the bitter end. Worst-case, we can hold 'em hostage if Earth ends up being difficult," Valerie had said with a too-bright smile.

"It won't come to that," Hart had said sharply.

"Course not. Everyone down there is all bark, no bite. Not like we'd actually hurt them. But they wouldn't know that, now, would they? The think pieces say I want to kill all men anyway." Valerie had waved her fork before sticking it in the silver pouch and stabbing a piece of barely warm vat-grown beef covered in thick, globular gravy. She'd been too impatient for a plate.

Lebedeva watched them all, eating her food in steady, even bites. "They are just bodies." She had given a shrug, lips turning down.

"Easy for you to say," Hixon had said. "You don't know them. Not like us. And especially not like some of us."

Naomi had kept chewing, eyes on her plate.

She'd had to come see them. Down in the Crypt, the light was dim, the main body of the ship cooler than the ring.

Naomi shivered and made her way to the storage containers. She passed over the quiet robots, powered down and waiting for their moment once they arrived on Cavendish to help them build the settlement. Her mother's inventions had provided the seed money that had turned Hawthorne into the multi-industry conglomerate it'd become. Naomi grabbed a spare LED lamp and then turned towards the cryopods.

They glowed blue in the darkness. Wrapping the cable of the lamp around her wrist, she moved closer.

Perhaps Valerie had also nixed the plans for the cryopods because she simply hadn't wanted to admit the danger of this mission: that if one of them died, they needed someone else to replace them. It was why now the women were on board, training continued, all of them learning from the others. Naomi would take on medical training from Hart. Not long after they'd taken off, Hart had walked Naomi through all the medication in their stores. What they were, what each was for. The proper doses for local anaesthetic, morphine, antibiotics. Making sure Naomi knew how to prep syringes and find veins to take blood or IVs. She'd made Naomi take her own blood every day for a week, conducting different tests on the samples, until Naomi could stick a needle in her own vein without hesitation.

Hart was learning more about piloting from Hixon and engineering from Lebedeva, and Valerie was teaching Hixon more about robotics in return for gaps in her mathematical abilities. And so on. Just in case.

The pods were laid out like coffins paned with glass, the inhabitants within little more than murky shapes in the liquid nitrogen. The readings on the panels on the outside of their cold coffins glowed red against the blue.

Technically, the *Atalanta* crew were guilty of abduction in addition to their myriad other crimes. The news had leaked to Earth, Valerie said, and Cochran's media bots were adding to the fury and fervour of reports on them just as he'd wished. They must be calling for the women's heads. Hixon had started referring to their escape as grand theft spaceship, which had brought some half-hearted smiles.

The backup crew had been selected from a shortlisted lottery of NASA active astronauts. Naomi, Hart, or Hixon had worked with everyone chosen. Colleagues, bosses, friends, more. At least if they came with them to Cavendish and woke up, maybe it wouldn't be as lonely.

Five men with similar skills and expertise. Unlucky enough not to be the main crew, which must have hurt their pride. What would they think if they knew that, compared to the five men stranded back on Earth, they were the lucky ones?

Lebedeva's analogue was Devraj Chand. Naomi hadn't worked with him directly, but he'd been at drinks after work a few times. She remembered him being very tall, polite, and quiet except for the occasional cutting remark that would make everyone blink and sit up and pay attention. Very fond of a pun.

The flight surgeon backup was Ryan Webb. He was blandly good-looking, brown hair and eyes, firm handshake. He'd looked after her health in her time at NASA. His specialism was internal medicine, like Hart, but without the same level of psychological expertise, which was another potential flaw in both the original proposed crew and the five men before her. Few had the same balance of skill as Valerie's choices. It was why she'd picked them.

The military test pilot and mechanical engineer was Josh Hines. He was one of those men that harkened back to the early days of astronauts, those Mercury boys with their swagger and machismo, who would drag race down freeways in the desert after half a bottle of Jack just to prove they could. A man's man, a little too familiar. He'd kept trying to flirt with Naomi and been very confused when she proved immune to his charms.

Dennis Lee was Naomi's own double. Another botanist, one of the team that had developed the strain of algae they'd be using in the greenhouse both for food and life support. It was Lee who had figured out the best place to store water would be in the hull of the ship to provide additional cosmic radiation shielding.

Dennis was the one she knew second-best. They'd worked together for two years at NASA, side by side, developing those in-jokes borne out of close proximity and long days in a lab that smelled of pond scum and bleach. He'd done consulting work for Valerie on her company Haven, as well. She drifted closer, peering at the blur where his head must be. He had a face Naomi could only describe as mobile—always on the verge of a laugh, a smirk, a frown. She had never seen him still.

And then the last one, the backup leader of the mission. He was such a celebrity, that First Man of Mars, that Naomi was surprised they hadn't put Cole Palmer on the main team to spearhead the mission like he had for Ares over a decade previously. His face had been familiar to her before she'd ever met him in person, his wide smile beaming at her from news segments, advertisements, the cover of his memoir in a bookstore. Even features, auburn hair, startling dark eyes. Those broad shoulders and tapered waist, his astronaut's helmet usually propped jauntily in one arm or against a hip. If someone were to build a man to be the face of space exploration, he'd be it.

"Hello, Cole," Naomi said, putting her hand on the cool glass, tapping it once. "You've looked better."

But he and the other frozen bodies were silent, waiting to be rekindled on a new world.

When she'd taken off and left Earth, she'd thought that'd meant she'd left her ex-husband behind.

CHAPTER FIVE

2.5 Years Before Launch

Catalina Island, California

Catalina Island rose before them.

Naomi clung to the handrail of the Hawthorne yacht as they passed the sea wall. It'd been built years ago to protect the island from harsh storm waves and rising tides. The rich had complained it blocked the views of Los Angeles, but the smog usually took care of that.

They docked in Avalon Bay as morning lengthened to noon. Naomi strode down the gangway after Valerie, her legs only a little unsteady beneath her.

White sails peppered the turquoise of the water. Already it was too warm, the air hot and close. Tourists decked out in hats and shades wandered the beach, lingering beneath the squat palm trees, the scrub-dotted hills of the island rising beyond the chintzy store fronts of the promenade.

Perched at one of the edges curving into the harbour was the Catalina Casino, with its rounded walls and its Moorish-inspired columned windows and terracotta roof. In a few hours, it'd be the site of Hawthorne's charity dinner. Ostensibly the dinner was to support climate change refugees, but it was also a means for Valerie to crow about Project Atalanta. To wine and dine the higher-ups in government and private companies to convince them to offer more funding for completion of her vision for Cavendish. The only viable long-term solution for humanity, she was certain, even if the men in suits didn't believe her yet.

It'd been six months since Naomi had moved back from windswept Scotland to sun-baked Los Angeles. Valerie had offered Naomi her old room, but she'd rented a studio near the office in Pasadena instead. She liked walking back home after the sun had set. The warm, muggy streets were cooler, quieter.

Back at Hawthorne, she wove together trellises of plants, a loom of lively green, or tended endless, long, skinny tubes of algae. Testing them, peering at samples beneath microscopes, seeing how to make them better and resilient enough for space and Cavendish. It meant a lot of experimenting with light and nutrient environments. She was developing a toolkit for genetic modification so that the algae could also be altered once they arrived on Cavendish. That way, they could survive with but not demolish the native algae-like cells already present in the planet's oceans.

The project was already behind schedule and over budget. Valerie appeared unconcerned, funnelling more of her seemingly endless personal fortune into the company and convincing other rich people to reach deeper into their pockets.

Valerie had insisted on making a day of it in Catalina, but as they wandered the shops and had lunch, Naomi was too lost in her head to enjoy it properly. Her latest crop of a strain of hardy, fast-growing sweet potatoes was proving promising.

She'd harvested and sliced them yesterday. Baked them into chips, sprinkled with oil, salt, and rosemary, chewing them slowly. They'd been good and grown entirely in soil that matched iron-rich soils on Cavendish.

They strolled along the beach, pausing at one of the breaks, their legs dangling above the water. Naomi's scars were bared to the sunlight. The Casino squatted before them. Valerie passed her a tub of pistachio ice cream—her favourite, though of course it wasn't made with anything resembling the real nut since the crops had failed. They sat in near-silence and took off their filter masks long enough to eat. The sugar and cold cream melted on Naomi's tongue as she looked over the bay to the concrete sea wall. It did rather spoil the view.

"You nervous?" Naomi asked.

"Never," Valerie said, sucking on her biodegradable spoon.

When they returned, hours later, the Catalina Casino was lit up from within like a jewel. Their dinner would be in the largest circular ballroom in the world. It had never been a place of gambling—the word technically meant "meeting place." People had not even drunk alcohol on the premises until after World War II. Built in the 1920s by Wrigley, of chewing gum fame, it was all art deco opulence. Tiles over the grand, curved entranceways depicted underwater scenes. Naomi paused, staring up at the larger-than-life, stylised mermaid. Her red hair streamed upwards like the seaweed in currents. It was as if she floated in zero G. The siren held her hands out in welcome, hips hinged dramatically to one side, legs morphing mid-thigh from pale skin to blue scales. The mural was muted, pastel colours save for the bright pop of a seahorse or a trio of small fish swimming along the seabed.

Valerie swept forward, a vibrant dawn to Naomi's more subdued midnight. Her bodice was red, segueing to orange at the waist and down to yellow and white at the hem. She wore red lipstick, her hair slicked back to a smooth cap. Her ears and neck were bare of jewels. She never saw the need to condense her wealth into hard rocks of carbon. She made rockets instead.

The ballroom was glorious, with its rose-hued walls, black and white cameos in relief above the windows lining the room beneath the scalloped ceiling and Tiffany chandeliers. They were the last to enter. Valerie loved to make an entrance.

Naomi made her way to her seat, annoyed at her dress—a sequined, dark blue affair, the tight skirt hobbling her into small, heeled steps. She'd never liked these fancy soirees. Valerie had dragged her to more than her fair share as a child. Naomi wished she was back at the lab. With a resigned sigh, she looked for her ex-husband. She'd rolled her eyes when she'd seen his name on the guest list. He never turned down an opportunity to come to these things.

Cole Palmer was seated halfway across the ballroom. His head was turned, and he leaned close to his new wife to whisper something in her ear.

Mel Palmer had the same colouring as Naomi, but aside from that they didn't look much alike. Her dark hair was twisted into a chignon and a sapphire glittered at her throat. They must have been married a year and a half by now. No longer newlyweds. They had a newborn boy at home. Mel had taken the governmental payout, quit her job as a journalist to stay at home with the child for five years. That was the end of that; in five years, she'd be too out of the game to pick up where she'd left off. Naomi didn't blame her—with the astronomical costs of childcare and the way women were being passed over anyway, Mel had chosen what many other women did when they birthed their first—and, because of the high subsequent children taxes, often only—child.

Naomi was meant to hate Mel, she supposed. Call her a man-stealing harpy or some other epithet. But Mel didn't take anything that wasn't already lost.

The Palmers made a handsome couple. She still remembered the first time she'd seen an interview of him on a screen, when she was twenty two and he thirty, fresh-faced and just returned from his mission to the nearest planet. The lines around his eyes were a little deeper now that he was nearing his late thirties, and there was a tad more silver sprinkled through his hair. He looked the same as he had the last time she saw him three years ago and she'd walked right out of his life. Cole caught her eye, not at all surprised to see her, and flashed that smile that had once worked so well on her.

Naomi dutifully curled her lips, her mind swirling with murky memories, both sweet and bitter. It'd have been easier, perhaps, to still be the one sitting next to him. Too late to wonder. Too late for regret.

Naomi twisted in her seat, the dress stiff, and introduced herself to the others at her table. She knew the Hawthorne employees, Liam and Bryony. Liam had the hangdog eyes of a beagle, and Bryony was over six feet tall and delighted in towering over others. Bryony was a doctor, working on astronaut health and immunology, and Liam was in public relations. The strangers were a hard-faced man from the Environmental Protection Agency named Bram and his much kinder-looking wife, Theresa.

Naomi spoke to Bryony primarily, as they'd at least worked together a few times. Bryony's eyes were bright, shining. "We're getting closer," she said. "Can't you feel it?" She'd always been an ardent supporter of Valerie's.

Naomi was spared from too much small talk when Valerie *ting*ed her fork against a glass, bringing the murmur of talk to a close. Valerie had taken her place at the head table.

"Welcome," she said, her voice carrying easily thanks to the acoustics of the room, "to the Hawthorne charity dinner. The proceeds tonight go to vital support services for those displaced by the growing pressure of climate change." A rough scattering of applause, a few smiles.

"I aim to help those in the here and now," Valerie continued. "But my vision has always been to the future. Fixing a root cause rather than slapping a band-aid over the symptom."

Some of the smiles in the audience dimmed. Naomi wondered how many people in the ballroom wearing designer suits and jewels actually gave anything resembling a crap for the refugees. People too poor to afford the subscription fees for a luxury like the internet, much less the even higher costs needed to live a comfortable life: dues to private police or firefighters or health insurance. So many lived in ramshackle housing little better than shanty towns. They didn't count as permanent addresses, so most couldn't register to vote. They were becoming increasingly invisible. Meanwhile, the people in this room showed up and donated pennies of their wealth to give the illusion they cared.

"We are working hard, at long last, to try and escape the damage we've done to Earth. First, we looked to the moon. Decades ago, men had taken their first steps there, which are still imprinted in the grey regolith. Robots went back next, and then humans added new footprints."

Naomi had grown up seeing photos of the base of bubbles like an unnatural growth on the pockmarked face of the moon.

"But we abandoned the moon when we'd realised how expensive it was for so little gain. So we turned our attention to Mars, inhabiting it with the descendants of Curiosity, Rover, Perseverance, Spirit.

"NASA, in conjunction with China, Russia, Europe, and Japan are doing excellent work on their terraforming of Mars. But that project will take decades, maybe even up to a century, and, frankly, we don't have that long."

A couple of titters and whispers, which Valerie ignored. She left the table and held her arms out once she reached the centre of the ballroom. Projections turned the pale scalloped shell of the ceiling into a map of the Milky Way. Gasps and murmurs made Naomi hide her smirk. Always one for dramatics, Valerie, but Naomi had to admit it was a good show. The people in the seats needed to be entertained enough to reach into their pockets.

The view pinpointed one star out of the thousands spackled across the ceiling. Formerly Epsilon Eridani, known colloquially as Ran, after the Norse goddess of the sea. Ten and a half light years away. The star was K2 class and eighty per cent the size of Earth's sun. It was cooler and would glow orange in the sky rather than yellow-white. The star was young, a sprightly billion years old, but it had taken half that long for Earth to develop life. It had taken Earth four billion years for something to crawl out of the ocean and colonise forests and jungles.

"Cavendish. Our new world. Our frontier."

Years ago, they'd found a gas giant, Aegir, named after Ran's husband, the god of the ocean. Aegir was too large for life—akin to Jupiter. The smaller planet was hidden behind it in the Goldilocks zone, or the circumstellar habitable zone. Not too hot, not too cold. The right temperature for water to be liquid on the surface given the right atmospheric pressure. For life to potentially grow.

The planet was brilliant blue and green, covered with swirls of clouds. Yet instead of grand continents, there were a few just big enough to be deserving of the name. Smatterings of smaller islands dotted the oceans, though plenty of them were at least the size of Great Britain. A planet of archipelagos. Its moon was even a similar size, creating tides in those alien seas. It had oxygen and rich biodiversity in the early stages of life, well enough established to have stable elemental cycles that could sustain agriculture. Humans could theoretically live there.

"I won't bother you with a list of the technical details, but Cavendish is closer to its star than Earth, so a year lasts one hundred and seventy-eight days. The sun is dimmer, but still warm enough to keep temperatures far more constant and habitable than Earth has become."

The view flickered to an artist's rendition of what it would be like to stand on the surface of Cavendish, overlooking the shore of one of the islands. It could be Earth, save for the fact that the sun was dimmer, more orange-red, and 1.6 times larger in the sky, for the smaller star of Ran had to be closer to heat Cavendish enough for life.

Naomi glanced at the audience. They'd all heard of Cavendish, of course, but it'd been a nebulous thing, still out of reach. With that artwork, they could imagine themselves standing on the shore. Free from a filter mask, from haze in the sky from smog or fire. It looked lush, primordial—like Earth back in the Jurassic era, before humans had come along to interfere.

The projection blinked to show our solar system, then Earth, rotating gently in a near mirror image to Cavendish, a sickly older sibling. Valerie gave the audience time to take in the differences between the worlds before zooming back out to a view of both Earth and Mars.

"Until relatively recently, we never thought we'd actually be able to journey to our neighbour stars and planets. Even Alpha Centauri seemed decades away. But with Hawthorne and NASA working together to harness negative energy and demonstrating that the Alcubierre drive is a workable concept, the universe is at our fingertips."

Whispers rustled around the room, less aggressive than before. Another flick of Valerie's manicured nails and the ceiling showed the warp ring around Mars, still under construction. The materials had been mined from Mars or nearby asteroids, built in situ on the planet by Hawthorne robots, then ferried up to the construction hub.

"I'm sure most of you here have been following the reports," Valerie continued. "The construction of our *Atalanta* interstellar spacecraft is ahead of schedule. Successful jumps of unmanned probes elsewhere in the solar system, and then out to Ran once we accurately calculated where we'd want a spaceship to appear on the other end of the jump. We've proved we can bring back biomatter from Cavendish, and we have successfully transported Earth specimens through the ring and back again."

Valerie neglected to mention that the first rounds of rats under Hawthorne supervision also returned dead as doornails.

Like Laika, who overheated to death above the Earth in the 1960s, another stepping stone in the space race. The plants hadn't fared much better. The soil and seeds from Cavendish had arrived still viable—a highlight of Naomi's career a few years ago, when she'd last worked at Hawthorne.

Yet they would need Earth plants to survive on Cavendish as it had no food crops. Every experiment they conducted with soil and light that mirrored Cavendish levels had failed. For months, the seedling kept dying.

Fortunately, following the changes in gene expression patterns over the time it took the last round of seedlings to die had allowed Dr. Dennis Lee to come up with a series of modifications to their developmental pathways. These accounted for the dimmer light and differences in iron concentrations and pH in the Cavendish soil. It was only the last few tests that had proved promising, so hopefully once they landed on the tantalising, lush, untapped world, they wouldn't slowly starve to death.

"The maths and the physics check out," Valerie continued. "We've done all the testing, but time keeps relentlessly ticking along—we haven't cracked time travel yet." A grin, a pause for a few chuckles.

"With your assistance, your shared vision of this future, we can finish the construction on the *Atalanta*. We can go to Cavendish within three to five years. Imagine—within a decade, all of humanity could have a fresh start. No more refugees. Just a world where we all thrive."

More murmurings. Valerie held her palms up, placating. "Naturally, I'm not suggesting we abandon Earth or Mars entirely. We can continue our efforts to undo the damage already done here and make our nearest neighbour habitable.

But it'll be a damn sight easier if not as many of us are around, pumping more carbon dioxide into Earth's atmosphere. Why have one or two or—God forbid—zero worlds, when you can have three?"

She beamed out at the audience. "We won't waste Cavendish. We will cherish it, and not repeat our past mistakes. I haven't been shy about my desire to spearhead the mission there. I want to bring you Cavendish. So let me help you. Let's save ourselves."

The ballroom erupted in applause. Among the clapping, Naomi spotted the still doubtful looks, the whispers out of the corners of mouths. Yet she also saw people gazing up at Valerie with wet eyes, clapping hard. Valerie didn't need to convince everyone in this room. She only needed to convince enough to finish building that ship.

Valerie kept her head high. As if there had never been protests verging on the violent when she showed up for speeches. As if countless think pieces hadn't called her little more than a pop-science feminist talking head. A woman with more money than sense. They said she was wasting a fortune on far-off possibilities rather than making a difference to the people on this rock. Naomi had feared for Valerie's safety a time or two. It'd only take one conference where security was too lax. It'd only take one angry man with a gun. But Valerie never seemed bothered. She was someone who photosynthesised limelight and controversy.

Cavendish remained on the ceiling, full and bright, a circle around the chandeliers.

Valerie made her way back to her seat, and the food arrived. It was good—as it should be, if people were paying upwards of thirty thousand dollars for a seat at the table. Wild mushroom soup, bacon-wrapped chicken—all vat grown—and scalloped potatoes. Fresh green salad, cold and crisp. Poached pears in wine with vegan Chantilly cream for dessert. Ingredients that were increasingly dear, not that anyone in this ballroom was struggling to afford it. Most of the people in this room probably still ate meat regularly—actual meat, grown on the hoof or claw.

Naomi ate her food, kept up her idle chit-chat. Her gaze would sometimes stray across the room, snag on the way Mel's hand rested on Cole's forearm. The softness of her smile as she looked at her husband. Naomi felt a brief pain, dulled by two years. Something like yearning, like relief. Naomi was not the woman she thought she would be when she married Cole. She was someone else. Not better, not worse. Different.

The waiters cleared the tables after the meal to ready the ballroom for the dancing. The guests clustered along the balcony, gazing out at the sunset over Avalon. Glasses of champagne, murmured conversation. Naomi slipped between it all, listening so she could report back to Valerie later. She sensed excitement, resentment. Many, she was sure, thought Valerie's goal would crumble and they'd relish the fall. They'd still pretend to support her vision. They'd run the Earth right into the ground, shrug, and live up on a privately constructed space station, gazing down at the world below them and sigh "isn't that a shame" before spearing another hors d'oeuvre and taking another glass of bubbly. She was annoyed at how much Hawthorne needed these sycophantic vultures to have a chance at their goal. To save everyone, not just the rich.

The glitzy attendees streamed back into the ballroom as the

stringed music began. Naomi took her time, nursing her drink, a wallflower near the rose-coloured walls. People paired off, the women's skirts belling as they swirled.

Cole and Mel danced, his hand on her waist. A night away from their child. Had they even been out since the baby's birth? The sitter or nanny would almost certainly be staying overnight, so this might be their first uninterrupted night's sleep in months. Or their first chance at privacy. She skittered away from that thought.

A year ago, seeing them would have ripped Naomi apart. Attraction still bloomed between her and Cole. It maybe always would. For all their faults, the physical connection had been one uncomplicated area of their marriage. When Cole met her eyes, she knew he felt it, too. She gave him a sardonic little salute, smirking when he was the one to look away first.

Valerie came over, bringing Naomi a new glass of champagne.

"Well done," Naomi said. "They're eating out of your hand."

Valerie surveyed the ballroom and gave a long, satisfied exhale. "They are, aren't they?"

By the end of the night, thanks to Valerie's charm offensive, there would be another round of investment. Mission accomplished.

They clinked glasses.

CHAPTER SIX

32 Days After Launch

94 Days to Mars

217 Days to Cavendish

The greenhouse was both the heart and the stomach of the ship.

When people think of space greenhouses, they think of them as more or less like the ones back on Earth. Or in science fiction films, an area of the ship that would essentially be an entire forest, with trees rising from soil on the ground, and false sunlight illuminating the trunks leading to the glorious glass ceilings that looked out on to the stars.

Naomi's domain was not green. It could be, if all the glowing LED lamps were turned off, and the normal pale lights throughout the rest of the ship turned on. Instead, everything glowed magenta. The combination of blue and red lights made the plants appear black as they soaked up the energy, nothing reflected. Naomi had long since started calling them her goth plants.

The lab was as small a footprint as possible to grow all that they needed. The walls were lined with two rows of glowing, horizontal glass tubes running across the wall in neat rows stacked from floor to ceiling, segmented every three feet so Naomi could slot the algae vials in and out as needed. She'd grown six batches of cyanobacteria so far, staggering the seven-day growth cycles.

She was often alone in her lab. Lebedeva would come in and check the hardware for the bioreactors or to service the harvester. The algae levels had to remain above a certain level, as they were part of the life support system, concentrating carbon dioxide from the air with machines and bubbling the CO_2-enriched air to the bioreactors. The algae grew faster as a result, which gave the ship a buffer on carbon dioxide and oxygen levels in the air.

Hart would be in more as the weeks progressed. Naomi knew plants, but Irene Hart understood bodies. Together, they'd conduct tests to ensure the five women on board were receiving adequate nutrition and had healthy gut flora. The walls and floors throughout the ship were already peppered with radiation detectors, which all showed normal levels so far. The shields were holding. But Hart would also run full biomedical scans to ensure that they wouldn't be riddled with cancer by Cavendish.

First, Naomi had to grow the food.

The GMO strains of spirulina were coming along nicely. She walked through the thin, purple corridor of reinforced glass tubes, checking the readings, taking down the segments with mature culture and putting them into the harvester machine that would turn them into pellets or powder. Mostly it created gummy nutriblocks the size and texture of Turkish delight but even more foul.

They could make a "savoury" flavour that tasted of a stale

pond, sometimes with added salt or chilli, or "sweet" flavours that were vaguely strawberry, vanilla, or cinnamon. Naomi had used some of the skills she'd learned back in undergrad, using vanillin or cinnamaldehyde, whose synthesis could be more or less automated in the nutriblock machine, as long as basic chemical supplies held out. They could continue synthesising more from the waste products of the algae itself once they reached Cavendish. Yet because it was still green and the wrong texture, and they had been unable to tone down the strong taste of spirulina without compromising its nutritional value, it was hard to associate the nutriblocks with any of the flavours.

Everyone was already tired of them, but it would account for seventy-five per cent of their diet. Pound for pound, algae was the most nutrient-dense food they'd found on Earth, full of protein with complete amino acids, some B vitamins, copper, iron, and omega fatty acids.

The rest of the lab was full of crops, to continue their research and provide the astronauts with some much-needed variety in their diet. Hydroponic greens—lettuce, spinach, bok choy—for crunch and texture. Small onions. A few herbs she'd tried adding to nutriblocks with quasi-disastrous results. The rosemary and peppermint ones in particular were like eating soap that had been left in stagnant water. Fruit was limited to actual strawberries, raspberries, blackberries, and tomatoes.

Some of her crops required soil pillows and mats. The left side of the lab had Earth soil and light conditions, and the right had Earth soil treated to mirror the nutrient and metal levels from the Cavendish probe samples, illuminated with Cavendish-level lights. She'd already planted the tubers like potatoes, sweet potatoes, and Jerusalem artichokes. Root vegetables such as beetroot and carrots—and they could eat their green tops, as well. She was attempting some dwarf strands of genetically modified wheat and rye, which grew particularly well in colder climates.

Naomi had already proved that Earth crops would grow in "Cavendish" soil back home, but on the *Atalanta* she'd grow crops at the same time, in the same amounts, and compare the Earth to the Cavendish specimens.

Over the years, Naomi had soaked up anything that would make her a viable astronaut candidate, but from early on, she'd loved plants the best.

She was bringing life to the inhospitable environment of space. This wasn't the first biome she'd created, but she knew the challenges of closed environments. Like everyone working in space horticulture, she'd studied Biosphere 2 and the challenges they'd faced in the early- to mid-nineties. A crew had volunteered to try and survive in a dome under the hot desert sun. At first, things had gone well enough. Then the bees died. Roaches appeared. A few times, those in charge of the project had had to pump oxygen into the enclosure, which was technically cheating, to stop those within from suffocating.

Everyone inside grew too thin, too hungry, bones stark against skin as they lost weight; chemicals that had been stored in their fat from pesticides they'd eaten had poisoned the air. They'd begun fighting. Friends became enemies. They grew depressed, irritable, hungry. The first mission lasted two years, but the second one was cancelled after less than a year. Those people could emerge, blinking, out into the hot desert, fresh air, life. If Naomi miscalculated, there was nowhere to hide. No reset button.

This type of long-scale isolation was called overwintering, named after long-term missions in the Antarctic. It'd been one of the main reasons Naomi had been so determined to go on her trip to the South Pole the summer before she graduated. She wanted to prove she'd be able to cope with that detachment from the rest of humanity.

She'd found the cold and the dark draining, as anyone would, and she mourned the fact that penguins could only be found in zoos. She'd also discovered pockets of pleasure. Drinking hot chocolate quick, before it cooled. The *aurora australis*. Keeping to her routine and finding her flow, the work its own form of meditation. Befriending her fellow scientists and playing board games to pass the endless nights. Picking up instruments and creating terrible but hilarious bands, with song lyrics full of science puns. Tips and tricks she'd take here on this ship. At least on board, it was warm.

Elsewhere on the *Atalanta*, all was clean, pristine, immaculate. In her lab, she could smell life, and the artificial sunlight almost felt real. The loamy scent of soil, the strong, oxidant tang of the spirulina. Once her work was done, she'd sit here, on her own, eyes closed, breathing it all in.

She'd allowed herself a small extravagance—zinnia seeds. They were small and light, and their life cycle was short. She touched the tiny sprouts with the tip of her finger. Once they bloomed, she'd take a couple to her room and feed them artificial white sunlight, so she'd be able to see the green stems and the orange flowers. Zinnias were one of the first plants grown on the ISS. They'd gone through the warp ring a few years ago and were officially the first interstellar flowers. The tomatoes and berries would bloom too, but it'd take longer.

Tucked within the cupboard of her lab, with backups down in the Crypt, were the seed vaults. Rows of three-ply foil packages, tidy and unassuming. They were backups in case her current crops failed completely, but they were also what they'd need on Cavendish. It was no Svalbard seed vault, that storage facility deep in the Nordic Arctic tundra, but it was still a mini ark of flora.

A tap at the door. Naomi stifled her annoyance at the interruption. Hart stuck her head into the lab.

"Mary, Mary, quite contrary. How does your garden grow?" she sang. On Earth, Hart had always worn mascara and dark red lipstick, her braids tied up into a high bun on the top of her head. With her short hair and bare face, she looked younger, almost vulnerable. But she'd seemed happy, these last few weeks. Space agreed with her.

"No silver bells or cockle shells," Naomi replied.

The smile stretched into a wide, white grin. "I just spent an hour in the observation room, staring out that window. Don't think I'll ever get tired of that view."

Naomi's face softened. She'd spent as much time in the observation room as she could get away with for the same reason. Spots of stars. Dark and endless. She'd fallen asleep curled up in the window ledge a few times. Woken up with a start.

"Dinner's in ten," Hart added.

"Can't wait," Naomi said without enthusiasm. The menu tonight was vat corned beef out of a packet, though they would be able to have a tiny salad of hydroponic lettuce to help freshen it up. Dessert was a strawberry nutriblock.

Naomi was isolating herself. Valerie or Hart would call her out on it soon. Space had been the goal, but she felt as though she moved through mud, her mind never clearing of fog. She kept thinking of Earth, wondering what she'd be doing now, almost as if she was mourning the life she'd elected to leave behind. If anyone else was doing the same, they knew better than to speak of it.

Naomi still felt nauseous, especially if she had to go down into the main body of the ship and lose her tenuous hold on gravity. As much as she'd loved floating weightless, the fear of retching up her breakfast in micogravity took the fun out of it. At night, strapped to her bed, all seemed steady enough, but her stomach still knew the ring rotated several times per minute, spiralling through the abyss towards their destination.

Naomi took a last look through her crops, running her fingers along their delicate stems and flat leaves. Promises she'd coaxed from seeds with light, water, warmth, air, and soil. She frowned, staring beyond the crops to the bioreactors against the far wall. A cluster of four cylinders began blinking, on and off, like a steady heartbeat. A sign that something within had gone wrong with the batch—too hot, too cold, a leak, or a contamination. As she watched, another two started flashing.

Naomi activated the comms panel. "Valerie?"

She'd anticipated problems from the crops, if anywhere. A plant infected with witches' broom, or fungus or aphids somehow getting through the contamination protocols. Algae was much easier to grow—especially the strand they'd engineered for space travel.

A crackle. "Lovelace." The use of her last name was a rebuke.

A reminder to keep to the command structure. No obvious favouritism that could lead to fractures in their group.

"Dr. Black," Naomi said, the slightest edge in her voice as another cylinder started flashing. "Houston, we have a problem."

CHAPTER SEVEN

42 Days After Launch

84 Days to Mars

207 Days to Cavendish

The batches of algae were leeching colour. In normal light they would have changed from a deep, verdant green to opaque and milky, announcing the algae was dead. It was happening quickly. Naomi would go to bed and return to the lab the next morning to find that viruses had exploded the cells within.

She'd flushed the first batch in case of infection—sending it out of the airlock instead of recycling it into fertiliser—sterilised the bioreactors, and grown a new batch from a fresh sample. It was holding, but its levels were still lower than she'd like. One of her older batches wasn't looking good either, and yet another showed normal growth and then sudden crashes. Lebedeva had double-checked the equipment, and all was functioning as it should. Temperatures were normal, nutrient feeds were good, and still batches were crashing in a matter of hours. So if it wasn't their environment, it was likely a virus. And that was not as easy to fix.

If it'd been the crops failing, it'd be a problem, but it'd mean all of their food would come from nutriblocks. If algae productivity dipped too low, it'd affect the bulk of their food and, of course, their life support.

Naomi was working until exhaustion, often falling asleep on the table. Her lab was no longer her quiet corner of the ship. Valerie would come in and narrow her eyes at the darkened cylinders full of cellular debris, as if she could bring them back to life with the sheer power of her glare.

Naomi put more of their healthy algae into the harvester. Out came more nutriblocks. They had enough food for an extra few weeks. They weren't at panic mode, not yet—Naomi had isolates of spirulina as well as a few types of chlorella in the vault that hadn't come into contact with the other strains—but she wanted to know what exactly was going wrong before she dug into her stores. If those isolates became infected, that was that. Endgame.

Naomi, with Lebedeva's help, centrifuged the cellular debris out of the dead culture and DNA-sequenced the remaining supernatant, which consisted mostly of the virus. So she had the virus isolated, at least.

Despite the stress, everyone else's space illness had passed. Naomi envied the others' easier shift from gravity to zero G if they went down to the bridge or the Crypt. Though they were all tense, they had found their rhythm. Hixon and Lebedeva checked the ship from top to bottom, working their way through systems diagnostics over the course of a few days only to start over again once they reached the end. Naomi would see them, heads together over some problem. Hixon would gesticulate wildly and Lebedeva would hunch her shoulders and focus.

Hixon and Valerie were working together to ensure they were on course as well as rechecking the Alcubierre theories, running simulation after simulation in the VR rec room. Hart helped Naomi with the crops while she battled the algae, kept tabs on everyone's health, and ran regular full physicals.

Valerie locked herself in the observation room, her de facto office, for hours at a time, working on urban planning for the landing site on Cavendish, building digital blueprint after blueprint. Catherine Lovelace had designed the robots and tech that led to many aspects of the spaceship thirty years on, but Valerie Black's first love had always been seeing how technology fitted into the larger whole. She loved designing buildings, cities, expanding Hawthorne into one of the few mega-companies with fingers in many industries. Tech, medicine, agriculture, distribution: so many tools that coalesced to help design a new base on another planet.

When she emerged, Valerie would flit through the spaceship, keeping an eye on everything. She sent word back to Evan every few days and asked for news updates and disseminated short reports to the crew.

Naomi was never sure if Valerie told them everything or filtered out the worst bits. The U.S. had tried to deny any responsibility, but the rest of the world wasn't looking too kindly on them. Under the Outer Space Treaty and subsequent amendments to it, NASA and Lockwood were responsible for the *Atalanta* by law even before they put it into orbit. The PR machine was in full spin; the women on board had made America look incompetent. Spaceship thieves, body snatchers. Scandalous enough to bolster sinking news-site hits.

"That's because they were inept!" Valerie had said, before snorting at an article. Conspiracy theories abounded. That the *Atalanta* was a distraction, so people would look up at the night sky rather than notice disappearing public money. Naomi had to admit, that one might hold water. Another theory she was less fond of, one that postulated that the U.S. had "allowed" the women to go because they didn't think it was actually safe enough yet for men. Writing the five of them off as bodies to be offered up on the altar of science.

"Horseshit," Valerie had added for good measure. "Then why did they put five men in the backup crew?"

Yet the article had reminded Naomi of something one of the Mercury 7 said in a press conference, when asked back in the sixties if there was room in the astronaut program for women. He'd cheesed it up and said they could have used a woman on the second orbital Mercury Atlas they had flown in 1961. In case they didn't get the joke, he went on to explain: "We could have put a woman up, the same type of woman, and flown her instead of the chimpanzee." The reporters had laughed.

"We'll send them a postcard from Cavendish," Hixon had drawled, but her eyes had flashed. Hart had taken her wife's hand, and Naomi had felt a pang at their intertwined fingers. Not jealousy, not quite, but a yearning for something as simple as touch, or falling asleep next to someone and letting the cadence of their breath lull her to sleep. She knew little of their relationship, other than Hart and Hixon had met in astronaut training—the last group to have gender parity in their ranks. They both applied to be on the Ares mission. When Hixon had gotten it and left Hart behind, it'd nearly been the end of them. Was it strange for Hart, to have Hixon outrank her as second in command?

Hixon rarely mentioned the Mars mission. If she did, it was only the relevant information to whatever task at hand they needed aboard the *Atalanta*. She never mentioned Cole, and Naomi never asked.

"There have been some protests and marches in support of us," Valerie had said, for a spot of good news. "They call us the Atalanta Five."

That had given them all a thrill. They all knew of the Mercury 13. In the mid-twentieth century, at the same time as the Mercury 7 had all the fame for being space flight pioneers, thirteen women had tested just as well if not better than the men on the aptitude tests. But they'd never reached space, even after bringing their case all the way to a congressional hearing. Eleven were still alive when Sally Ride was the first American woman in space in 1983. When Eileen Collins was the first woman to pilot the space shuttle in 1995, seven of them attended the launch, and ten attended her first command mission in 1999. Women had clawed their way into NASA only to be edged back out by the governmental policies that saw women as threats.

As Naomi wrapped up the nutriblocks—they had the unfortunate side effect of collecting any speck of dust in a five-foot radius—Valerie watched her work, leaning against the only spot of wall bare of bioreactors. Naomi could feel her stare as she watered the crops, which were thankfully doing all right. The Cavendish crops were peakier than the Earth ones, which was something to worry about once the problem of the algae was solved.

"Do you know what's wrong with our pond scum?" Valerie asked.

"Yep." Naomi grimaced. "It's a cyanophage."

"A virus?" Valerie asked, intrigued.

"Take a look." Naomi gestured to the microscope on the lab table. Valerie pushed her back, peering through the eye-piece.

"It's subtle, but it's there. It shouldn't have gotten past the checks." Teeny little cyanophages, with icosahedral heads and a little tail that had landed on the cell surface and pumped their DNA into the cell.

"I think we can probably bioengineer a fix. There's a good amount of stuff on cyanophages here on the drive, but not as much about genetically engineering algal resistance to this one specifically, and I need to double-check some data." She took a breath. "I also need to talk to Evan directly. His work in immunology means he might be able to help as well."

Valerie's eyebrows rose. "Volunteering to speak to Evan? Has hell frozen over? God, you used to be at each other's throats every goddamn holiday."

Naomi rolled her eyes. "We weren't that bad."

Valerie scoffed. "Sure. Came a time I thought one of you would end up killing the other one. Though I guess you ended up playing nice enough in college before you decided you hated each other again. Then I gave up."

"I see you trying to pry and I'm not falling for it, Dr. Black," Naomi said. "I'll send him some questions tonight, if that's all right."

Valerie's soft laugh was just shy of mocking. "Sure. After dinner. Ask him for anything you think might be useful. We'll only be able to talk to him until Mars, after all."

As Valerie turned the doorknob to leave, Naomi thrust out the bag of freshly-pressed nutriblocks. "These could hitch a ride to the kitchen with you."

Valerie wrinkled her nose, but she took one out of the bag and popped it in her mouth, grimacing and chewing. "So gross."

After the door slammed, Naomi's plastered smile fell.

"I have to talk to Evan," she said to the little zinnia flowers. "Fuck."

Naomi shifted on her chair in the VR rec room—the large console doubled as the main comms point. She hadn't spent much time in here, even as Valerie kept reminding her that yes, downtime was essential, algae emergency or not.

They could watch films or play a few games. They could also exercise in here instead of the gym, running in place and pretending they were jogging through forested trails or along the beach, the pixellated landscapes a pale stand-in for the real thing, even if the floors, walls, and ceiling were made with a flexible, programmable material that could raise false rock croppings or nearly whatever they desired.

Naomi put her fingers on the keypad.

> Atalanta: *Evan, it's Naomi. I'm going to send you the DNA sequence of the phage that I've isolated. First, can you search GenBank to figure out what phage this is by matching the genetic sequence to the ones on file? Then I'll need you to blast it against the database and tell me which receptor and which part of the receptor the phage targeted. At that point, I can use gene editing to change the shape of the offending receptor. Voila. No more virus.*

She added a few specific databases and authors that would be good starting points. There would be a small delay before

Evan got her message. He should be at the comms hub—it was ten at night in California—but he might not respond immediately.

The further away the ship flew from Earth, the longer the delays would be. The position of the planets would also have an effect. It could take anywhere from three to twenty-two minutes for a signal from Earth to reach Mars. With current positions, it'd be about four minutes, so a minimum of eight minutes between messages. Once they jumped through the ring, it'd take months. Communications would have to be sent through the rings via probes, like messages in bottles. Twenty minutes later, she had her first reply.

> Earth: *Hello from Earth,* Atalanta. *V told me about the algae trouble. I'll look through those and send you anything else I find on what these phases are targeting on your spirulina. Any other search parameters?*

Naomi focused on the task at hand. She sent him everything she needed, terse and factual. She didn't let herself imagine him hunched in the tiny underground comms base, his dark eyes staring at blue screens, lips pursed. Despite spending his days in a lab, he always struck Naomi as uncomfortable indoors—he was active, his half-Chinese skin tanned from hours outdoors on long hikes or runs.

No one knew the base's location save Evan and Valerie, not even Naomi, though she'd seen the pictures and schematics. Satellites sprouting from the roof, screens surrounding the interior. A desk. A bed. A bathroom and kitchen. It was a little bigger than Naomi's cabin on the *Atalanta*. He had to be careful coming and going. If people found the bunker and suspected he was in contact with the ship, they'd take him in. Valerie had been repeatedly ignoring any official message from Earth.

It was strange for Evan to agree to do this in the first place and put himself at risk. If there was one thing Naomi knew about Evan, it was that he was a little mercenary in his approach to life. That didn't mean he was selfish to the point he wouldn't do the right thing, but he was always angling to make sure his actions directly benefitted himself in some way. Or he'd take action for the opportunity to learn something interesting rather than because it was moral. Why offer to help? Or had Valerie not given him a choice?

He'd delighted in frustrating Valerie's plans for him. He'd been the rebellious one and Naomi the one who did what she was told.

Once, Evan had been dropped off at Valerie's mansion in a cop car. Evan had sauntered up to the front door, unbothered by his mother's fury. He'd broken into a nearby lab just to prove he could. He didn't steal anything, just peered at all the different medicines, the animals in their cages, taking it all in. They'd been experimenting on the vaccine for Seventh Disease, or *erythema varicella*. It was a new childhood disease, a mutation of the same virus that caused chickenpox and shingles, that affected children intensely but barely touched adults. It had only taken a few years to engineer a new vaccine.

The lab didn't bring charges against him, in no small part due to who his mother was. They were impressed, despite themselves, that he'd been able to get in so easily. They ended up hiring him to help with their security, then given him an internship that eventually led to him studying immunology. It'd stopped him going down the road of seeing what he could steal for the pure thrill of it, at least. Naomi had no doubt he still unpicked a lock that struck his interest from time to time, to prove to himself he still could.

How did it feel, to know that Naomi and his mother had gone and stolen something far bigger than he ever could?

It took ages to send the information back and forth. While she waited for his responses, Naomi had scrolled through the existing information on the remote drive. Once she found the fix, she could stamp out the virus and continue with her crop experiments. Perhaps she was overthinking it, and there was a simpler way to fix the cyanophage. After all, even with cases as virulent as Seventh Disease, there were always a few children who were naturally immune and unaffected.

The astronaut mantra snaked its sneaky way through her head: expect the best but prepare for the worst.

Naomi rose and stretched, heading to the canteen for a cup of coffee before heading back to the comms centre. Black and bitter. She'd be sad when it ran out. They'd have to start adding caffeine pills to mint tea or something, but it wouldn't be the same. She'd try to grow coffee on Cavendish.

When she returned, another message from Evan waited for her.

Earth: *How is it up there? Never sure if V is telling me everything. I mean, why start now?*

Naomi paused, her fingers hovering over the keypad. So much on this ship was automated. Records of how long everyone spent in each room, their locations easily drawn up on a map. Useful if anyone wanted to know where one of the other crew members were. Not as useful if you wanted privacy. The logs would be automatically saved—any of the others would be able to access this if they desired. Naomi was almost certain Valerie had read her childhood diaries, especially during her silent years.

Atalanta: *They're all settling in. It'll be easier once we know the algae levels are stable.*

She hesitated, then sent another message.

Atalanta: *What're the updates on Earth? V just gives us the highlights, including that one article that said the U.S. was offering us up as guinea pigs and didn't expect us to survive. That was a cheery one.*

She sipped her coffee as she waited for Evan's reply. Valerie would be annoyed with Naomi asking Evan for news—that was beyond her remit. But her curiosity was high enough she thought it worth the risk.

Evan's response took longer than usual. He was choosing his words just as carefully.

Earth: *Officials are livid. Politicians have condemned you. The usual. Has she told you that they're starting construction on another ship? Just announced: the* Atalanta II. *They won't be able to launch for two years at the absolute soonest, but they'll be following you.*

They weren't even creative enough to give it a new name. The coffee made her jittery. She perched on the chair, one leg drawn up to her chest, resting her chin on her knee.

Atalanta: *Well. At least we'll have a bit of time on*

Cavendish before they arrest us. That's something. It was worth being a part of the resistance.

Whoever crewed the new ship would likely put the women's skills to work once they arrived. The five of them were still valuable. But they'd be punished, one way or another, to set an example. Cavendish would become their prison.

The word "resistance" stared at her from the screen, worming its way into her mind. A tiny fraction of the spirulina she had on board was probably resistant. The crew of the *Atalanta* were only five women out of all of humanity, but they could still found a whole new place for humans to flourish. Sometimes you only need one tiny proportion of the population to enact change.

Earth: *I'm sorry, for what it's worth, though I know that's an empty thing to say. How are you doing? I mean, no bullshit. Is outer space what you thought it'd be?*

Naomi hated it when he tried to be nice.

Atalanta: *I'm fine. Send through the stuff when you have it, and thanks for the help. I might have an idea of what could work. Goodnight.*

She didn't want him to keep talking. To risk him bringing up their last conversation on Earth and all the baggage that came with it. Plus her mind was buzzing. Resistance.

Mutations and evolution. She might not even need to bioengineer the algae. It might have already started solving the problem on its own. Life was stubborn.

His message snuck through just before she shut down the console.

Earth: *Good night, Naomi.*

She finished her cooling coffee, mindlessly scrolling through the various VR locations as she kept thinking. Her fingers paused on somewhere she'd been, interrupting the flow. She bit back a curse. It'd take her ages to pick up the edges of it again. She stared at the words: the Natural Bridges State Beach in Santa Cruz. She tapped it.

She'd camped there, her freshman year at Stanford, for a weekend trip called Living on the Edge for geo-sci class. The teacher and a few older students from Earth, Energy & Environmental Science acted as guides, taking them around local beaches to point out landforms and illustrate how the Earth had folded upon itself, the history fossilised in layers of rock. She'd known Evan had chosen Stanford too—with a delayed start after travelling the world on a gap year funded by Valerie—but she hadn't expected him to show up as one of the guides, since he was only a sophomore. She'd been so successful at avoiding him those first few months.

They'd chosen a campsite near Natural Bridges, under the juniper trees, and everything smelled like sharp berries, badly barbecued veggie burgers, and smoke.

Evan had kept off to the side, watching everyone chatting around the fire. It was early in her freshman year, and Naomi hadn't made much effort to get to know anyone. Evan, weirdly, was the most comforting option. At least he was familiar.

She had gone up to him and passed him a singed burger and held out her hand for his water bottle. He'd passed it to her, wordlessly. She'd sat next to him and unscrewed the metal cap, taking a swig.

"This is shit vodka," she'd said, as she fought not to sputter.

"Yep," he had agreed.

It'd been the first time they'd properly spent time together without Valerie's imposing presence over them. To her surprise, they hadn't devolved into their usual bickering. They'd snarked about professors, kept the conversation light, but something between them eased that night. She'd still found him a bit of an asshole. But he'd been an interesting asshole.

Naomi "walked" along the beach for a few minutes. The rock bridge was topped with the dark dots of birds, and the blue of the sky turned haze-orange at the horizon. The sound of waves and bird cries was convincing, but the white foam of the waves always stopped just before they reached her still shoed feet. No sand, no smell of salt or brine. Nothing but an echo of an echo.

She turned it off in disgust and went back to thinking about the power of a few resistant individuals.

CHAPTER EIGHT

8 Years Before Launch

Bay Area, California

When Naomi told Valerie she'd gotten the crushing voicemail, Valerie wouldn't let her mope.

"I'll be in northern California tomorrow," she'd announced when Naomi answered her cell phone. "Come to the Hawthorne airfield at noon." She'd hung up without saying goodbye.

Naomi had groaned and fallen back into the pillows. The next morning, she'd dutifully showered, brushed her teeth, and changed into actual clothes. She'd prided herself on her resilience, and she'd had her fair share of rejections. But this one? This one had hit deep.

She hadn't cried when she listened to the message. She'd sat in the dark of her apartment and realised that for the first time in years, she didn't have a plan. Everything she'd done up until this point had been with the hope of getting into NASA and it'd all unspooled in her hands.

When she'd gone to the interview in Houston, Naomi had been confident she was a reasonably clever person. Then she'd been thrown into a room with dozens of people just as smart, if not smarter, and discovered she wasn't that exceptional. Everyone else was equally determined.

Over twenty-five thousand people had applied. She'd made it to the top 120, the first round of interviews, and into the top fifty for the second round. She'd been one of the youngest candidates there, at twenty-four up against plenty with more than a decade of experience on her. There were people with doctorates when the ink on Naomi's master's degree was barely dry.

Naomi hadn't made the final cut. Others were better. That was that.

When the names were revealed, they were all men.

Valerie stood in the bright sun waiting for Naomi, brown curls tied back from the wind, eyes hidden by mirrored aviators, her transparent filter mask barely obscuring her nose and mouth. Valerie had gained her pilot's license years ago and kept it up to date. She'd been Naomi's instructor for some of her flight hours. Naomi had expected something large and loud, but when she saw the zero-G plane emblazoned with Hawthorne's planet-and-star company logo parked on the runway, her mouth had dropped open.

"Seriously?"

"Seriously," Valerie said. "Being CEO has its perks. Though I'm not going to fly it."

Their pilot walked across the tarmac, face half-hidden by her own shades and mask, but Naomi still recognised her. Jerrie Hixon—pilot to the Ares mission to Mars, the firecracker who would rip any interviewer to shreds if they made some tired reference to her red hair in the context of the red planet.

"I'm not your Mars pin-up. And the planet isn't even red! Not truly," Naomi had watched Hixon exclaim on a morning talk show with some far-too-perky hosts. "Under the dust it's green and caramel and sand and grey. Not red." She wasn't invited on talk shows much anymore. She didn't play the game.

Hixon was out from Houston to visit the NASA Ames Research Center in Silicon Valley for work, Valerie explained, and so she'd called in a favour. Later, Naomi would learn that Valerie was already courting Hixon for Project Atalanta. She'd spent over eight years gathering information on her proposed team before offering them jobs.

"No need to twist my arm to fly one of these on a day off," Hixon said, grin splitting wide as she took in the gleaming craft. Civilians buying extortionate tickets for a ride on one of these was one of Valerie's highest profit cash streams.

Naomi shook Hixon's hand, but seeing the pilot didn't help with her shame. Here was an inspiring woman with an illustrious career—she'd been to Mars, for Christ's sake—and Naomi was the imposter who'd just been told she wasn't good enough.

They climbed up the stairs and into the cockpit. Jerrie Hixon strapped herself into the pilot's seat, working the controls with practised ease. With her flight cap, freckles, and devil-may-care grin, she reminded Naomi of old photos of Amelia Earhart. Valerie and Naomi lay down in the body of the plane. The floor was padded, the white walls smooth, and the only window was on the door.

The engines rumbled to life, so loud they drowned out Naomi's thoughts. She was grateful for the distraction. Hixon raced the plane along the runway, gathering speed. Naomi loved the moment of flight when the wheels lifted off and you knew you were no longer Earthbound. If she were at the window, she'd watch the ground grow distant as they rose over the grids of houses, the swathes of freeway like grey ribbons, and Mt. Tamalpais would look like little more than an inexpertly moulded pile from a child's sandbox. Hixon pushed up, up through the lower atmosphere, speeding to the upper stratosphere at a forty-five-degree angle.

Naomi should be proud she'd made it to the second round of interviews. Objectively, she knew this. She hadn't lost her nerve during questions designed to poke at her weaknesses or show the cracks in her psychology. She'd proved her physical fitness—swimming, running long distances on the treadmill interspersed with all-out sprinting, the ever-present monitor tracking her heartbeat. She hadn't panicked when they'd put her in the sensory deprivation chamber, floating in water the exact temperature of her skin, time ceasing to have any sense of meaning.

Naomi had thought she'd performed well in the tests. No, she knew she had.

But what do you do when your best isn't good enough?

"Ready?" Valerie called.

Hixon reduced the thrust and lowered the nose of the airplane, creating the perfect parabolic arc relative to the centre of the Earth.

Naomi felt it—that first sense of her body lightening as Hixon brought them over the apex. The candidates that were chosen wouldn't have a chance to go up in one of NASA's vomit comets for ages yet. She'd beaten them to this. Sure, it was only because she'd grown up with one of the richest people in the world, but still. She'd take her victories where she could. Naomi's back arced as she rose.

"I didn't get into NASA my first time," Hixon said, her voice amplified by the speakers. Naomi twisted, staring at the back of the pilot's head. "I think that was my first heartbreak."

Naomi darted a glance at Valerie, who kept her face very innocent. Naomi should have known Hixon was going to be a part of the pep talk.

The craft began its downward pitch. Hixon adjusted the controls, pulling the nose up at the bottom. Naomi floated back down to the ground, not gracefully, and Hixon immediately began another upward trajectory. Naomi swallowed down the nausea.

"What did you do?" Naomi called back as she rose again.

"Went backpacking around the Andes and yelled really loudly at the top of mountains. Startled the shit out of some llamas. I screamed until I lost my voice. Then I came back and got back to work."

Naomi had to admit running away to mountains sounded very tempting.

Valerie floated closer to her.

"This is only the beginning," Valerie said. "In two years, you try again. You'll have more knowledge, more experience. Tomorrow, you'll get back to it, find another way. You have so much at your fingertips to help make this happen."

They entered another brief period of anti-gravity. Valerie's hair was around her, her eyes unblinking and dark. "They did you a favour, saying no."

Naomi's head jerked back as they fell.

"You've had less rejection than most. I'm partially at fault for that, I'll admit it. You work hard, but my money's opened doors you never even realised were locked."

That hurt. But Naomi knew it was the truth.

"This is your first big setback. How are you going to react to it? That's what'll show your mettle. Not the failure, but what you do next."

Naomi's shame twisted into something different. Here was a woman who had been told no over and over again. Who had been raised in abject poverty in a small, dusty little town in Texas.

Valerie had been knocked up at sixteen by the son of an oil tycoon. He'd stuck by her, much to the surprise of many, and Valerie had access to money that got her into university. Catherine Lovelace had been Valerie's robotics teacher.

On the first day, Valerie had proclaimed in her white-trash drawl, six months pregnant, that she was going to make spaceships. A few people had exchanged incredulous looks. But Catherine had leaned forward and said, "Yes, you will."

They fell again, and Valerie grabbed Naomi's hand in a vice-like grip.

"Success will never be linear. Success is illusive, it's a mirage. What you learn, what you do, how you react—that's what matters. Are you actually sad about the decision, or are you angry that they turned you down?"

Naomi's lips pressed together. She was angry. Yes, she'd been young, yes, others had more experience, but she had proved herself. "I'm mad at myself, and I'm mad at them. I want to prove them wrong."

"Good. Don't be afraid of your rage. It doesn't have to be weakness. It'll make you do anything. Get angry. Channel it."

As they rose again, Valerie's chin turned up in a silent dare.

Naomi rose and fell as gravity took and released its hold.

She spread her arms wide, far above the ground, and promised she wouldn't let failure define her. She would try again in two years. And again two years after that.

She'd try until they couldn't say no.

CHAPTER NINE

46 Days After Launch

80 Days to Mars

203 Days to Cavendish

Naomi slept in too long and was late to her physical with Hart.

She cursed, jumping into her coveralls, chewing a couple of vanilla-ish nutriblocks on her way to the med bay, her stomach still protesting as she struggled to wake up. Her circadian rhythms had been hopeless since they'd taken off.

Naomi was the last of the women to submit to Hart's pokes, prods, and ministrations. She'd delayed the inevitable. She made her way to the opposite side of the ring from her lab and sleeping quarters.

Hart called for her to come in when she knocked. She had a stylus stuck behind her ear and was frowning at something on her tablet. Naomi perched on the spare chair, crossing her ankles, shoulders hunched. The room was the same size as Naomi's lab, and nearly as crowded. A covered autodoc centre in the corner looked eerily similar to the cryopods down in the Crypt. It'd run scans, perform minor procedures, and was their backup in case Hart herself became ill. She did some initial tests, looking in Naomi's eyes with a light, down her throat, taking her pulse. More for the familiarity than anything else.

"Sorry I'm late. Overslept," Naomi said.

"You seem nervous, Lovelace," Hart said.

"I'm fine."

"Nausea still troubling you?" Hart asked, eyeing her critically. "You've lost weight, and you were on the slim side to start with."

"It comes and goes. Stress and boring chow don't help." She couldn't quite meet Hart's eyes.

"Here you go," Hart said, passing her an empty cup.

Naomi took it to the bathroom in the corridor. There was no way to collect it gracefully, though at least gravity made it easier—no peeing into a hose with a cup on the end like astronauts had once done on the ISS. Her heartbeat hammered in her ears as she washed her hands. She came out with the small plastic container.

Hart put it in the tray to the right of the autodoc, selecting a few commands on the screen. "So are you planning on telling me or will we let the machine do that for you?"

Naomi stood stiff, arms wrapped tight around her torso. She sucked in a breath. "I…I don't know for sure."

Hart gave her a look. "I'm not surprising you, though, am I?"

Naomi clicked her tongue against the back of her teeth, then shook her head. "How long have you suspected?"

Hart rested a hip against the glass of the autodoc. "About three weeks in, when you were still having trouble keeping food down. Plenty of other signs. That cramp in your foot at dinner two weeks ago. Stiffness in your lower back. Rather moody, too, no offense."

Naomi grimaced. "Do the others know?"

"Hard to say with Lebedeva—can't tell what she thinks about breakfast, much less anything else. But I don't think so. Jerrie hasn't said anything to me. Black? Another who knows."

Naomi swallowed.

"Let's see if we're right, shall we?" Hart drew up the results. Naomi leaned forward.

Human chorionic gonadotropin (hCG): Present

"Shit." Naomi exhaled the word. The cover of the autodoc slid open and she sat on the white, ergonomic cushions, her legs swinging. She hunched over her stomach.

"How long?" Hart asked.

"Sixty-one days."

An arched brow. "That's exact."

"It's easy enough to pinpoint."

Hart snorted but, mercifully, didn't press for more details. She could do the math. The night before they left for quarantine. "Eight weeks is more than early enough for a scan."

Naomi hesitated. "You need to scan me anyway, don't you? Might as well." She inhaled through her nose. "Don't put it on official records."

Hart pursed her lips. "Dr. Black will definitely find out sooner or later," she said with a pointed look at Naomi's still flat stomach.

Naomi said nothing.

"All right. Fine. Lie back."

Naomi complied. She lay on the ergonomic cushions, hands at her side, staring up at the white ceiling. Hart lowered the door and the screen came over the glass, blocking the doctor from view. Naomi closed her eyes as the machine mapped out her insides. Eventually, the cover pulled back, revealing Hart and the too bright lights of the med bay.

Hart helped her up, and she projected Naomi's body double on the white wall across from the autodoc. There were her muscles, her veins, laid out as if she had been flayed on the table.

Hart zoomed in on the womb.

There it was. A clear image; no grainy static of an ultrasound or strange, knobbly 3D scans. As big as a sweet pea. A tiny blob that looked like it could become anything. That early, a chicken and a human embryo were much the same. The bulbous, earless alien head, the lattice of veins like a leaf, the small buttons where the eyes would form. Nodules that would elongate into legs and arms. Its minuscule heart beat twice as fast as Naomi's own. A small, doomed tail curled around the C-shaped body, an evolutionary leftover. All tethered back to her through the umbilical cord. An unexpected seedling that should never have been able to take root and could still float away like a blown dandelion.

Make a wish.

Naomi reached for Hart's forearm. "The first day. The spacewalk. The radiation protection isn't as good in the EMU. Could it...?"

Radiation was a sneaky thing. She remembered reading about the girls at the turn of the last century who dipped their paintbrushes into glowing green radium to paint watch dials, then licked the tip of the brush to a point to do it again, each watch face ticking away at the time they had left. They'd paint the radium on themselves for a lark, swirls of green along their skin, luminous dust shaken off their dresses at night. They were told it was healthy, and the radium girls glowed right up until their jaws disintegrated and they spat their teeth into their palms.

Hart put her opposite hand over Naomi's, giving it a reassuring pat.

"There's no need to tell anyone, is there?" Naomi asked. "It's happened before. I didn't make it past ten weeks. I'm—I'm meant to be infertile." She kept her gaze even, her shoulders square. "There's no reason to suspect this'll be any different."

"Well, at present, it's healthy," Hart said. "You've passed the window with the highest chance of miscarriage."

Four to six weeks. Naomi glanced away from the tiny, pink-veined cluster of cells.

Hart turned off the projection. "If you don't want to wait for a potential miscarriage, I can help you," she said. "It's your choice to make."

Her voice held no judgement, as if what she offered wasn't illegal in all fifty states. Women were meant to carry their first child and then be fitted with their IUD, with very few exceptions. Any subsequent children resulted in the additional child tax, which was at least six months of the average salary, and no birth bonus. Enough to financially devastate most families.

Naomi swallowed. "I'll think on it," she said. "Thank you. Do you need anything else from me?"

"No." Hart's eyes held pity Naomi didn't want and wouldn't stand for. "I have what I need for the reports."

Naomi gave a curt nod and left. She made it to her room without coming across any of the others. She climbed back into bed, staring up at the ceiling.

She should have known better. That last night before they

flew out to the launch site, she'd looked up at the moon, two hundred and fifty thousand miles away, and known she'd be going light years beyond it. She could have ignored his knock. She could have left it at that first kiss. Pulled back, softened her rejection with a smile and another sip of wine. The whole time, she'd known that it was a mistake to look for comfort from him. He was not hers.

But she was too much of a coward to spend her last night of her old life on Earth alone, counting down the hours and minutes until she flew out for quarantine and left it all behind. So she'd reached for him.

Another selfish wish.

CHAPTER TEN

61 Days After Launch

65 Days to Mars

188 Days to Cavendish

They gathered in the rec room to celebrate the Fourth of July and the fact that Naomi had successfully solved the problem of the algae. In the end, she hadn't even needed to bioengineer the receptor.

She used evolution instead. She isolated the contaminated crops into hundreds of small samples with one cell of culture in each and waited. The spontaneously resistant cells did their work, and she isolated those cells and regrew. Three batches in a row had held. Even if it came into contact with the virus again, it was now immune. Life support was stable, and they had all the nutriblocks their hearts desired.

Naomi had scienced her way out of the mess, and she was relieved. And frustrated that she didn't foresee the problem sooner. Cyanophages were common, and they should have been prepared for some form of contamination. Going forward, Naomi saw it as an indication that she needed to think through ways of systematically dealing with biohazards on the new planet. She wished she could be proud, but she was mostly sheepish.

Hart had stressed the importance of holidays, of carving out a routine, marking time. Otherwise, they risked a lack of varied stimulation, and everything would blur together. Naomi was already having trouble remembering what day of the week it was back on Earth.

On the *Atalanta*, the air always smelled the same, except for in the canteen or the greenhouse, and even that didn't deviate day to day. The ship's small bots sucked up the dust so it wouldn't catch in filters and recycled everything back into the fertiliser. It was always the same temperature. When she'd been down in Antarctica, she'd been able to leave the compound, feel the bite of the cold. She'd been able to phone people back home, check the news regularly uploaded to their local server. She'd still understood the shape of events and felt a part of the world, even hunkered down at its southern pole.

But Earth was further away each day, and not simply in terms of distance. Headlines could not affect them out there, unless it had to do with the threat of *Atalanta II* on Cavendish's eventual horizon. She'd skim the information Valerie disseminated from conversations with Evan, but it was difficult to spare it more than a second thought. It was callous, perhaps, but protective.

Naomi had continued to speak to Evan as she worked on the spirulina problem. They kept to practical matters. Naomi had also begun the vat-grown meat experiment, and she kept him updated on it. A corner of her greenhouse had been relegated to a Dr. Frankenstein lab. It wasn't so different from growing plants. Prep the starter cells in the growth medium and program them to grow along their lattices—thin tendrils that would thicken into corded, artificial muscle within the incubator. Meat. It wouldn't be much, but the few grams here and there would help bolster their protein and give a much-welcome break from endless nutriblocks.

Evan asked her opinion as one of his colleagues was looking into an outbreak of sickness from suspected wheat rust in local crops. She recommended the company where she'd done her first summer internship, Argaine.

That brought back memories of that summer between freshman and sophomore year. Those long days, fingertips growing calloused and dirt under her fingernails. The farmer's tan on her arms despite the sunscreen. Walking down to the end of the farm to the gas station to buy an ice cold soda, holding the can to the back of her neck, her temples, before sucking it down by the time she got halfway back to the office.

Evan and Naomi were too stiff, too polite, aware that every word they typed could be read by anyone on the ship.

Hart had set the background of the rec room to a park—green grass and crusty barbecues next to wooden picnic tables, complete with weathered, carved initials in lopsided hearts. No matter the detail, it still paled compared to Naomi's memories of past Independence Days—hot, sticky nights, the blaring of "Star-Spangled Banner" from old speakers, the smoke from the charcoal grills and spent fireworks tickling her throat.

Hixon passed her a plate. They'd raised comfortable chairs for the crew from the malleable floor of the rec room. Naomi stretched, her spine easing as it moulded to the shape of her back. The crew was marking the first meal made almost entirely from Naomi's crops. An entirely nutriblock-free meal.

Their protein was from some of their last packets of vat steak in gravy—her own crop of vat meat wasn't quite ready yet—but they had a side salad of lettuce, spinach, and tomatoes, and potatoes and Jerusalem artichokes with rosemary. The salad was still peppered with ten grams of spirulina for an extra micronutrient burst, but at least they didn't have to chew it in gelatinous form.

Hart pressed a button on the controls, and the fireworks began—bright carnations of red, green, blue and white flickering out, leaving a ghostly imprint behind. They were mercifully quiet. Naomi had loved the fireworks displays as a child but hated the noise—she'd always stuck her fingers in her ears, which did little to block out the gunshot booms. She'd turn from the fireworks and read the lips of the adults. She'd taught herself how, watching people speak about her when they assumed she couldn't hear.

Naomi carefully layered a bite of steak, potato and salad on the tines of her fork. She tasted it, chewing slowly. Was it the best meal she'd ever tasted? No. Was it satisfying and palatable? Yes. The rec room filled with that reverent silence as the women ate and watched the silent fireworks.

Hixon had a smear of blue ink on her cheek, like another freckle. She liked to calculate longhand on a sheet from their precious store of paper using a particular pen—said it helped her think better. Hart noticed and leaned over, wiping the spot away. Hixon made a face but put up with it.

Lebedeva watched the fireworks with a half-smirk. "It is strange, to celebrate patriotism to a country that wants us behind bars for what we did."

They all took this in.

"Did you ever feel patriotic towards Russia?" Hixon asked.

Lebedeva's gaze went distant. Naomi thought she wouldn't answer. "Once I did," she said. "This is new for you—your country thinking of you as a traitor. Give it time. It gets easier." She poured herself a glass of mint tea, clearly wishing it was something stronger.

Of the four other women on board, the Russian was the one Naomi knew the least about after more than sixty days in space. Lebedeva had struck up a friendship with Hixon, but kept the rest of them at arm's length, preferring the company of machines. Naomi knew Lebedeva had spent time on the ISS, and not long after she'd returned, she'd left Roscosmos and Russia before landing at Hawthorne. Naomi had begun to suspect Lebedeva had been kicked out and forced to flee. She'd left behind a husband, but there seemed to be no love lost there. Valerie had ended up sponsoring Lebedeva's work visa and scooped her up for Project Atalanta.

Dessert was berries, a sweet potato, and a scoop of peanut and hazelnut butter from their stores. Naomi really, really missed chocolate.

She picked up one of the raspberries with her fingertips, biting down on the sweet tartness, grinding the seeds between her molars.

"I've never been good at patriotism," Hart said. "The U.S. was too big, too diffuse and diverse to really understand what it meant to be American. Was I proud of the good things we'd done? Sure. But I'm ashamed of a lot of other things. That we did. That we still do."

"I used to be proud," Hixon said, her mouth twisting as she stared at the remnants of her sweet potato. "In the military, I was honoured to have that flag stitched across my chest, representing my country. I was one idealistic little recruit, plucked right out of the cornfields.

"Took me too long to realise the country would rather I shut up, sit down. Don't be too loud about who I loved. Move aside and make room for someone new. I already went to Mars—how selfish was I, to want to go up again?"

"They never said that to Cole," Naomi said, thinking of him down there in the Crypt. Waiting to wake up. "They were constantly courting him to go back up."

"Well, he's straight, white, and has a dick." Hixon folded her legs and rested her chin on her knees, watching the fireworks.

"He only got backup for this mission," Naomi pointed out.

"Yeah. Guess they found Shane Legge shinier this time around. Cole still got on the ship officially over us."

Naomi could say nothing to that. It was still strange to think of him down there. There and not there.

Valerie's face had remained still throughout the conversation. "Forget America. Forget Earth," she said. "We've got Cavendish."

"We won't for long." A thought occurred to Naomi. "How does it even work, if we get there first? We're not a sanctioned U.S. vessel anymore."

"We can't claim it," Hart said. "I looked into it, out of curiosity. The Outer Space Treaty covers all celestial bodies, including the moon and exoplanets."

"But," Valerie cut in, "that means America can't claim it either, much to their consternation." Valerie poured herself more tea. "Cavendish is what space law called a *res communis*, or a thing belonging to all. Think of space like the high seas."

She popped a raspberry into her mouth. "No one needed to ask permission to move through it. So even if the *Atalanta* set down, and we plant a flag—whether American or one of our own making—officially, we would only have jurisdiction over ourselves and the ship. The ground underneath the base would still technically belong to all of humanity."

"I like that," Hixon said. "Don't you? People owning or claiming land hasn't exactly worked out well historically, has it?"

"America is still coming for us," Lebedeva pointed out. "And we still stole American property."

"They're legally within their rights to reclaim their stolen ship, that's true." Valerie seemed unconcerned. "But it's worth noting that not every country has agreed to the treaty or ratified it into law, and the UN isn't terribly strong anymore anyway. It's difficult to enforce things from ten and a half light years away. I can't imagine it'd be worth the effort as long as we're not building a military base and planning to attack Earth." She drained the last of her tea. "If we could make Cavendish our world entirely," Valerie said, leaning forward, her face animated, "if we could build it from the ground up, set the rules for everyone, how would you want it to function?"

"You're asking us to build a utopia?" Naomi asked.

"Sure. Thought exercise."

"No such thing as utopia," Lebedeva said. "People mess it up."

"Or one person's utopia usually means someone else's dystopia," Hart agreed.

"Come on," Valerie said. "Try, at least."

They thought about it as the fireworks kept up their slow dance.

"Well, if the ground belongs to all of humanity, then there shouldn't be borders," Hixon said. "No nationalism getting in the way of things. Freedom of movement."

"Not sure we'll be able to shift humanity's penchant for tribalism so easily," Hart said. "Can we throw rampant capitalism out the window? Not saying we need to go full communism, but the whole desperate reliance on growth and inflation, the bubbles and the pops of the economy—that can go."

Valerie held up her hands. "As an ardent capitalist myself, sure. Though most of my money's gone now, anyway. Liquidated as we speak."

"Free education," Naomi said. "And placing emphasis on art and creative play as well as science."

"Good one," Hart said.

"No plastic," Lebedeva said. "No fossil fuels. Eco-friendly from the beginning."

"No factory farming or meat industry," Hart said. "I mean, we're basically all vegan once those meat packets run out anyway, if you consider meat grown without a nervous system vegan."

"No men?" Hixon joked. "Though I guess that plan is already kaput with the backup crew."

"We don't have to wake them up on day one of landing," Valerie said. "We can have a few weeks of a women-only planet, I'm sure." Her tone was teasing.

They drank more tea and kept building their idea of utopia. It was a nice way to spend an evening. They changed the VR background to a rainforest, the sound of rain dripping through green leaves and the caw of now-extinct birds soothing.

Some of their ideas might come to pass. Once you're capable of harvesting exotic matter and building a warp drive, it's hard to imagine everyone gleefully using fossil fuels and coal again. But borders would be drawn. Not every community would be able to produce everything they needed—trade and some form of currency would be required. The Outer Space Treaty could be broken. Instead of grand, large countries, due to the planet's islands and small continents, perhaps it'd be more like the city states of ancient Greece. People would find ways to disagree, to squabble, to fight.

They all knew that their rosy picture of Cavendish was just that—a fantasy. And so much of the inequality would happen before the ships came. Earth had so far only managed one interstellar ship and was in the process of building more. Valerie had sent them plans for the ark ships, but it'd be impossible to build enough for everyone on the planet.

So who went?

The tickets weren't going to be free. Hawthorne had been planning on a sliding scale—a percentage of income.

Lockwood would do no such thing. Tickets were going to be dear, most people going into debt to the government or whatever company built the ships. And what of those who couldn't afford the ticket?

They'd almost certainly be left behind.

CHAPTER ELEVEN

7 Years Before Launch

UN Climate Change Conference

Orange County Convention Center, Florida

Naomi stood in the middle of Cavendish.

Well, not quite.

She'd created two biomes. The larger one was in her lab at the Hawthorne headquarters in LA. Once a week, at least, Valerie threatened to move it into the lobby. She wanted everyone who passed through the doors of her company to walk through the tunnel, gazing at the alien plants like people stared at sharks gliding over the walkways through aquariums.

"I'm not going to do my work with a bunch of people gawping at me," Naomi had said, and she'd compromised by creating this smaller one that usually stayed in the lobby but was portable enough to bring anywhere.

Valerie insisted on taking it to the UN Climate Change Conference that year, in the convention centre not far from the Kennedy Space Center, and that meant Naomi had to tag along, looking after her biome.

Naomi's smaller creation was the size of a large living room. A six-foot-tall tunnel led to a round centre big enough for five or six people to stand comfortably under the dome of Perspex. They couldn't touch any of the plants, walled off as they were, but they could stare at them through the glass for ten minutes, taking in the tiny echo of the new world. There had been a waitlist all day.

Hawthorne had shut down the biome for the evening, and most people had already left the main floor, streaming to the large auditorium for the keynote speech. Crowds of people had eddied around the various stalls, peering at what was on offer, networking, and pretending there was still enough time to stop what they all knew was coming. They walked around with easy smiles, as if the Florida coastline wasn't barricaded by high sea walls. As if the hurricanes that descended on the state yearly didn't grow stronger every year. The Kennedy Space Center was thinking of packing up and relocating to an area where the high winds didn't cancel launches more often than not.

The crush of the people hadn't overwhelmed Naomi, but as someone used to the relative silence of her lab, the constant noise and having to shoulder her way through the throng—who would stop like pebbles in a stream—was exhausting.

Naomi let her hands fall open in her lap as she tilted her head up, breathing deeply, emptying her mind.

She and Valerie had spent the day introducing the public to Cavendish. Naomi had been on a couple of panels that day, knowing her face was being recorded, her words quoted and dissected from every angle. Sent out in out-of-context or paraphrased bytes on social media. Her face hurt from holding a polite smile.

Some of the panellists had been more diplomatic than others, but Valerie had, without fail, gone into one of her impassioned speeches, any attempt the others made at candy-coating the future washed away by Valerie's acid.

The artificial sunlight in the biome was as orange as Ran's would be. Naomi had grown four types of vascular plants that were similar to Devonian-era flora on Earth, like ferns and lycopods, in her larger biome from seeds brought back through the probes. For ease of transport, her portable biome only grew one.

The ferns weren't radically different at first glance. The fanned, striated leaves were still green, though tinged closer to teal. Instead of fiddleheads, the ends spiralled sinuously in a way Earthen ones never did. The ground was a rich, loamy soil, softened with a blueish moss. Between the orange sunlight and the odd shade of the greenery, Cavendish would likely look like a world on the edge of perpetual sunset.

Naomi had spent the last year studying the reports from the Cavendish probes until her eyes crossed. When the first bit of blue-green had emerged from Earth soil treated to be like Cavendish's, she had felt a fierce satisfaction.

That little sprout would be her ticket to NASA.

Naomi was late—she should already be in the green room. Valerie's keynote speech would begin soon, but it almost hadn't happened. Protests. Petitions. Valerie Black would not represent what the UN stood for in this conference, they said. She was too loud. Too radical.

Too female.

She was branded a bitter feminist who couldn't accept how the world had changed. Even that early, the murmurings were there, if Naomi had bothered listening. Women were being gently urged towards retirement, passed over for promotions.

Cochran was on the horizon for the presidential run even then, building on his work in the Senate to limit abortion and introduce the additional child tax. He was whispering poison about his running mates, especially the women.

Global temperatures were already at projections for 2060—decades too soon—up two degrees Celsius. Carbon emissions, and Brazil deciding to sell off the lungs of the Amazon—what hadn't burned—one tree at a time, was worth the money. The deforestation was coupled with a massive release of methane during the rapid tundra melt of the 2020s, which caused a larger positive feedback in warming than any of the pre-2025 models had accounted for.

In the green room, Valerie would already be sipping lemon- and mint-infused water. To anyone else, she'd look perfectly calm and in control. But Naomi would see the way her long fingers would smooth non-existent wrinkles on the trousers of her dark purple suit. The way she'd blink just a little too long, as if centring herself for the extra half a second.

"Naomi?" came a voice from outside.

Naomi's lips thinned. Evan. She hadn't seen him since Christmas and hadn't spoken to him alone since the night after her master's graduation. She stood, leaving the orange light and locking the entrance to the tunnel.

The crowds had thinned, but people lingered near the stalls, the dark-clad security guards slowly ushering them towards the doors.

"Valerie was asking for you," Evan said, keeping his distance. His features were as hard for her to read as ever. They'd gone to a graduation party and he'd told her about his new job at NASA in astronaut health at the Kennedy Space Center.

The job was junior as he'd just started his PhD, but NASA were even helping a bit with funding while he worked. By all accounts, despite working and studying he'd end up finishing his terminal degree in record time.

She'd drunk just enough that she hadn't been able to temper her response. She'd been an asshole, but hadn't known how to apologise, and the time between had lengthened into an awkwardness that couldn't be breached. Even now, seeing him with that NASA badge emblazoned on the chest of his polo shirt was still a reminder that, though she loved her job, she still wasn't where she wanted to be.

"Thanks," she said, annoyed at her own curtness.

Evan made to leave. Froze. Naomi saw it a second after he did.

A crowd had gathered on the other side of the biome. Murmurs and whispers grew louder, like the buzzing of bees. People raised phones cupped in the palms of their hands, snapping photos by blinking their eyes.

Evan and Naomi pushed their way to the front. A few edged away from Naomi when they recognised her as Valerie Black's shadow. She felt their eyes on her as she took in the ugly, red graffiti scrawled across the biome's smooth exterior.

VAL BLACK = FRIGID CLIMATE CUNT

In another context, she would have laughed. Naomi stared at it, unblinking. The intent of this was malice, belittlement. She wanted to jerk back from the force of it. Reducing Valerie and her education, her company, her work, into a four-letter word. The rudest insult they could come up with. The condescending use of the nickname. That equal sign, as if this was a logical equation. A foregone conclusion.

Naomi's eyes darted around the hall at the crowd. How many pictures had already been taken? It must have happened while she was in the biome collecting herself. The idea of someone looking in and spray-painting this while staring at the back of her head through Cavendish ferns unsettled her. Was the person who did it one of the crowd?

"Did you see who did this?" Naomi asked them. A few scattered, embarrassed to be caught gawking. Others shook their heads. Still more were already craned over their phones, uploading their snaps, pithy captions at the ready. Stone-faced security guards broke up the crowd.

Naomi put her finger out to touch the last T of the graffiti. The paint was still tacky. Her gaze flicked up to the cameras. Their positions meant it'd be hard to get a clear shot of whoever did this, and they'd doubtless have worn a hat or a filter mask. Part of her wanted to demand the footage, but a far larger part of her wanted these words gone and off her work. Right now.

Naomi grabbed one of the large, standing Hawthorne posters, dragging it in front of the lettering to hide it from the last of the onlookers. She rummaged in the depths of the stall and found the cleaning solution she'd used first thing that morning to make the biome shine. After hours of curious hands, it was smeared with fingerprints.

Evan disappeared, returning with extra tissues liberated from the bathroom.

Naomi sprayed the letters, gritting her teeth so hard her jaw ached. The red dripped pink rivulets over the glass of the dome. Evan started scrubbing. The paint was oily, smearing into a mess.

Naomi snuck a glance at Evan as they worked side by side. His hair was longer, falling into his eyes, still that shining black. He'd just turned twenty-eight and had settled into his features. For most of her undergrad degree, they'd formed an alliance. They'd studied together, alternating who brought the snacks. Evan had taken her to her first college party and held her hair back the first time she'd drunk too much. They'd been friends, for a time. And she'd let that go.

They scrubbed harder, dousing the glass with more cleaning solution.

"I never apologised," Naomi said. "For what I said that night."

"That's not why we really stopped talking. You know that."

"Ah." It was what had happened not a half hour before her outburst. She kept wiping, even though that section of the glass was already clean. "Nothing to apologise for there, right? It was just a kiss."

The party the night of graduation. She'd tied her tassel to her wrist, watched it flutter each time she moved. He'd tasted of Sprite—he had stopped drinking by that point. Said he didn't like the crutch it'd become, or who he became when he drank. They'd broken away, both shocked and not at the same time. He'd changed the subject, told her about the job, and she'd lashed out. She ached with embarrassment as Evan kept scrubbing with more vigour than necessary. The red was gone, the surface of the biome clear. As if it'd never happened.

They gathered up the stained, crumpled napkins. They said nothing else as they put them in the trash, moved the screen back to its original place, and made their way to the auditorium. She'd kept Valerie waiting.

Evan parted before she could say goodbye, making his way to an empty seat in the crowd. Naomi went behind stage to watch. Bryony was there, the doctor from Hawthorne, giving a presentation on astronaut radiation protection the next day, her eyes panicked.

"Had she heard about it?" Naomi asked her, head tilting up at Bryony.

"Haven't been brave enough to ask. Is it still there?"

"No. Me and Evan cleaned it off."

Bryony let out a breath, bobbed her head in a nod. "Good." She flitted away, head already bowing over her phone.

Naomi opened her own phone, holding her breath as she searched the platforms. Already the news was cascading. Photo after photo, the ugly red stark against the soft orange of her created, miniature world. Whenever Naomi gave a talk or showed her biome to the masses again, those words would be branded across people's memories.

Valerie came to stand next to Naomi, surveying the audience. Her lipstick was freshly applied, her hair its usual dark corona.

"Valerie—" Naomi began.

"I know already," Valerie cut her off.

Before Naomi could say another word, Valerie stepped on to the stage, head held high.

Valerie began; her speech easy, appearing unrehearsed. She'd been up half the night practising; not a word uttered by accident. She spoke as if she didn't give a damn what people out there were saying, sharing. That she didn't know those red words would be thrown back at her face time and time again. That her inbox and platforms wouldn't be inundated with even more hate mail than before. That she wouldn't have to strengthen her security detail against the inevitable death threats.

Naomi turned off her phone.

Projections of the probes and the schematics of the Alcubierre warp drive that would become so familiar to Naomi swirled above Valerie's head.

Naomi searched for Evan in the crowd. She found him, his elbows on his knees, staring up at the screen. It had been the first time he'd really been confronted with what Valerie and Naomi were trying to do. And it'd been the first time he must have realised just how much they had up against them.

Naomi wanted to go to NASA so that she wasn't only Valerie's ward and the daughter of Catherine Lovelace, working away in the company that her mother and adopted mother started. She needed to prove herself on the government side, make herself invaluable to both, so that when the time came to pick a crew to go to Cavendish, she'd be one of the first names they listed.

Valerie paced slowly on her black pumps, her voice taking on a deeper timbre, an almost hypnotising cadence and rhythm as she one by one lured them all closer to Cavendish.

CHAPTER TWELVE

71 Days After Launch

55 Days to Mars

178 Days to Cavendish

It started with the lights blaring too bright, then flickering, then darkening. Naomi woke up from a deep sleep, disorientated, before everything snapped into focus.

Alarm lights blinked as violet as the grow lights of her labs—red, it had been decided, would inspire too much panic. Dread still lurked within Naomi as she stepped into her coveralls.

Years of training took over. On the way to the bridge, she checked on the greenhouse. The alarm lights were yellow there, the other end of the spectrum from purple. The backup lights for the spirulina were on—they ran on a separate generator with a double backup in case something like this happened. The air was cooler than she'd like, but it shouldn't affect the crops short-term. It was puzzling, though. The alarms were going off, they were on backup, but none of the trackers had registered anything odd. There weren't any detectable radiation spikes on the monitors.

She climbed along the long spoke to the centre of the ship. Her hair had grown out enough that she could feel it rising from her skull like a bristle. Hixon and Lebedeva were there, alert and working on the main controls. Valerie and Hart floated in just as the lights stabilised again.

"Radiation spike is my guess," Hixon said. "Leaked through the shields enough to mess with the systems."

"Not in my lab," Naomi said.

"Somewhere else, perhaps. See to it," Valerie said, voice tight.

There had been little else Naomi could do, so she'd floated back up to solid ground and spent a few hours in her lab before catching a handful of hours of fitful sleep.

By the time she'd woken up again, Lebedeva and Hixon had run full diagnostics. All looked fine.

Yet over the next two days, alarms dinged through the ship. Oxygen levels started to dip, slowly and inexorably. Naomi, Hart, and Valerie helped Lebedeva and Hixon with the checks. They'd checked the ship again from top to bottom but couldn't find a fix. The filters were fine, as was the shield. No one was panicking yet, but it was similar to when Naomi's algae was infected—if a solution wasn't found soon, they were scuppered, to use one of Naomi's father's favourite sayings. No one spoke much. The full wattage of the team was focused on solving the problem.

Lebedeva found the issue on the morning of the third day—a subsystem in the main body of the ship was leeching power, affecting both the life system and fuel efficiency. Hixon was isolating each subsystem to find out more detail.

Valerie had delegated communication with Earth back to Naomi as she helped Lebedeva and Hixon. Evan had sent through what additional information he could, but there wasn't much that wasn't already in the repair manuals and detailed diagnostics on board. He kept saying he wished he could do more. She'd dryly responded that she wished the ship would stop trying to kill them.

The lower oxygen left the crew sleepy and sluggish, with heavy limbs and constant headaches. Those on the ISS or the Gateway had suffered lower levels and been fine, but Naomi went to the medical lab and gave herself another scan in the autodoc, alone, just in case.

At twelve weeks, it was a foetus rather than an embryo, her body easing from the first trimester to the second. The thing inside her was now the size of a peach, forming into something more concrete—bones and cartilage and buds of teeth.

She'd avoided looking at herself too closely for the last few weeks, but in the lab, she unbuttoned her coveralls, peeling the top half back. She ran her hand over her stomach. There was a slight roundness to her lower abdomen, but no different than if she was bloated with cramps. Veins of blue criss-crossed against her pale skin, always visible but now thicker, rising above her sports bra and down her abdomen like tree branches. Subtle changes. She wouldn't have long.

Hart came in as Naomi was buttoning up her coveralls.

"I was going to make you come in for a scan today," the doctor said. "You beat me to it."

"Sorry not to ask first. I just needed to know."

"It's fine. I get it." She drew up the scan, peering at it.

"Still healthy, right?" Naomi asked.

"Perfectly. No abnormalities. If the oxygen dips much lower, you'll have to go on supplemental oxygen."

Naomi grimaced. "How would I explain that?"

Hart gave her a pointed look. "I know this is not the best time to ask, but have you made up your mind?"

"What, abort or let it suffocate?" Naomi said, wrapping her hands around her stomach.

"It wouldn't come to that." Hart put a hand on Naomi's shoulder. "This is a stubborn ship, but it's full of even more stubborn women."

Naomi gave a weak laugh. "That's true enough." A hitched breath. "Do you think it's ridiculous, to even entertain keeping it?"

Hart considered it. "It'd be a challenge. Someone else would have to take over your duties when you're nearly at term or have an infant. But you'd have access to a full medical lab and a damn good doctor, if I do say so myself." She fluttered her eyelids. "If we were in microgravity, it'd be more dangerous, but the ring solves a lot of potential problems and complications. I don't know. I support you either way. It'd be a hell of a thing, though, wouldn't it? The first baby in space?"

"It would. I'll let you know in a few weeks. If I haven't—or if we haven't—" She hated stumbling over her words.

"Sure," Hart said, gentle.

Hart gave Naomi some easy tasks to do in the med bay to take her mind off things. They'd just settled into a rhythm when Valerie's clipped voice came over the comms.

"Crew. To the bridge."

Hart and Naomi exchanged a look.

"That doesn't sound like good news," Hart admitted.

As they walked down the dimmed hallway, Naomi wondered if they were about to be told this was it. The end. No way to recalibrate the systems. They could fill the emergency shuttle with as much nutriblocks and water as it could carry and speed back to Earth and hope they made it in time. With a clench, Naomi realised that would mean leaving the backup crew behind.

But they might be too far gone for that to be an option. Valerie could be summoning them to ask if they wanted to die quickly or slowly.

Naomi kept one foot moving in front of the other. If they did have to take a shuttle, Naomi would have to take Hart up on her offer. A miscarriage or other complications on the *Atalanta* would be dangerous enough—on a tiny shuttle they'd be deadly. The choice would be taken away.

She took the rungs of the spokes one at a time until her feet floated and she gently rappelled towards the main craft of the ship.

To sacrifice this much to get this close and have to turn around . . . to never see Cavendish.

Valerie's face was grim. She floated above the captain's chair, reminding Naomi of the mermaid in the mural over the Catalina Casino. Naomi's breath stayed even as she prepared herself. Lebedeva held on to one of the handholds near the window, staring out. Hixon had strapped herself into the pilot's seat, staring intently at the plotted course to Mars on one screen, then swivelling to the readouts of the ship on the next. Hart and Naomi both found handholds. Naomi crossed her ankles.

"I'll start with the good news. We found a solution," Valerie said.

"And the bad?" Naomi asked.

Valerie tapped her teeth together three times—one of her few anxiety tells.

"The cryopods are leeching power," Hixon began. Her pale fingers were fully smudged with blue. "Lockwood made an error in the calculations. Underestimated power requirements by the tiniest fraction of a per cent, but that's enough."

Naomi let that sink in. "Lockwood cut corners. First the cyanophage got through the contamination procedures, now this." They were on a defective ship. Who knew how many other problems could crop up between now and Cavendish?

Naomi remembered a quote from Mercury 7 astronaut John Glenn, the first American man to orbit the Earth, when asked how he felt listening to the countdown for lift-off: "I felt exactly how you would feel if you were getting ready to launch and knew you were sitting on top of two million parts—all built by the lowest bidder on a government contract."

Valerie nodded, simmering with rage.

"The chambers are becoming progressively less efficient," Lebedeva said, her accent clipping the words. "Incremental, but we already see the effects."

"So that means..." Naomi let the words trail off, unwilling to finish voicing what she already suspected.

"If we don't pull the plug, we won't make it to Mars," Valerie finished. Her jaw jutted forward. Her features were sharp in the dim light of the bridge, as if they'd been sketched with charcoal.

"Are you sure?" Hart asked.

"I've run the numbers so many times," Hixon said. "I can't find another way. Even if we divert the chambers to the lowest setting, we'd go dark before Mars. And—" she squeezed her eyes shut—"the original glitch was a surge of power directly to the cryopods. I don't know how to say it, but—"

"—they partially defrosted," Hart finished.

Naomi kept her face very still.

"Yes," Hixon said, wincing. "The inhabitants are almost certainly damaged. Irene, will you check them over?"

The inhabitants. Did Hixon realise she was already using distancing language?

Hart nodded. "Of course I will. But if the cells have crystallised...you can't undo that."

Naomi tried to order her thoughts into something like logic. Cole was in the storage bay. Either still asleep or already dead.

Like her, he'd sacrificed to be on this ship. He'd left behind his new wife, his son, knowing he wouldn't see them for half a decade or more. He knew what he risked. That space was as unforgiving as the ocean.

And it wasn't only him. She'd known every man in those chambers. Lee's face, reverent, as he showed her the half-grown vat meat specimens in his lab. "It's not that different, growing tissue compared to plants," he'd told her. Twenty-odd years ago, Lee had made some of the early breakthroughs that had led to cloned organs that Valerie had almost turned into a thriving company before it'd been made illegal.

Josh Hines and his infuriatingly cheerful flirting. Devraj Chand standing proud as he presented his findings on life support systems to the team at NASA. Ryan Webb declaring her fit as a fiddle when she was a trainee.

All gone or soon to be.

Hixon's face crumpled like one of her discarded calculations. Her eyes met Naomi's in silent apology. Hixon had spent months in a tin can with Cole, following the same flight path they were on now. She probably knew things about Cole that Naomi had never discovered. Understanding passed between the two women—an instant of apology, of horrible finality.

Hart had disappeared, floating into the storage bay next door to inspect the cryopods and their readouts. Valerie went with her. The rest of them waited in the bridge, in silence. Lebedeva was twisting, round and round, her lips moving as she silently counted each turn in Russian.

"If they are undamaged... we can't wake them up, can we?" Naomi asked the bridge.

"Not unless you know how to feed twice as many people on nutriblocks for an extra fifty-five days," Lebedeva said from her spinning. "Or make them exhale less carbon dioxide so they do not upset the life support equilibrium. Or produce less waste that is difficult to expel. Or drink less water."

Naomi knew this before she'd asked, but it was still a gut punch to hear it.

No way to send them back on the shuttle. This far out, if something went wrong they were meant to land on Mars to wait in the *Atalanta* for rescue. Even if they could spare the supplies, there wasn't enough power to keep them cryofrozen until home. No way to keep the pods powered on the surface of Mars, either.

There was no lifeboat on this ship.

Hart floated back into the bridge, followed by Valerie. Naomi knew even before Hart shook her head. "It's not looking good. The surge was big enough and there was enough brief defrosting that it's almost certain the inhabitants are irrevocably damaged."

Again, that word. As if they were inert things instead of humans who had lives as strange, complex, and messy as their own.

Cole was dead. The thought throbbed in her mind like a drumbeat.

"You say you're almost certain?" Naomi asked.

"I am about ninety per cent. There's a small chance the defrosting was minor enough that one or two of them are still viable."

"We can't feed an extra one or two, can we?" Valerie asked.

Naomi had done the math. They could feed an extra body—if it was an infant. Not a fully grown man, who with more height and weight would have higher calorie needs than any of the other women.

"And if we wake them up and discover all five of them survived?" Valerie continued. "If they realise that's what's happened, they could decide to take over the mission and kill us so they could survive."

"They wouldn't," Naomi said.

"They might," Valerie pressed. "They'd be torn up about it, sure. But if they thought it was the right thing? The only choice?"

Naomi closed her eyes, did some desperate mental math. "We could maybe feed one extra, if we all took reduced rations, but it would mean we would have no buffer if anything went wrong. One more malfunction and that's it."

"I don't trust Lockwood enough for that, not now," Valerie said. "Do you?"

"So what? We just let them all die, even if we could technically save one?" Hixon asked. "This is bullshit."

Valerie's eyes flashed. As second in command, Hixon shouldn't publicly disagree with her.

"This is survival," Lebedeva said. "Do not think they would give us the same courtesy."

"Goddammit," Hixon said, but for all her hand-wringing, she knew as well as the rest of them that this ship was designed for five people. Not ten. Not eight. Five.

"I don't like this either," Valerie said. "It was another reason I took out the backup crew in my final version of the schematics of the ship. Even if there hadn't been a surge, the pods are a drain on fuel efficiency. Yes, it'd be good to know that if something happened to one of us, someone with equivalent skills would be able to take up the reins, and it'd be useful to have a few extra hands once we landed on Cavendish. Cryogenics is hard on the body, though—it's not without its own risks."

"No, it's not," Hart said. "Sacrificing five lives to save our own. It's hard to balance with the Hippocratic Oath, I have to admit."

"If it's five instead of ten, you're saving five people," Lebedeva pointed out.

Hart glanced at Naomi.

Five lives and something that could become a sixth.

Lebedeva continued. "Yes, I do not know these men. Not like you. I do not like this, but they are dead either way. We cannot send them back. We cannot drop them on Mars. They cannot stay here. They are already dead, whether their brains would refire again or not."

Hixon's shoulders slumped. She was so used to solving problems, to finding the solution no matter how tricky it was.

Their conversation floated around Naomi, growing more

distant. Cole. A man she'd loved. A man she'd hated. A man who, near the end, she'd come to understand, if not forgive.

"It's like we're being punished for what we did," Hixon said.

"Don't you dare start with fate or God or any of that," Valerie said. "If you want to blame anyone, blame Lockwood. They're the ones who fucked up the numbers."

"This scenario would have happened with the original crew, if the plan had gone ahead," Lebedeva said. "They would be the ones doing this instead of us, that is all."

"Do you even care about this? They're just strangers to you, aren't they?" Hixon demanded.

"It is unfortunate."

"Unfortunate—"

"Hixon," Valerie interrupted. "Stop."

Hixon's nostrils flared, but her flame of anger snuffed out. Hart went to her, wrapping an arm around her wife's side.

Valerie caught each of their gazes. "This is hard. I recognise this. The right decisions can sometimes be the hardest. We'll do it tomorrow morning. We will give them a funeral. A hero's send-off." She stared at Naomi, unblinking. "There is time for you to say your goodbyes."

CHAPTER THIRTEEN

72 Days After Launch

54 Days to Mars

177 Days to Cavendish

Naomi said she'd go down to the Crypt last. She waited in the observation room while the others flitted out, one by one. She rested her chin on her knees as she stared at the expanse.

Even Lebedeva had spent some time in the Crypt, whispering Russian Orthodox liturgies over them. "Just in case," she'd said when she'd emerged.

After Hixon had come up, her eyes red-rimmed, Naomi finally asked her what Cole had been like on the Ares mission. She wanted to know. Needed to. Some part of her still felt like this was all happening to someone else. The skin on her face was numb.

Hixon folded herself on to the other side of the windowsill, resting her forehead against the reinforced glass, gaze focused on some distant star. They could both be staring at stars that had already died long ago, their light still reaching the craft thousands of years later. "He was a good commander, all things considered." Hixon sniffed. "One of those ones where, if you were falling behind, he'd be the one to keep pace with you and urge you forward. Even when things went tits up, he always stayed calm until the crisis was averted. That's when the temper might come out."

Naomi gave a mirthless laugh. "Well do I know."

"Yeah, I suppose you would," Hixon said, wiping her face with the back of her hand. "He was young. Bit impetuous. He always talked about his hopes for what would happen when we made it back home. He loved Mars and was as desperate as the rest of us to get there. But when he set foot on it…I don't know. It's not that it disappointed him. I think he was as awestruck as the rest of us. It's just, I got the sense what he really wanted was to go back to Earth to be a man who had gone to Mars."

Each of Hixon's words fell into place, echoing the picture of Cole that Naomi had long since put together. "Yeah. That."

"I'm sorry for you," Hixon offered. "We knew all of them down there but still…"

"We said our goodbyes long ago," Naomi said. A half-lie. "But thank you."

Naomi stood, making her way back to the spoke leading down to the Crypt.

She took her time, clasping each rung carefully, letting her body adjust as she descended into zero gravity again.

When she reached the storage bay, she floated over the pods. In zero G, there was no up or down. Her brain recalibrated no matter which direction she faced.

She reached down a hand to rest on the blurred, opaque outline of each face. She said her goodbyes, one by one. She spoke out loud to them, her voice soft but unwavering. Sharing her memories, thanking them for what they had learned, what they had taught her. If they could speak, would they accept their fate? Or would they beg, plead, fight for the same chance at life?

Up above, Hixon was probably still running numbers, hoping for an eleventh-hour save, a way to bend the impossible to her will. Naomi saw what was in front of them, just as Valerie and Lebedeva had. Hart knew, as a doctor, but she'd be hoping for a miracle, if partly for her wife's sake.

There was no other way. If there was, one of the five of them would have found it by now.

They hadn't introduced the flaw to the system, but it was difficult not to feel responsible. Especially when it was people you knew. Emotion clouded logic.

She said goodbye to Cole last.

She remembered marrying under the fake stars of the Hayden Planetarium in New York, eight months after she'd met him. She still didn't know why she raced towards marriage so quickly and why she'd agreed to such an expensive wedding. It'd been a beautiful ceremony underneath shifting nebulae in greens, blues, pinks, and purples. A kaleidoscopic projection tinging the faces of the attendees—most of whom were Cole's friends and family rather than hers.

Valerie had walked her down the aisle. Naomi had constellations sewn into her dress—the Hydra serpent; Andromeda, the girl rescued from the sea creature; Cygnus, the swan; Lyra, the poet and musician. At the bodice, Ran, Aegir, and Cavendish had been stitched in silver thread for luck.

Cole had been sharp in his tux, backlit by the false galaxy. Valerie had officiated as well, leading them through their vows. Naomi thought she'd been telling the truth, that she was promising to stay with him until the end. Thick and thin and all in between. Naomi had worn a ring of meteorite—she'd left it back on Earth, of course—and Cole one fashioned from a piece of the aluminium composite from the scrap metal of the *Ares* ship.

"That was the problem, wasn't it?" she asked him, softly. "In the end, we loved our careers more than each other. Or you wanted to stay married to your work and you were only too happy to let me divorce from mine. You wanted to trot me out as an astronaut's wife, but that's not all I wanted to be."

He'd been annoyed she'd refused to take his last name. But Lovelace was one of the few pieces of her family she had left. She liked the sound of it, the delicate image it painted in her mind. The fact it was the same as Ada Lovelace, one of the earliest programmers, who may or may not be one of her ancestors. Naomi Palmer had never felt like a name she could claim as hers.

Naomi grabbed the wall, moving herself closer. Had the surge fractured the molecular bonds or membranes in his cells, disconnecting synapses, erasing the memories they'd both shared that only she would go on to remember? If he wasn't gone, he would be soon enough.

There was so much she could say. The sick sense of failure that they couldn't make it work. The hatred that had somehow morphed into something almost like fondness, despite everything. Maybe they should have had one last dance on Catalina Island.

Naomi's head turned as she heard the distant sounds of someone coming down the ladder.

Valerie closed the hatch behind her, swimming towards her in the blue darkness.

"This is hardest for you out of all of us," she began. "I wanted to check in."

Naomi didn't say anything. Her hand was still on Cole's pod.

"He was a good man," Valerie began, then stopped.

Naomi smiled wryly. "He is as good or bad as anyone," she said. "No more, no less."

If he'd been chosen for the core crew, he'd still be on Earth. Home with his family, waiting for the replacement ship so he could catch up to her. Through sheer luck of the lottery, he was here with the other unlucky souls.

"It feels awful, deciding their fate for them," she said, voice low.

Valerie's face was smoothed by the cool light from the pods, making her look younger, more like the woman Naomi remembered from her childhood. "I know."

They sat there, in silence. Naomi didn't cry. She thought she would have. But the longer she stayed with her hand on the cold glass, the more she hardened. The choice had been made, there was no going back. No point railing against it. Even after switching off the pods, getting the life support back into its symbiotic balance with the other systems on the ship would be difficult. They'd all be working twelve-, sixteen-hour stretches. Naomi welcomed the work and the distraction.

"I've told the others I'll be the one to do it," Valerie said. "As captain, the responsibility falls to me." Her hand floated towards Naomi, as if she'd touch her, but at Naomi's stiffness, she drew back. "I'll take care of them. Of him, Naomi. As best I can."

Naomi tilted her head towards the black ceiling of the storage bay. The next time she came down here, the humming of the pods would be quiet. The light would change to the pale white of artificial sunlight if it was the "daylight" hours on board, or the amber lights of "night."

Naomi had planned to be strong and bottle up the swirl of her emotions. But Valerie had once told her not to be afraid of her rage. So why be afraid of frustration? Of grief?

Valerie's arms reached wide and Naomi floated into them. They were tethered to each other, suspended, twirling slowly with the momentum of Naomi pushing up to reach her. Naomi had rarely hugged Valerie, growing up. A few memories of stiff, unyielding embraces, especially in public. Down here, there was no one to see. Valerie's touch was light as she stroked the space between Naomi's shoulder blades.

"Thank you," Naomi whispered into Valerie's shoulder.

Valerie squeezed her tighter, then let her go.

CHAPTER FOURTEEN

6 Years Before Launch

Singapore

Naomi shifted from foot to foot on the boat as it neared the sea burial site.

She hadn't known Evan's father well—only met him a handful of times. She remembered him as tall, brusque, handsome. His cultured Chinese-Singapore accent had blurred from years spent in America. He'd always smelled of sharp cologne, just that little bit too overpowering.

For all she and Evan were still not speaking, Naomi wanted to support him, and so she'd flown to Singapore for the first time with Valerie in her jet, grateful to leave California behind for a time. Back home, the horizon was constantly hazy from the summer wildfires. Flames licked through the kindling of golden grass, the cypress and oak trees blackened.

The air was cleaner here. She could stay outside without a filter mask for up to two hours. Naomi wore black sunglasses, the lower half of her face exposed. By the end of that summer, wearing masks outdoors would become a legal requirement in California, rather than strongly recommended. A bare face in the Golden State was the equivalent of smoking two packs of cigarettes a day without even the nicotine buzz.

The problem was, it was also unbearably hot. She wore a cooling gel around her neck like the rest of the people on board, but her dress was sweltering. Her tights were borrowed from Valerie—too tall, tight at the hips but bunching at the ankles and knees. Her feet hurt from the heels she rarely wore. The water vapour fans blew chilled air that barely seemed to make a difference.

The burial party was small, despite Evan's father's influence. Daniel Kan had inherited his father's oil empire and recognised the competitiveness of wind, solar, and geothermal energy. He kept producing oil—gallons and gallons of it—but invested most of his profits in renewable energy and battery research and development, preparing for the shift. Singapore was motivated to create zero-carbon cooling options to remain habitable, but only a few governments were able to push through legislation to replace fossil fuels quickly enough. So he kept pumping out more oil. Evan stood near the chanting priest, holding the biodegradable urn of ashes. His face was tight. Around him, people held joss sticks, ghost money, and small bags of flowers. Most of them were in designer jeans and white tops, meaning Naomi felt overdressed and yet un-chic at the same time.

Naomi knew little of Taoist ceremonies, so she hung back, an observer not wanting to overstep but wanting to pay her respects. Valerie did the same. She said nothing. Naomi wondered if Valerie mourned her ex-husband. Growing up, Naomi had heard the raging fights on the phone, turned up the music on her earbuds to drown it out.

The priest finished his chanting, and Evan stepped forward to place the urn in the water. It was painted to look like a shell. It'd float for twenty minutes or so before the water broke down the paper and the ashes would ebb away in the currents. Whenever Evan visited the ocean, even if it was over in Cape Canaveral, he'd be able to pay his respects to his father.

The mourners threw the ghost money and the flowers into the water. Yellow and white chrysanthemums and purple irises bobbed along the surface of the water.

Evan didn't speak to her until they were back on land. The wake was in the roof garden of Evan's father's apartment, a lavish penthouse in a skyscraper overlooking the city. It was still warm and humid as afternoon lengthened to evening. The garden smelled of night jasmine.

Evan greeted each of the guests, taking their white envelopes with thanks and giving them his own in return.

Naomi offered him her gift, but he gave her the same bland thank you as everyone else. She opened the envelope he'd given her. A Singapore dollar and a sugar sweet. Naomi followed Valerie's lead, continuing to hang back. It was only after the feast, with dessert eaten first to bring sweetness to the sad occasion, that Evan came up to her.

Every time Naomi saw a snap of that red graffiti still circling around the drain of the internet, she remembered him scrubbing away at it, the muscles of his forearms rippling against tanned skin, his tendons taut with suppressed rage. The way Naomi had been unwilling to pick open their past.

"I'm sorry for your loss," she said, reflexively.

He snorted. "Everyone says that."

"Yeah. Always sounds hollow. But what else is there to say?"

"True enough." He stared out at the people gathering in remembrance of his father. Evan had seemed close to him.

Daniel could be exacting, but he had also been warm in a way Valerie never was with either of them, but especially Evan.

"Do you remember much about your parents' funerals?" he asked.

Naomi's throat tightened. "Not much." She had been nine for one and ten for the other. She remembered two pristine coffins, on two different days, and both times thinking it seemed a waste for something so shiny and new to go down in the dark for no one else to see. Her father's had been closed casket. Her mother's had been open, but she wished it'd been shut.

Naomi only started speaking again a few months after the second funeral. Valerie had always said Catherine was travelling for work. It'd taken Naomi years before she'd realised her mother had gone to a mental health institution after the fire, unable to cope with the loss of her husband and home. The pressure of a company, of a daughter, had been too much on top of the grief.

Naomi had been the one to find her mother's body when she was on weekend release from the centre. Sometime in the night, her mother had gone out into Valerie's garden. Stumbled over the edge of one of the steep steps of the landscaped levels. Broke her neck, right at the C3 vertebrae. It had been quick, they said, painless. That image was burned into Naomi's retina for years. In some ways, it was worse than the memories of the fire.

"I've been lucky, I guess," Evan said. "Here I am, almost thirty, and I haven't really lost anyone before."

"Burying your parents is especially hard," she said. "And grief is strange, so don't be surprised by that. You'll feel sad, then all right again, then guilty for feeling all right. Then the weirdest thought or memory will be the one that gets to you. Sometimes even years later." Naomi was still sad every time she smelled pancakes because her dad used to make the best ones.

Evan made a noise in his throat, taking everyone in. "Does the number of people who turn up show how much of an impact you left behind, do you think?"

Naomi shrugged a shoulder. "Think it depends more on if they're actually mourning rather than appearing to."

Evan winced, and Naomi realised she'd just implied everyone here was only pretending to care about his dad's death.

"That came out wrong." Naomi took another sip of wine. "I just mean people are selfish. I'm sure there are some people whose funerals are more about the living wanting to appear to mourn. Or hoping to impress someone else who might attend." Naomi nodded towards Valerie, who was surrounded by a small gaggle of "mourners."

"I take your point. How long before Valerie pitches Cavendish to the people here?" He scoffed. "What am I saying? She probably already has. I mean, the Man of Mars is here. Poster boy for the new world, surely."

Naomi craned her neck to see better. She had clocked him on the other side of the boat. "How did Cole Palmer know your father?"

Evan's mouth turned down. "Business. Sponsorship. Who knows."

Naomi reached out for his hand. He started, looked down at their clasped fingers, then at the other people in the room. Pulled his hand away. Her palm smarted, as if burned.

They'd both spent years with outsiders viewing them as siblings, even though they hadn't been raised together and weren't related by blood in any way. Over the past year, she'd thought about that kiss, time and again, and wondered why she had been so worried about what people might have thought. Evidently Evan hadn't come to the same conclusion.

Another mourner came up to Evan and she used it as an excuse to slip away from him. She moved towards Valerie and those caught in her orbit. Naomi saw Valerie's lips form the words Cavendish and she stopped, as if hitting the transparent wall of her biome. Evan had been right. Even here, at her ex-husband's funeral, Valerie wouldn't stop the hustle.

Naomi took another glass of wine. Across the rooftop garden, Evan's expression was shuttered. Naomi left the rooftop, heading back into Evan's father's apartment. She skulked through the rooms, an interloper, until she found a quiet, back sitting room. It was as smooth and minimalist as the rest of the penthouse, the walls lined with large, framed prints of the universe captured by the James Webb telescope. Daniel Kan had been taken by space as well, it seemed. Or his interior decorator had.

She'd finished her wine when the door opened. Naomi didn't startle.

She expected Evan, but Cole Palmer paused, his hand still on the doorknob.

"Sorry," he said. "Thought it'd be empty."

"It's all right," she said. "You can sit, if you want. Escaping everyone wanting to meet the First Man of Mars?"

"Got it in one," he said, with that megawatt smile she'd seen on countless news feeds, documentaries, and photos. It was always strange, to see someone in the flesh you'd only seen through the lens of a camera on a pixellated screen. But that was a real smile instead of the one put on for strangers knowing it'd be captured for the masses.

He'd just turned thirty-four, two years after his journey to Mars, and his clean-cut image was marred only by the beginnings of a reddish five o'clock shadow. He had a few faint lines at the corner of his eyes, no hint of the grey that would soon start to grace his temples, forcing out the reddish brown.

He perched on the opposite sofa, hands holding his near-empty wine glass. They both stared at the prints. She didn't ask him those same questions everyone asked him about Mars. They spoke instead about the pictures, about science and space and the universe. Then they lapsed into silence, standing just that bit too close as they took in the art. Naomi sensed his attraction, and she ended up not regretting the dress and the way it hugged her. Naomi leaned close to him, paused, raised her eyebrows. He gave a hopeful "yes?" and she drew him in for a kiss. His fingers tangled in her hair.

Eight months later, they were married.

CHAPTER FIFTEEN

84 Days After Launch

42 Days to Mars

165 Days to Cavendish

The *Atalanta* sped ever closer to Mars.

Naomi couldn't get the image of the five wrapped bodies in the airlock out of her mind. They'd used rubber sheeting meant for lining her soil planters. Horribly, she'd spent a split second wondering if they should keep the corpses for fertiliser, or, even worse, as emergency calories. But she couldn't. She just couldn't.

They had looked like tarred mummies. Small. Diminished. She hadn't been able to tell which one was Cole. One of those bodies she had once known as well as her own. That body had lain next to her at night. She'd memorised every scar, every birthmark. She'd learned to read every expression that face had made, searching for the clues to show what he meant versus what he said. She'd been able to pick out the timbre of his voice, his laugh, from the other side of a crowded room. She remembered every line of those hands that had held her close or slammed doors after their fights. A funeral had started their story, and now another ended it.

Cole would have liked the thought of being buried in space, though he'd probably rather have been buried on Mars.

The five women had gathered, shoulder to shoulder, staring through the porthole of the airlock. Everyone had said a few words. Naomi couldn't remember what she said at the time. It had been inelegant but heartfelt, she knew that much.

Valerie pressed the button. The bodies were there, and then a blink, a release of pressure, and they were gone. Cole floated out there, somewhere, left behind with his crew mates. Man overboard. Naomi's eyes still stayed dry.

They had a wake in the rec room. Hixon played ukulele—it was small enough she could justify bringing it among her personal items—and Lebedeva sang, her voice surprisingly good. Naomi wished she'd considered making vodka moonshine with some of the potatoes. She wanted that sharp bite, the burn against her tongue.

Twelve days later, the life support had stabilised. No more flickering lights, no more falling asleep wondering if they'd never wake up. Food supplies were steady. Now that the cryopods were dark, fuel efficiency had improved. They had slipped back into their routine, the rhythm of monotony. Yet the five women tiptoed through the ship, as though afraid to disturb ghosts on board, even if none of them were superstitious.

It was easier to distract herself with her algae and crops. Lebedeva was teaching the others to make Russian food with what they had—borscht with beets, carrots, and onions. Perogies with the potatoes and their dwindling supplies of powdered cheese and milk. Everything was sprinkled with copious amounts of dill, which tasted like liquorice to Naomi.

Beneath the shapeless coveralls, Naomi's body changed, day

by day. Her centre of gravity had shifted. Her stomach had always been flat, her body spare and muscular, and the new softness was strange. She'd press her fingers against the flesh that gave at her hips, her thighs, tracing the curve of her belly. She'd thought she'd hate it, from years of swallowing the message that women shouldn't be too big or too much. She didn't mind taking up a little extra space.

Each morning, she wondered if it would be the day she'd miscarry. If what was hidden inside her would uproot. It still clung on, and the window to make her decision was closing. Neither direction was clear-cut. She'd be arrested whenever the *Atalanta II* arrived. They might still utilise her skills, but that gave no promise of clemency. No promise that she'd be able to stay with her child and watch them grow up.

She imagined the child going from a nebulous thing, this bulbous foetus, to a person. To watch them grow, to see an echo of the child's father in the tilt of their eyes or the curve of a lip. Or to see her own features embedded in another's DNA.

It'd be a hard life for a child on Cavendish. And lonely. Children weren't scheduled until the third wave, once infrastructure was established.

But her child could still grow up on Cavendish. A world without Earthen rules, at least for a little while.

Her fingers curled spirals across the skin of her stomach, and she knew she'd made her decision.

"Grow," she whispered.

Naomi spent more time in the rec room, watching old films or toying with the various landscapes. It was still like eating artificial gummies when what she craved was fresh fruit. She'd open the console and send Evan messages every few days, even though she technically no longer needed his help with her work. She was hungry for information back home, even if it wasn't good news. Cochran's party had already swept the mid-term elections, and his re-election was almost guaranteed. His base was still so strong he might even, horribly, have a shot at a third term.

Stories about the Atalanta 5 were still vicious. Digs at Valerie's age, at Lebedeva's past, snide homophobic remarks about Hart and Hixon. Naomi was still painted as a nepotism pick. Naomi was the last person to pretend access to Valerie's money and connections hadn't put her in a position to be here. She'd still worked damn hard to make sure the opportunity didn't go to waste.

Naomi knew there was still anger back home, deep and pulsing, about what they'd done. The Atalanta 5 had taken action against men who had told them they knew best.

Not everything Evan sent was negative. He knew she'd want to see the development of a new type of algae that could absorb more carbon dioxide, which could give Earth a few more years of habitability. San Francisco had successfully lobbied for higher taxes for the wealthiest, pledging the money towards environmentally friendly and sustainable housing to help combat rising homelessness. Yet it all felt too late.

Naomi sent him a message that evening when she knew Evan was more likely to be online.

Atalanta: *It's N. No specific queries from the crew. Requesting a general status update.*

She scrolled through some of the medical training documentation Hart had given her, only taking in half of it, as she waited for his message to come through.

Earth: *Sorry for the delay. Work's been mad. Doing research to try and determine why there was a higher than usual resistance to the flu vaccine last year to see if that helps our approach for this year. Long hours.*

She could feel his exhaustion, even from there. She wasn't sure what to say beyond empty commiserations. She hadn't been able to bear bringing up what had happened to the backup crew, and she wasn't sure if Valerie had told him in her communications. A quick opening of the logs showed she hadn't.

Earth: *Construction on the* Atalanta II *is continuing.*

Naomi inhaled slowly, then exhaled.

Atalanta: *We'll still have Cavendish, for a little while. And women will still be the first to step on that planet. That's something they can't take from us.*

The symbolism of that would be undeniable. It could fracture the new status quo.

They'd seen what Cochran was doing with the old world. What would he try to do with a new one?

Unsure what else to say, Naomi changed the subject, asking Evan how he was. He gave a terse "fine," but she teased it out of him. He was isolated, though to a lesser extent, of course. Unable to tell anyone what he was up to, the secret eating him up. She knew how he felt, but her pity was limited. At least he could go grab fast food—what she wouldn't give for a hamburger—if he wanted, or go for a hike to clear his head.

The long hours were gruelling, and only the beginning before his second, secret shift started. In a little over a month, he'd be done. The *Atalanta* would be through the warp ring, ideally speeding towards Cavendish, unable to reach him for weeks, months. Would he be relieved?

Naomi didn't even know if Evan wanted to board one of the earlier ships or wait for the last one out. Early, she'd guess. Think of the hiking trails on Cavendish, just waiting to be explored. He'd be able to take deep lungfuls of air.

Naomi's hands floated over the keys. For a moment so intense it hurt, like looking into a bright light, she wanted to set the secret down before him. She typed it out: *I'm pregnant.* Stared at the words. Pressed backspace, deleting one letter at a time, until the cursor blinked on a blank screen.

The crew deserved to hear it from her, directly, not by accident if they scrolled through the chat logs. That was what she told herself, in any case, before she said her goodbyes to Evan, knowing he'd be yearning for sleep.

She stood, stretching, leaving the VR console and heading back to her lab. After she had finished the last of her work for the day, she leaned her right temple against the glass of one of the thin tubes. She closed her eyes but still felt the almost warm glow of purple against her skin. She breathed in and out, long and slow. For the first time in days, she felt almost at peace.

Time to take the others out of the dark.

CHAPTER SIXTEEN

92 Days After Launch

34 Days to Mars

157 Days to Cavendish

The rest of the crew rarely entered Valerie's quarters. Her room was large enough for a desk and a couple of screens, but she still stole the observation room when she could. Couldn't beat the view.

Naomi knocked, waited.

"Come in," Valerie called.

One screen showed blue lines criss-crossing black—a skeleton of the base buildings seen from above. On another, Valerie had zoomed in on one of the heating systems, touch-screen calculations scrawled in the margins.

"Yes?" Her tone was polite, but the frown line that appeared between her eyes betrayed her annoyance at the interruption. "I still need a name for our base. It hasn't come to me yet. Maybe we have to see it first."

Like when people didn't name their child until they held the squalling, wrapped bundle. Naomi stifled her laugh. She hadn't even begun to consider names.

"Two years isn't a long time," she said instead.

"Mmm," Valerie said, as if it didn't bother her.

"Aren't you worried?" Naomi asked.

"I have a plan to get them off our backs. Don't worry. I know how to play it." She gave a slow smile.

Valerie had always put up a brash, unbothered front for the media. She was good at making it seem like everything she said was honest and off the cuff. Naomi had lost count of the times she'd watched Valerie get people to agree to something that they thought was their idea in the first place. Naomi had to hope it'd still work ten and a half light years away. She wanted to ask what Valerie meant, but knew better. Her mentor was in one of those moods where she'd only say, "Wait and see."

Valerie cocked her head, bird-like. "You're not here for that. You've got something else chewing at you."

Naomi stepped into the room, closing the door behind her. She tapped one of the thumbnails of the Cavendish probes on a screen and expanded it. A photo of the proposed site for the base, in grainy definition. The gymnosperms were the same ones she'd grown in the larger biome. Far older, their roots sunk deep. It was on the shores of a freshwater lake, the sand a pale pink from quartz. They'd chosen an area near the equator that would be temperate. On Cavendish, seasons changed every forty-five days. On the base, they'd be imperceptible temperature changes, but nearer the poles, seasons could swerve from 30 degrees Celcius to minus twenty degrees in a month or two.

Naomi squinted at the screen. This was where she might give birth. A toddler could run across that beach, kicking up the sand. Making castles and stomping them down only to build them up again.

"I've kept something from you," Naomi said. "I needed to be sure."

Valerie leaned back in her chair. The body language brought Naomi back to her teen years, needing Valerie's permission for a school trip or asking for new supplies for her makeshift lab in the shed in the garden.

"Out with it, Naomi." Her gaze had sharpened to a point.

She may as well be direct.

"I'm pregnant. Almost four months."

Valerie's face was inscrutable—only the tiniest flicker of an eyebrow and a glance at Naomi's midriff gave her away.

Naomi pulled the fabric of her coveralls tight, showing the small bump. Valerie leaned forward and placed her hand on it, just for a second, before her hands dropped to her lap.

"When?" she asked.

Here came the questions she really didn't want to answer. There was a particular embarrassment of skirting around the subject of sex with the person who basically raised you. "The night before quarantine."

An exhalation. "Do the others know? Hart?"

"Just her. She guessed before my first medical. I asked her to keep it to herself while I decided. If I'd keep it."

"And I take it you are. Is the child healthy?"

"Yes."

"Who's the father?" Valerie asked, point blank.

Naomi swallowed. "Someone I really shouldn't have slept with. Someone who isn't mine."

Valerie steepled her hands over her mouth, elbows pressed together. Naomi could almost feel the power of her mentor's thoughts as she worked through it all. "God," she said, blanching beneath skin that had already lost its Earthen colour. "I pulled the plug on the child's father, didn't I?"

Cole would have gone into cryo just after Naomi left for quarantine. Naomi chose her words carefully, rolling them in her mouth. "Cole was already gone."

"Fuck."

Naomi looked down at Valerie. She rarely stood over her mentor like this. At five-foot-ten, Valerie had always towered over Naomi's five-foot-four frame, but beyond that, she always seemed larger than life, a magnetic force that attracted any energy in the room and knew how to manipulate it.

"Are you angry?" Naomi asked. "I can often never tell with you."

Valerie stood, and there was the put-together woman Naomi knew. "I'm rearranging everything in my head. We'll have our work cut out for us, if you're to give birth after we land." She gave a laugh. "I'll have to design you a nursery, for a start."

Naomi blinked quickly. The tears snuck up on her, but she kept them back. A tiny part of her had worried Valerie would tell her there was no way she could keep it. That doing so would jeopardise the mission. She wasn't sure if she'd be strong enough not to bow to the pressure, if Valerie exerted it. Valerie knew, more than anyone, that Naomi wouldn't have made this choice lightly.

"The child might end up calling you Nana, you know," Naomi said, striving for lightness. Yet the words gave her a pang. Her child would never meet their grandparents. Wouldn't even be able to visit the graves. Naomi only had a handful of photos of them, deep in her files.

"Like hell she will," Valerie said, pulling a face.

"I don't know the assigned gender yet." She'd avoided finding out the physical sex—she didn't mind either way. She would have cared, if they were still back on Earth. Where having a girl meant she would be born into a world where her chances of doing what she wanted with her life were smaller and shrinking each day.

Valerie snorted. "I'll say 'she' until you know for sure, then. I will maybe—maybe—concede to Nan." She squeezed past Naomi and strode out of her room. Their meeting had concluded, but she was all business. "Come on, then. Time for you to tell the others."

Later, Naomi went to her room, leaving the others to discuss it among themselves.

It'd gone smoother than she'd hoped. Hart had long suspected Naomi would keep the child. Hixon and Lebedeva seemed surprised. Hixon was delighted; Lebedeva markedly cooler at the news.

"You'll need more food," she'd said. "Did you calculate this?"

"Two extra nutriblocks a day. Well within parameters." It wouldn't have been, if they had defrosted the backup crew and one had been viable. She shoved away any guilt.

Hixon had held up her hands. "Eat as many of those bricks as you like."

Lebedeva had shrugged, gone back to her meal, and that had pretty much been the end of it. Naomi had no desire to be a fly on the wall. Hart would anticipate how the news would change the balance of the interpersonal relationships and be there if anyone needed to talk to her. Naomi had no idea if Hart and Hixon had ever wanted children.

Despite living on top of each other in a ship hurtling through space, they had avoided a lot of personal questions. They were wary of sparking fights or unintentionally opening old wounds when they needed to try and rely on each other. At the same time, if they let things fester, they were bound to bubble up at some point.

Naomi lay back on the bed, pressing her feet together like the pages of a book, letting her knees fall open. It helped ease the pressure on her lower back, but she was never comfortable. She'd have some relief if she went down to the main body of the ship, if only she could bring herself to.

She'd needed supplies from the Crypt for days but kept putting it off. The cryopods were still there, a stark reminder. She had to stay strong and focus. Cole was gone. She'd said her goodbyes.

Yet it still felt unfinished. Or unfair. Cole Palmer had been the Man of Mars, the Martian, the Red Man. Cole's story was meant to end on a grand finale—making it to over one hundred, dying on a bed somewhere on Cavendish, his reddish hair pure white, surrounded by generations of his family. He was meant to leave the universe as a patriarch who had left his mark. He had always wanted a family. A giant brood of children so his progeny would carry on. Once, Naomi had thought she wanted that. Eventually.

"Five years ago, neither of us could have imagined where we'd be," she said aloud, face pointed up towards the ceiling, eyes closed. It felt good to speak to him. Like they were both still back in their old apartment, after dinner, when they held those thick-bottomed blue-green tumblers she'd bought from a thrift store one day on a whim. She would have gin and he had whisky. The news would be on, but muted, flashing lights against the living room. Their conversation had meandered, or they'd lapsed into silence, waiting for the day to end.

"You were a good father to your son. I'm sure of it," she said, opening her eyes. She reached her arms out, as if she floated in a pool rather than her small bed.

"If I'd stayed. If you'd stayed. You would have been a good father to our child."

She let her gaze fall to her belly. She was still so tired, all the time—she let herself drift into that liminal space between sleep and awake.

Even in her tiny, empty room, she couldn't bring herself to say the next words aloud. So she stated them in her head, each word clear and loud as a bell.

But this child was never yours.

CHAPTER SEVENTEEN

6 Years Before Launch

Houston, Texas

Naomi knew as soon as her phone rang that she'd made it into NASA.

She'd flown back out to Houston and aced both her interviews. She gave them a presentation on the Cavendish biome, watching the panel's eyes grow increasingly round. Most of the details of what she'd grown in her larger biome hadn't leaked to the press, and Naomi hadn't yet written many papers on it.

One of them had asked why Naomi wanted to come to NASA and leave behind a corporate sector that gave her such opportunities. Naomi said she knew that for NASA to travel to Cavendish, they'd need to partner with companies like Hawthorne, and they'd need three main things:

1. Better fuel efficiency through ion drives for relatively short distances.
2. To crack the Alcubierre equation now that they'd discovered negative energy for longer distances.
3. The ability to grow food and keep the crew fed, both on the way and once they arrived.

Naomi couldn't help as much with the first two, but the last had become her area of expertise. NASA needed her more than Hawthorne did at present.

It had been risky, to be that brass-necked and state that *they* needed *her*. She'd channelled her inner Valerie Black. She wasn't sure she could get away with it, or if the all-male panel would decide she was too arrogant. But it'd paid off.

Naomi packed up the rest of her things and officially moved in with Cole, who was already based out in Houston. They'd dated long distance for eight months, then gotten married. Even after marriage, they'd scandalised Cole's parents by staying long distance until she got the job with NASA.

The week before training started, as she tidied away the last of her things, she realised her period was almost two weeks late.

She hadn't thought much of it. Her cycle had rarely been regular. At the first sign of extra stress, it'd disappear for months at a time, then return when life calmed down. But for the last few months, she'd been regular within a week or so, even if her cycle was longer than the standard twenty-eight days.

The day before training, she slunk into a convenience store on the other end of town, a cap over her hair and her most opaque filter mask over the lower half of her face and bought a pregnancy test. Just in case.

She jiggled her knees as she waited for the results.

She did the mental math. She was maybe two weeks late. She and Cole were finally living together and the novelty still hadn't worn off. When he came home from work, she'd reach for him almost as soon as he was through the door. He oversaw astronaut candidates in the Neutral Buoyancy Lab, training them for spacewalks in the vast underwater pool. He always smelled of chlorine, his hair brittle beneath her fingertips.

They'd been careful. Cole had agreed to go on the male contraceptive pill, as hormones had never agreed with Naomi even if they regulated her cycle. They deeply affected her mood. They had still used condoms.

Cole must have forgotten to take it one morning with his orange juice and coffee. That and a broken condom was all it took.

It could be the stress of starting training had thrown her off again. This wasn't the first time she'd taken a pregnancy test, just in case. Previous ones had always come back negative. This one shouldn't have been any different. Naomi called herself a fool a dozen times as she stared at the little stick with its accusing blue lines.

Her training started tomorrow. She'd have to postpone her place (if they even let her), and decline the goddamn governmental birth bonus because otherwise she'd have to pledge giving up work for five years. She and Cole would have to scramble funds for childcare. Naomi would have to hope that by the time she could return to the workforce six months to a year after birth, some other expert in astro-hydroponics didn't sneak into the spot they may or may not hold for her. Especially if said new expert was male and wouldn't be leaving a babe at home. She wouldn't stand a chance.

Naomi threw the stick against the shower tiles. It hit with a smack and clattered into the tub. She paced through her new apartment, in a nice part of Houston, half an hour's drive to Clear Lake and the Johnson Space Center.

Think. Think. What are my options?

She'd bought the test with cash, kept her face away from the cameras as much as possible.

It didn't make sense to bring a new child into the world when Earth only had thirty, forty years left. Naomi had gone to her high school friend Lynn's baby shower the previous year. She couldn't help but ask Lynn why she'd gotten IVF. Lynn had shrugged a shoulder, her stomach already distended—she was having twins. She'd have to pay the additional child tax on one of them, which wasn't cheap. The IVF would have been a pretty penny, too.

"Earth has been thirty years from dying for twenty years," Lynn had said. "It's going to stay thirty years off forever, just to scare us into recycling."

Lynn had been surrounded by other expectant or recent mothers, children playing in the shade out back. Naomi had felt out of place as the one attendee not even dating anyone at the time, much less married or thinking about kids. It was as if Naomi had blinked and everyone her age was having children. Like there was some sort of unspoken pact Naomi had broken.

If you were reading the signs closer, Naomi had wanted to say, *you would realise this time, thirty years is likely the best-case scenario.* Wars had broken out due to the ever-increasing waves of people displaced by climate change, with many countries shutting down their borders through force. Refugee aid programs were cut left and right, leaving philanthropists like Valerie to plug the funding gaps. Naomi didn't have the heart to tell Lynn that if things didn't change, those babies in her belly might not make it to middle age.

So many went about their day-to-day life with the vague unease that things were sliding past the point of no return. It was easier to push it away, to focus on the problems that could be solved. What to have for dinner. Fretting about how to pay for that leak in the roof. Those in power can worry about the larger things—that's why we voted for them. What can one person do?

Naomi needed to move. She fished the pregnancy test from the bottom of the bath, wrapped it in a plastic bag, and shoved it into the pocket of her hoodie. She paced through her nice, boring suburban neighbourhood. There had been a cold snap—gooseflesh shivered across her skin until her furious pacing warmed her up.

It'd been easy, in the end, for Cochran to borrow enough from religious rhetoric to overturn *Roe v. Wade* but only for the first child. Population control was still a necessity, so they reluctantly also increased sex education in schools. They still espoused the virtues of monogamous marriage, but birth control was readily available. This had the benefit of convincing left-leaning voters, such as disenfranchised libertarians, to support Cochran. And of course, it was a death knell for vat-grown wombs like Valerie's Haven.

Naomi walked faster.

With the additional child tax, the poor were unable to afford more than one child, the middle class were largely content to stop at one, and the rich continued to illustrate that having a brood of children showed just how rich they were. All in the name of population control and the good of the country, the world.

Naomi threw away the pregnancy test in someone else's

trash half a mile from her apartment. She wove her way back, thinking it all through, weighing up her options.

When Cole returned from work, he drew her close, his mouth on hers. They took a shower together, and she tried not to think of that *thwack* of the plastic against the tile. It hadn't left a mark. She ran her hands down the muscles of his back and tried not to resent that he couldn't remember to take a damn pill every morning.

Naomi had grown up wanting children, but later. Much later. Five years, maybe ten. When she'd had time to finish training and go to space for a tour or two. Save up the money to turn down the bonus and keep her career, or hope the political situation swung back towards progress. Why have children unless she could be sure humanity would actually last longer than a few decades?

A tiny part of her wondered if Cole's happiness at being a father would outweigh what it meant for Naomi. If he'd realise the extent of what she'd have to give up. In his mind, she would have no choice but to keep it. That was the way things were, now.

The next morning, Naomi reported for training with her fellow astronaut candidates. She threw herself into every task. She was the only woman.

When she had her first free weekend, she flew back to California, to Valerie, to ask for her help.

CHAPTER EIGHTEEN

119 Days After Launch

7 Days to Mars

130 Days to Cavendish

Day by day, Mars grew larger. Naomi would find excuses to go down to the observation room to watch it. When they neared the warp ring, it'd spread below them like Earth had. Naomi could just make out Mars' two moons: the larger Phobos and the smaller Deimos.

She wished they had the time and ability to stop and set down. Naomi could walk, heavily suited, along the planet Cole had been to not long before they met. She'd see the pale blue sky turned rusted orange at the horizon. She'd kick at the reddish dust to find the true colours hiding beneath.

One day, people might live there. If the terraforming took root, shifting the planet green. At her job in Sutherland, she'd focused on growing plants on Mars as well as on the ISS and the Gateway. She'd found ways to chelate the calcium perchlorate in native Martian soil so they instead formed harmless crystals so any plants grown weren't poisonous. There would still be the challenge of dealing with the fact that plants often concentrate heavy metals, but Naomi had been working with some of the plants used in bioremediation around the mines on Earth. She'd carefully created cassettes of genes that could be integrated into crop genomes that would allow them to survive in high-metal soils. She'd figured out how to concentrate the metals in nodules that could be removed mechanically—cleaning the soil and making the plants safe as a human food source.

It was doable, but UKSA and ESA couldn't access the funding they'd needed to make Naomi's work there a true success. They needed a Hawthorne with deep pockets. They needed a Valerie Black.

The *Atalanta* had come all this way only to see Mars from orbit. A rock that so many stories had been written about. So many myths and fears and legends.

Then they'd fit themselves into the warp ring for the test jump. The ring would help ensure the ship was an exact location for the equation and give parameters for the warp bubble for utmost accuracy.

In one week, Naomi and her crew mates would test the warp drive and see if they could indeed drag their destination closer to them through space-time. If it worked, they'd slot themselves back into the warp ring and away they'd go again. All the way to Cavendish.

That evening, as she finished work on her tablet in her lab, she heard a ping. For half a minute, it didn't register as bizarre, until she realised it was a specific notification she hadn't heard since Earth.

She drew it towards her, frowning. There it was:

New message.

Evan Kan: *Hey.*

Her frown deepened. She typed the first words that came to mind.

Naomi Lovelace: *What the fuck?*

He'd timed it for a shorter window of communication. Five minutes passed as the signal swung its impossible way back to Earth. Another five minutes for his reply.

Evan Kan: *It worked. I'm sending this through the main hub but encrypted and rerouted to your tablet. A buddy taught me how. I wanted to talk to you before you went through. Actually talk to you. This should be secure.*

Naomi Lovelace: *I suppose I should take advantage of this, then. I've been wondering how to ask you, but not wanted to put it on the official records—do you by any chance know if Earth is still sending the* Atalanta *messages?*

It was something that had been niggling at her. They'd sent messages the *Atalanta* had ignored from lower Earth orbit, but they knew the ship's location and projected path. It'd be easy to send further missives, but Valerie hadn't mentioned anything. Naomi had asked Hixon, but she hadn't heard of anything either, and seemed annoyed about it.

Evan Kan: *Funnily enough, that's what I wanted to ask you about, too. Earth is definitely still sending messages, and V is ignoring each and every one. I've urged her to at least see what they're saying or if they're offering anything, but she's refused. I don't know what's in them, but you'd be able to access them from the hub.*

They still save on the drive. A little hard to access, but doable.

Naomi rubbed her lower back, easing the tight muscles. A conversation that could have taken a few minutes had already stretched out to almost an hour.

Naomi Lovelace: *That would be crossing a line I can't come back from. It'd be undermining her and Hixon at once. I'm technically lowest ranked on this ship. Maybe I should just trust her.*

Evan Kan: *Are you really okay with not knowing? It could be they're offering clemency. Or that there's more to this mission than you know.*

A thread of unease wound through her. Why wouldn't Valerie tell them what Earth had said? Naomi would previously have stated their mission had always been clear. Naomi sometimes feared that Valerie had already lied to them once—had Valerie found out about *Atalanta II* and not passed that on to the crew? Naomi could have explained it away, that the distraction would have only caused stress and opened them up to making errors when they needed to focus. Could she say the same again? It was an uncomfortable pattern.

More minutes of delay. His next message told her it was up to her if she wanted to read them and gave her instructions on how to access the subfolder.

Evan Kan: *If there's one thing we both know about my mother, it's that she never leaves anything to chance. There is always a contingency. If she's read them and not told you, they are saying something she doesn't want you to know. You know this as well as I do, but it's up to you what you do next. Send me a goodbye before you go to the warp ring.*

Then he was gone.

She swallowed several times in quick succession, as if that would ease the tight knot of guilt.

It was late on Earth—nearly two in the morning. Naomi should have been in bed ages ago. She went back to her room, the amber lights leading the way, her tablet held tight in her hand.

As she brushed her teeth, she thought about the day NASA had told Valerie they were firing Hawthorne from Project Atalanta, a year before launch. Valerie had stood perfectly still in the centre of the lab as people tiptoed around her, packing their things. Everyone had that same blank expression. As if a bomb had just been detonated and their ears were ringing as they waited for shrapnel to fall.

Naomi spat into the sink, rinsing her mouth out with water that had been recycled through the systems—and their bodies—countless times since they'd taken off. The potable water had once been their urine, sweat, even water in their breath. It was all distilled and cleaner than water back on Earth, but it was carefully rationed. God, she wanted a shower. They always helped her think, the warmth chasing away the stress of the day. She was tired of sponge baths.

Naomi had only seen Valerie that furious a handful of times in her life. She'd known, with certainty, that Valerie would make NASA pay.

She sat at the little desk by her bed, too agitated to sleep. She unwrapped one of her extra nutriblocks, forcing herself to chew the gummy stuff.

Evan was right. Valerie never left anything to chance. She was always one, two, three steps ahead. Even when they'd been thrown off Project Atalanta, it hadn't been long before she'd approached Naomi with her plan to steal the ship. Naomi had thought she'd been joking, but she had every step planned out. She'd put in the manual override on the ship long before NASA had thrown Hawthorne off the project.

She'd known she'd have to take it on her own terms. To reach Cavendish and have a stake in it at the start.

The women on the ship could make no claim on the exosolar planet. Not for longer than two years. As soon as the *Atalanta II* touched the surface, that was the end of any chance of making their utopia a reality.

But Valerie had been told she couldn't do something over and over again, and that hadn't stopped her. What was an outdated treaty that hadn't been ratified by all countries of the world?

It was late. All the women on the ship would be asleep.

Naomi ghosted through the curved hallway and slipped into the rec room.

It took her a few tries to find the subfolder. She stared at the list of messages. They were all marked as read. Should she start with the most recent one, or the oldest?

It mattered little, in the end. Most of the messages were

more or less the same. In the early ones, they were official, with all the pomp and circumstance:

> *By the authority vested in me as President by the Constitution and the laws of the United States of America, and to ensure the safety and integrity of its citizens, in accordance with other major world leaders,*
> *it is hereby ordered as follows:*

...and so on. Demanding they return at once or face the consequences. Citing the specific laws they had broken. Berating them like they were a group of errant children. Small wonder Valerie had ignored those.

Naomi should find the messages frightening, but way out here, it was hard to feel intimidated. She couldn't help but read the missives in Cochran's voice. He had a peculiar intonation—in his speeches, he tried for gravitas but ended up speaking with that untethered transatlantic accent from old movies. Cochran was a desiccated hard-boiled egg of a man—hair too white to be from anything but a bottle, pale skin spotted with freckles. His dark eyes, blond eyebrows and eyelashes gave him the look of a skinny, naked mole rat, but with perfect, Chicklet teeth. He'd been handsome, once, but time and hatred had bleached him.

The later missives had their hot air punctured. They were more informal, with an edge of desperation.

> *Your takeover of the Atalanta is in violation of uncountable laws. This is fact. We understand your frustration that Hawthorne was taken off the project, and we recognise that your work made much of the*

Atalanta possible. I could continue to threaten you, but what is the point in that? I will admit we should have handled this better. We should have worked with you instead of cutting you out.

Naomi blinked. By virtue of silence, Valerie had gotten the President of the United States to admit he was wrong. And they said miracles couldn't happen.

Not that she was entirely convinced he wrote it. More likely, Vice President Thomas was the one who drafted it. He was usually the more temperate of the two.

We know we cannot easily decommission the warp ring, and that you could instead calculate your way to Cavendish from a different starting location, but that would risk the ship. So we have listened to your proposed plan. We discussed it at length. What you ask for we cannot agree to. I am sure you can understand why. The next ships will arrive with the originally proposed inhabitants.

Naomi's shoulders clenched. Valerie had sent a missive back to Earth and demanded something. What?

We ask that once you land on Cavendish, you revitalise the backup crew—

Naomi glanced away, grimacing. Valerie obviously hadn't shared that bit of news with Earth yet.

—and establish a base on the surface. We will arrive as soon as is feasible with the Atalanta II. We cannot give an exact arrival date at this point, due to several unforeseen delays.

Naomi snorted. "That's because you don't have us helping you with it, you ghoul."

You will acquiesce to our PR statements and send missives back to Earth showing life on Cavendish.
Once we arrive and the base is in good working order, you will welcome the exodus ships with hospitality and camaraderie. In return, we will pardon your crimes.
If we do not hear from you by the time you jump through the warp ring, we will assume you have turned down our offer, and when the Atalanta II arrives you will be arrested and transported back to Earth.

I think that, considering the circumstances, you will consider this more than fair.

We await your reply.

FRANKLIN M. COCHRAN

Naomi sucked her lower lip. She couldn't find any outgoing missives. What had Valerie sent them? What had she demanded?

It was a laurel leaf. Grudgingly offered, likely poisoned. The government had no real reason to hold to it, once the *Atalanta II* was on the ground. This missive had almost certainly not been released publicly, and was likely classified. Valerie must have seen it for what it was—a way to keep them obedient long enough for the next crop of settlers to arrive. Valerie saw through that. She wouldn't cave so easily.

The proof was still before her: Valerie was keeping secrets. From the crew. From Naomi.

CHAPTER NINETEEN

123 Days After Launch

3 Days to Mars

126 Days to Cavendish

Mars was growing ever closer. Naomi was running out of time. By confronting Valerie, Naomi would be revealing that she and Evan were speaking privately.

She couldn't let the other women do the test jump and then go to Cavendish without realising what the U.S. was offering. They deserved to know the truth, and Valerie was in the wrong for hiding it from them.

Bringing it up in front of the group with no warning would only trigger Valerie's anger. The morning of the third day before the jump, an hour before breakfast, Naomi knocked on the observation room door, where Valerie had locked herself in to work.

"Yes?" came Valerie's voice.

Valerie had clearly already been up for hours. Her eyes were bright and clear, the blueprints back up on the screens, the universe spread out before her.

"The others deserve to know," Naomi said without preamble. "That the U.S. has offered us clemency."

Valerie's only response was a slow blink. If she was surprised Naomi had found her out, it didn't show.

"What message did you send back to them?" Naomi asked. "What plan have they rejected?"

"I know what I'm doing here, Naomi," she said.

"That's not an answer."

Valerie stood, and Naomi had to tilt her head up.

It would have been easier, to pretend not to see. To go through the ring, let the offer expire, keep her head down. Her heartbeat had risen, but she refused to back down.

"You don't like me confronting you, any more than I like questioning your judgement."

Valerie's gaze flicked at the blueprints. "Look. I didn't mention it because it's an empty promise. Do you really think that they'll land and let us carry on as we want, without repercussions? Don't be so naive. I raised you better than that."

Naomi's neck stiffened. "We'd have documented proof they offered us a pardon. And if we're there from the beginning, we can change things. Set the groundwork. I'm asking again: what plan did they reject?"

Valerie took a few moments, leaving her desk and staring out the window, and Naomi fought the urge to back down. To acquiesce as she had so many times before. Standing her ground before Valerie was a new and terrible, uncomfortable experience.

"I'll tell you all at breakfast. Lay it on the table, discuss next steps."

The taut rope of tension between them slackened.

"Thank you," Naomi said.

Naomi made to leave, and Valerie's hand snatched out,

catching her shoulder in a vice of a grip. Naomi fought the urge to recoil.

"Watch how you go, Naomi," Valerie said. "You can question me, but do not undermine me."

Naomi kept her back to her, her chin high.

The others were bleary, still waking up. They each had three nutriblocks on their plate, dotted with a few berries for colour.

"Do you think they'll still feed us nutriblocks in prison, once they arrest us?" Hixon asked, poking at one listlessly. "It'd be a form of cruel and unusual punishment."

Naomi hadn't touched her food. She stayed still, alert. Hart noticed, sending her a questioning look that Naomi ignored.

Valerie cleared her throat. "Before we jump, there is something we should discuss. America has offered us clemency. Their offer expires once we pass through the warp ring."

All at the breakfast table went silent.

"What's the catch?" Hixon asked.

Valerie rose an eyebrow in Naomi's direction as if to say: *See?*

She gave them a summary of Cochran's last message.

Lebedeva made a disgusted sound. "His offer is—how is the word? Ah. Hogwash. It's hogwash, yes?"

"I don't believe he'll give us immunity any more than I believe he'd go to Hawaii for three weeks and come back with a tan," Valerie said.

"As resident redhead, I agree," said Hixon.

"I'm more worried about that bit about agreeing to the PR spin," Hart said. "That's an implied threat that if we don't play nice and say whatever he wants, we'll face arrest anyway. That's how he'd get us."

"He has no reason to want us free," Naomi said. "What kind of message does it send to his base that he let five women get away with what we did?"

Hixon rested her elbows on the table, her nutriblocks forgotten. "So, what, do we just agree to get them off our backs, jump through, and hope for the best?"

Valerie tapped her teeth together, the sound of enamel on enamel loud in the relative quiet of the canteen. "Whether we agree or not, the end result is the same. They follow and bring along humanity unchanged. Cavendish will end up being another America. Another Earth. They'll throw out the treaty, draw the lines in the sand. Like we all talked about. Our version of Cavendish will stand no chance."

"It never stood a chance," Naomi said. "We were just being fanciful."

"It'll take decades to move people across. Having to leave people behind as Earth continues to heat up could shock people into being better. To not wasting a second chance," Hixon tried.

Lebedeva laughed, the sound hard. "Maybe for a few years. Not for long. People are good at forgetting."

Valerie placed her fingertips on the table, her face more animated than Naomi had seen in days. "What if it wasn't just a passing fancy? What if we could make Cavendish what we wanted? Fair. Prosperous. Peaceful. Somewhere humanity could actually thrive."

The silence lengthened.

"Like we said: utopia can't exist," Hart said. "And you're

way too much of a capitalist to make it some socialist paradise." She softened the words with a regretful smile.

Valerie flicked her wrist. "I used capitalism to get me where I needed to be. My wealth is gone now, all spent. What do I need it for? Money was never my true purpose. I want a world where people don't grow up hungry like I did. Where women aren't being pushed out of the spaces they worked so hard to enter. I'm tired of the -isms they love to use to break us down."

"You don't think we'll simply find something else to divide us?" Hixon mused.

Hart rolled a blackberry on her plate. "Probably. But what can we do? Go through, stick a flag of our own making in the soil, and you declare yourself Queen of Cavendish?"

Valerie gave a laugh, high and almost girlish. "Something better than a monarchy. President sounds nice. Or Warden."

"We could say Cavendish was ours all we wanted," Naomi said. "But declaring it so would make us a military base, wouldn't it? Then the treaty is void. We're a hostile force. All of Earth could band together to remove us. We're only five women. What have you been planning, Valerie?"

Valerie's gaze was a knife. Naomi was pushing too hard, but this had been building in her for four days.

What did you ask them to do, Valerie?

"If they don't agree to what we propose, we don't build a Cavendish warp ring in orbit," Valerie said. "That means it takes longer to arrive and is way more expensive. We could journey back to where we originally arrived in Ran's solar system and destroy the atomic clocks, too. That'd make it very difficult for them to know where to jump from Mars."

Naomi couldn't blink. Hixon jerked back in her seat. Even Lebedeva shifted uneasily in her chair.

"You would trap them on Earth?" Hart asked, horrified.

"That...that would definitely be considered a military stance." Hixon's voice was faint.

It'd taken Earth over a decade to set up the atomic clocks, ferried across as close to the speed of light as they could, with gold-sheeted sails propelled by solar wind and lasers. They'd sent them after they discovered negative energy but before they understood the Alcubierre drive, in the hopes that one day it'd be a reality.

"We would delay them," Valerie countered. "Upset the power dynamic. They'll agree to what I propose."

"Which is...?" Naomi asked.

"Send a ship of children first, plus some selected caretakers. I've already thought this through and sent a list."

Silence.

"A list? How'd you come up with a list?" Hart demanded.

"Haven. I had to close it down a good fifteen years ago, but before I did, I helped a lot of women with infertility conceive through vat-grown wombs." She gazed out ahead, eyes distant. "They signed over their data rights to the company—people were so much sloppier about that sort of thing back then—so I had access to a huge database of women who wanted to be parents. A few years ago, when I realised Project Atalanta was progressing well and we actually had a shot, I ran big data analysis and came up with a list of those who are sympathetic to what we are trying to achieve. Politically, ethically, morally. There are five thousand names. They can bring their partners and children on the first ship."

"And they all just kept silent about this for years?" Naomi asked, feeling sick.

"Of course not. They have no idea they've been selected. But I'm confident at least eighty per cent of them will jump at the chance. Their personalities are adventurous enough. We'll have our pick. A ratio of ten climate change orphans to one caretaker, plus their own offspring, should be sufficient.

"So we welcome the first exodus ship, get them settled. We'll be able to raise them without the influences that had shaped previous generations. A few years later, when the children are nearing adulthood, we'll allow another few ships of children. Repeat. In roughly fifteen years, the rest of humanity can arrive into a world with existing infrastructure. Fewer country allegiances. Open borders. Everything we've discussed."

Naomi let out a breath.

"Can you think of another way?" Valerie asked. "This isn't some whimsy. I have been running scenarios in my head for years. If we bring over the adults in large numbers first, there will be the usual scrabble for power. New versions of old countries. They won't even change names, they'll be so lazy. Imagine a Nova Nova Scotia." She gave a bitter laugh. "We mix everyone up. Teach sciences and arts. Keep their wonder and curiosity. Think about what it could be."

Naomi had no idea how to feel. She should be horrified, but she could see the reasoning. It did almost make sense. A chance to truly start anew. Her hand strayed to her stomach. It meant her child wouldn't grow up alone.

"You can't," Hart said, but even she sounded unsure.

"I can't, no. But we can." She leaned forward, eyes so wide they showed the whites. "We could have the upper hand. Finally call those in power on their bullshit. Break it all down. Build it all up again. They can think of it as boarding school, if they like. Or an orphanage a hell of a lot better than any they'd be shunted off into back on Earth. I like the idea of orphans being first in line instead of last."

She met their eyes, one by one, unblinking. Naomi dug her fingernails into her thigh but didn't look away. "We always say the next generation are the ones who will fix the problems of the past," she continued. "So let's get out of the way and let them do it. I'm open to other ideas, other plans. You'll all come back to the same realisation."

The lights caught the edges of her hair. She tilted her head up towards them, closed her eyes. "This is how we truly save humanity."

CHAPTER TWENTY

126 Days After Launch

0 Days to Mars

123 Days to Cavendish

In a few hours, they would slot into the warp ring.

None of them could bring themselves to accept the U.S.'s version of clemency. They knew it for the trap it was.

Throughout discussions, Naomi had kept Evan updated. He hadn't been appalled by Valerie's plan, to her surprise. He had to admit the logic of it, but he thought Valerie was wrong to take measures into her own hands. Naomi was still conflicted, but she and the rest of the crew were coming around, as Valerie had known they would.

Perhaps leaving the adults to cook on Earth for another ten to fifteen years would shock them into behaving better on Cavendish. Arriving to a world populated by people in their twenties who had spent years on equal footing, without the same allegiances and biases. Would that work?

Hart was concerned first and foremost with the children's physical and mental well-being of coming across, whether they left their families or not. Lebedeva sided fully with Valerie and thought it a fine idea. Hixon was somewhere in the middle.

She'd grown up as poor and hungry as Valerie, but she wasn't entirely convinced it wouldn't devolve into *Lord of the Flies* if anything went wrong.

"Not sure I expected going to an exosolar planet to be a babysitting gig," Hixon had said one night. Naomi had to agree. Raising her own child seemed intense and challenging enough. Naomi kept her reservations to herself.

Public sentiment was turning, ever so slightly, against Cochran. The summer wildfires were worse than ever, entire towns disappearing into flames despite the best efforts of public and private firefighters. Naomi's throat ached as she read. She'd been lucky. She'd gotten out, even if her father hadn't, and her mother's body had, though not her mind. Naomi told Evan not to go to the press yet when he asked if he should. Valerie would send Earth a missive before they jumped through the ring, and if they hadn't acquiesced by the time they planned to jump to Cavendish, Evan was to broadcast it wide. Let the public decide what they should do with their own children. Let the children themselves decide.

In a few hours, they'd be jumping. Naomi had begun a message to Evan several times.

He'd looked as lonely as she felt when he knocked on her door the night before quarantine. She'd let him in. She'd known what would happen. Their last chance to give up, give in to each other like they'd wanted to since that one kiss at the graduation party. Since that night under the juniper trees, if she were honest with herself.

They loved each other, but that didn't mean they were in love. That night, they were two magnets tired of repelling.

Was it a kindness to tell him? If the *Atalanta* jumped and

never made it back out, he'd gain a child only to lose one again a few hours later. Even if they survived, he'd still be over ten light years away for years unless he bartered a place on the first ship.

He'd miss the birth, first words, first steps. She didn't know if he even wanted a child. Much less a world of children. To tell or not—which did less harm?

Valerie had always posed those sorts of questions to her. Or her and Evan, to spark spirited discussions at the dinner table. Naomi had once asked Valerie about the trolley problem when she came across it in some article. It was Thanksgiving of her sophomore year at Stanford, when Naomi and Evan were closer. They'd had an unspoken agreement not to let on to Valerie how friendly they'd become.

Evan hadn't heard of the trolley problem. Naomi had explained the philosophical dilemma: "A trolley is pummelling down a track towards five tied-up people. You can pull a lever and redirect the trolley to a side track but there is still one person there.

"Which do you choose? Do nothing and five people die, or pull the lever, but still kill one?" Little did Naomi know that, in a few years, she'd have to make that choice with five cryogenically frozen people.

Valerie had asked Evan to answer first. He'd taken his time, puzzling it over as he moved bits of his vat turkey around his plate. His hair fell across his forehead, and Naomi resisted the urge to brush it back from his eyes. He'd deliberately worn his oldest T-shirt and most frayed jeans to annoy his mother. Naomi liked it. He looked just as he did on those countless late study nights, as they worked together in silence. The last study session, Naomi had grown too tired to stumble across campus to her own dorm. She'd ended up staying over, sleeping in his bed while Evan took the sofa. She'd borrowed one of his T-shirts to sleep in and wear home and hadn't yet given it back.

"I'd have to pull the lever, I suppose," Evan said, slowly. "Smaller level of overall harm." The corners of his lips turned down. He took a sip of Coke.

"What about you?" Valerie had asked. Her eyes darted between them. Naomi had felt like Valerie was pitting them against each other, and it hadn't sat well with her.

"I reject the premise that those are the only two options," she had said. "There must be some engineering fix. Or I could be really selfless and throw myself over and let my body stop the trolley."

"I like that better. Can I change my answer?" Evan had asked.

"No. Too late. And is that what you'd do?" Valerie had asked Naomi. "Sacrifice yourself for the greater good, if it really came down to it?"

"I'd like to think so. But I can't pretend when faced with it, I wouldn't be selfish and let someone else take the fall for me."

Over the years, Valerie had asked Naomi and Evan variations of the same question—the transplant problem, the loop and the man in the yard variation. Eventually, Naomi had asked her to stop. She never knew what answer Valerie wanted her to give.

Evan Kan: *This is it. How long until the jump?*

Naomi Lovelace: *Two hours. I'll message you once I'm through. Feel better.*

Evan Kan: *Go forth and disappear. I'll be here when you get back.*

I'm pregnant, she typed. Deleted it again.
I'm a coward. Deleted it again.
I'm sorry. Delete.

Naomi strapped herself into her chair on the bridge. Her belly swelled above the waistband of the seat belt, the shoulder straps pressed her against the back of the chair. Hart had given her another scan, a snapshot to compare to once they were through. Still there.

Hixon flexed her fingers. Her red hair had grown out since launch, and it drifted up from her skull like fire. Over the past 126 days she had run the Alcubierre simulation at least 126 times.

Naomi counted her breaths, tucking away the nerves that had no place here. The others were equally determined. Hart twisted her wedding ring round and round again. This was nearly the halfway point to Cavendish. It'd be four more months of travel once they jumped. They couldn't jump too close to the planet for the same reason they couldn't jump too close to Earth—just in case something went wrong. This test was the last step, and then it would be time to leave the solar system behind—to fling themselves further than any human had ever been.

Naomi clenched her toes. She'd left them bare, her socks and shoes tucked up neatly underneath the bed of her cabin. Unlike the launch from Earth, she wanted to be able to feel everything. The engines were still so silent, but the thrumming beneath her soles comforted her.

Satellites around Mars had captured the *Atalanta* for the last few days, streaming grainy photos and videos back to Earth. On their home planet, whether they hated the Atalanta 5 or not, everyone would be glued to screens, waiting to see a spaceship disappear.

The greatest magic trick. To an outside eye, it'd be there one minute, gone the next.

"Ready?" Hixon asked.

"As we'll ever be," Valerie replied.

Naomi reached out across the distance and clasped Valerie's hand, giving it a squeeze. Valerie's gaze flicked to hers, the corners of her mouth turned up.

The launch sequence started. As the numbers counted down, Naomi found her voice.

"Now you see us!" she called.

Three. Two. One.

Now you don't.

CHAPTER TWENTY-ONE

6 Years Before Launch

Pasadena, California

Valerie had arranged all of it.

The day after Naomi had flown to Valerie's house, she realised that had all been for nothing.

She had started bleeding on the plane. Light spotting. She'd known that could be normal, thought nothing much of it, and it soon stopped. The next morning, not long before the doctor was to visit under the guise of giving Valerie her biannual check-up, the bleeding returned. Heavy, dark and almost grey. Too much. Naomi was bent double in pain, clutching a hot water bottle. Valerie's hand brushed Naomi's forehead medicinally, reminding Naomi of when she'd stayed home from school with soup, pillows and bad TV.

Valerie frowned at her fever and asked the doctor to come sooner.

She was a tiny woman, under five feet tall. The doctor didn't give her name and kept her filter mask on the entire time to ensure her anonymity. Naomi remembered a soft, Indian accent, dark hair in a thick braid to the middle of her back, and gentle eyes.

Naomi knew before the doctor said anything that she was

losing the baby, and that she was bleeding enough that the doctor was worried. Instead of a conversation where the doctor walked her through her procedures and made sure she was sure of her decision, the abortion done on the plastic-lined teenage bed of her old room, Valerie drove her to the hospital herself. Naomi's memories fractured at that point, from the pain and the drugs that followed as soon as she was through the double doors.

She remembered the chill of the metal forceps. The coolness of the jelly for the ultrasound. The same doctor was in the hospital, waiting for her. Her filter mask was discarded, anonymity gone in the shape of her nose and mouth, the stitched name tag declaring her Dr. Pillai. Her eyes were sharp with a warning not to let on that Naomi had just seen her at Valerie's home. It was an act of trust, for the doctor to see to Naomi herself rather than passing her on to someone else. Naomi groaned with the pain, a low and ugly animal sound. She still nodded her understanding.

Naomi listened as the doctor said that her embryo was a blighted ovum, which sounded strangely poetic to her. She'd treated how many plants in her life that had been affected by blight? Leaf curl, or the fire blight of pears, apples, or raspberries. Fungal or bacterial pathogens burrowing deep into healthy plants or fruit. Seven weeks into her pregnancy, the gestational sac was there, but there was no sign of the foetal pole on her ultrasound. The egg had never developed into an embryo. It was lost.

Yet the sac had still implanted on to the uterus, and for all the blood, it wasn't releasing. A missed miscarriage, they called it.

Dr. Pillai walked her through her options. Naomi could go home, rest, and hope it eventually loosened and released on its own. If it still hadn't shifted in two weeks, she'd have to return and have a dilation and curettage—essentially, a legal abortion, as the embryo had been established as no longer viable. Naomi would pretend that she'd never even known she was pregnant and was in town only to see Valerie.

Naomi opted for an immediate D&C. She couldn't wait for two weeks while NASA training continued. She wanted this over and done. Her body had beaten her to the inevitable conclusion. That was all.

Valerie had hovered, then disappeared, probably to call Cole. Would he fly out? Did Naomi want him to?

Naomi swallowed pills to soften her cervix. Valerie returned, asking if she should stay, but Naomi shook her head. Valerie gave her hand a quick squeeze, told her Cole was flying out, and then she was gone.

Naomi lay on the bed in the hospital room that smelled of antiseptic and the psychosomatic scent of blood. She wished Valerie hadn't told her Cole was on the way. They'd put her under, and Naomi couldn't wait for the room to go soft, like she was wrapped in eiderdown. Her tongue was dry. She kept asking for water, but the nurse gently told her no. Not yet.

There was another exam, the feeling of the doctor's hands on Naomi's belly, between her legs. As the medicine took hold, all grew fuzzier. Naomi floated away as the doctor opened her up, reached within, and withdrew a tiny cluster of cells that were already dead. In five minutes, it was gone. Naomi's life trajectory had been realigned to where it was seven weeks earlier.

Naomi came to gradually. Valerie had paid for a private room, and Naomi was absurdly grateful. She lay there, a heating pad on her belly, her eyes on the ceiling.

She would have gone through with the original abortion. She knew that. She wouldn't have regretted it. Nevertheless, she was oddly relieved the choice had been taken from her. What had happened to her seemed selfish and not at the same time. If the condom hadn't broken, she never would have had to ask herself these questions. But it had.

Naomi never asked Valerie how much it cost to have Dr. Pillai come to her house. Or how much the visit to the hospital cost, paid out of pocket so Naomi wouldn't have to go through NASA healthcare and potentially answer questions she didn't wish to. Naomi was all too aware that most women didn't have the access or resources she did. Some of the financially privileged ones, if they needed an abortion, could go up to Canada, or down to Mexico. Or fly to Europe and pretend they were having a restful holiday near Lake Como. For so many, it was out of reach. Child number one, then an IUD, and that would be that.

Dr. Pillai came to her, first thing the next morning, alone. She said that the blood tests indicated that she had previously undiagnosed polycystic ovarian syndrome, or PCOS. That explained the irregular periods that often disappeared for months at a time. Naomi had always put it down to stress and the amount of exercise she did, but it turned out her hormones were off-kilter. Slightly higher androgens. It'd been surprising she'd fallen pregnant in the first place—often women with PCOS had fertility issues. Dr. Pillai told her to keep using contraceptives, but with her symptoms, there was a low chance it would happen again without treatment. She probably only ovulated once or twice a year, at most. There were pills she could take, to regulate her cycle and hormones. IVF would be an option if, down the line, she changed her mind, though there were no guarantees.

Naomi pressed her lips and nodded, taking it all in. She hadn't wanted a child, not then. It was strange, to know the choice could be taken away from her. A pity Haven had been shut down. Having the knowledge that she could have grown a baby outside her own body would have been reassuring.

Cole arrived hours later and took her home from the hospital. His face was pinched, wan. He was the one who cried, strangely, even as Naomi's eyes stayed dry. He kept apologising, over and over. Naomi grew tired of saying "it's all right, it's not your fault." Why was she the one offering comfort?

He held her hand the whole plane ride, and his palm was clammy. She resisted the urge to pull it away.

He carried their bags up to their apartment in Houston and helped her on the stairs. She leaned on him. The pain was lessening, but every step still echoed in a stab in her abdomen. She wanted to sleep, to forget. Cole hovered, offering her drinks, or food. When she snapped at him to leave her alone, his face shut and he closed the door with a slap. She opened her mouth to call after him to apologise, but she was too grateful to be alone.

She slept more than she ever had in her life. Over twelve hours a day. A few sleeping pills to chase away consciousness when she was awake long enough for her mind to start spinning again.

A week later, Cole urged her to sit up, to dress. It was their one-year anniversary—he'd made the reservations months ago. Wouldn't a good meal help?

She squeezed herself into a black dress, painted her lips blood red. Cole was in better spirits and kept up a steady flow of conversation as Naomi picked at her pasta and drank one too many glasses of the expensive, thick red wine.

When they were back at home, alone, she opened her mouth to tell him. That she'd known about the pregnancy, that if her body hadn't rejected it, she would have ended it the same day. She should tell him about the diagnosis, warn him that years later, their expected path might not be as smooth as they'd planned. Before she could, his mouth was on hers, his fingers trailing down her arm, her torso. The bleeding had stopped, only the barest tenderness remaining, and so she let him unpeel the dress, let it crumple on the floor. Lost herself in the lines of his body. If Naomi was honest with herself, those wordless moments had always been the best part of their relationship—their bodies understood each other. It was the words that got in the way. The expectations.

Naomi went back to training, desperate to catch up after her recovery. She pretended she'd contracted a virus, and no one questioned her. Naomi would come back from the Johnson Space Center long past sunset. Each night, she'd stare at Cole's sleeping back, silently promising him that tomorrow would be the day she came clean. The days kept passing, one after the other, until she'd left it too long. The silence became its own lie, one she was unable to unpick. She often wondered, over the next few years, how he would have reacted. Back then, she'd hoped he'd have been supportive, that he'd understand. Much later, she suspected she had been right not to tell him. That her intuition had been its own warning.

No one at work knew. None of her friends from undergrad or grad school, most of whom had already drifted away, since Naomi was terrible at keeping in touch. A pregnancy that ended before it could truly begin. A missed period that turned into an ellipsis of a promise, then an interrupted dash.

How many women had kept their lips tight over stories of abortions? Farmers' wives who knew one more baby would mean her other children going hungry. Another with narrow hips whose first birth had nearly been the death of her. Women who could barely afford to feed and house themselves, much less someone else. Those who had faced violence or had abusive partners who would use a child as a weapon. A trans man who would have found pregnancy distressingly dysphoric. A woman who felt the movement within her grow still, but there was still technically a heartbeat. Or women who, plain and simple, didn't want a child and knew their own body, their own mind, best.

The only one who knew her secret was Valerie. It didn't occur to her until much later that, if Valerie had wanted to, she could have used that information against Naomi like a knife.

CHAPTER TWENTY-TWO

126 Days After Launch

5 Days to Mars

123 Days to Cavendish

If they'd gone through a wormhole, they would have technically died. So would her child. So would everyone else on board. They'd blink into nothing, shifting from one point of the galaxy to another in an instant. The blueprints of the women and everything on the ship would reassemble in an instant, using new matter, new cells.

If someone were watching the ship from the outside, it would seem as if the ship disappeared, as it moved through space faster than the speed of light. Yet inside, it was all strangely anticlimactic.

They'd closed the covers over the window for additional shielding, but it didn't feel as though they were going any faster than they had since they'd reached full ion acceleration. Inside the warp bubble, it was exactly the same. It was the universe outside that shifted.

Naomi thought her body would still recognise that something fundamental had occurred. She almost wished they could blink out, splinter their matter, devolve into negative energy just for an instant. Like being reborn.

When they arrived at their destination, the warp bubble devolved. Again, they felt nothing.

Hixon raised her fist in triumph, peering at the screens. "We've done it. All systems nominal," she said, with an attempt at composure, but her voice was tight with excitement.

Lebedeva slumped in relief, though she also seemed curiously disappointed by the lack of fanfare. Hart offered Hixon a smile. "You did it, Hix."

"Our location?" Valerie asked.

Hixon's face was smug. "Right where we want to be, according to atomic clock projections. Five days' travel back to the warp ring."

Valerie had clenched her left hand into a fist, which she released. Naomi's mind caught up with her body, everything slotting back into place. Her hand went to her belly.

Hart unstrapped herself, floating over to Naomi unsteadily. "We'll check, don't worry. Right after—" She grabbed an emergency sick bag from beneath Naomi's seat and twisted, retching. The smell reached Naomi and threatened her own stomach.

Hixon drifted over. "You okay, babe?"

Hart nodded. "Just nerves. I'll check myself over, after Naomi."

"I also feel queasy," Lebedeva admitted, and the rest of them blinked at her in surprise. She must have felt absolutely wretched to admit that much. Naomi had a bit of nausea, but not much more than she had throughout the pregnancy so far. Perhaps at some deeper level, their bodies did know they'd moved thousands of miles in a few minutes.

"I'll scan myself," Naomi said. "You rest, Hart."

"If you're sure," Hart said, faint.

Valerie's voice was sharp, authoritative. "Hixon, Lebedeva, run diagnostics again. Hart, when you're settled, look over everyone's vitals. We'll meet at eighteen hundred hours. We deserve a damn good meal after this. I'm busting out my chocolate reserves."

"You've been hiding chocolate from a pregnant woman?" Naomi asked, mock hurt. "That's just cruel."

Valerie was buzzing, hardly able to stay still. It was infectious—they were the first humans to successfully navigate a warp drive. To travel thousands of miles in an instant. Naomi smiled through her nausea.

Naomi left to the sound of Hart retching again.

Once she was back on the ring, Naomi counted each step to the med bay to distract herself. She wouldn't stress until she knew if there was something to stress about.

The autodoc scan made its whirring noises. She lay in the tube the same size as the empty cryopods in the storage bay. The nausea faded to a dull ache.

She had no spotting. No cramping. She felt exactly the same as she had on the other side of Mars.

The other side of Mars. Jesus.

A corner of her mind still feared that now she'd decided to keep it, even though she wasn't the superstitious sort, fate or the universe would find a way to play its trick on her.

The machine beeped. Naomi counted down from ten, preparing herself. The cover of the autodoc pulled back. She rose, the slight swell of her stomach already making her move awkwardly.

Naomi loaded the facsimile of herself, then her womb.

Twenty weeks, almost twenty-one. The foetus moved, from time to time. At night, if Naomi was very still, she could sense the shifting.

On the scan, the chest contracted and relaxed, almost like breath. The room filled with Naomi's slow, sure heartbeat and then beneath: the faster fluttering. The foetus was halfway through gestation. There were ten fingers, ten toes, tipped with soft nails. The whorls of fingerprints had formed. The eyelids were translucent, and the face showed the barest hint of eyebrows and eyelashes. The child would have dark hair, between Naomi's brown hair and Evan's black.

Six and a half inches long. Ten whole ounces. The little thing would fit into her hand like a kitten.

Naomi bowed her head in relief.

"Congratulations," she said to her belly. "You continue to boldly go where no baby has gone before."

Naomi had the right angle this time—she could see the sex. There was no hidden Y chromosome on board. The foetus would be assigned female at birth. Valerie had guessed correctly.

The door to the med bay opened. Hart's head poked in, her temples damp with sweat. Her eyes went to the scan and she visibly relaxed.

"Still there," Naomi said. "Not lost in space."

"Thanks for that horrible mental image." Hart took in the angle. "A girl."

"Yeah, looks like. I didn't mind either way. But I guess the all-female mission continues."

"Got any names picked out?"

"Nope. Not a one. Think I'm still afraid of jinxing it. How are you feeling?"

"Better. Not exactly looking forward to voiding the contents of my stomach once we do the proper jump, though."

Naomi exhaled. "Five days. Then goodbye, solar system."

"I thought I'd be ecstatic, but I'm all deflated," Hart said. "I know it's just the adrenaline comedown. I'll rest in here, so I can come back kicking at dinner. Don't want to dampen Jerrie's moment."

"Hixon will understand," Naomi said. "This is strange for all of us."

"What...what do you think Earth will do?" Hart asked.

Naomi let out a breath. "I don't know. I think they'll have to cave, won't they? If Valerie threatens to interfere with things on the other side."

Valerie wouldn't threaten to destroy the warp ring near Cavendish until moments before the jump, when it would be too late for Earth to interfere. They'd have to send through a probe.

"I'm still horrified but I'm also..." Hart trailed off.

"Weirdly hopeful?" Naomi finished.

Hart's shoulders rose, then dipped. "Yeah. I want a break from Earth and all its bullshit. I want a chance to make things better. Why let Cochran come in and take the credit? As soon as there are boots on the ground loyal to him, with all the colonial baggage that implies, that's it. There's too much money to be made." Hart jumped up on the autodoc, sitting cross-legged. "They'll push us out of the way." She counted on her fingers. "Valerie for stealing and being too damn rich in the first place, you for basically being her daughter, Lebedeva for being a foreign national of an enemy state that would also just love to lay claim to Cavendish, Hixon for being gay, and me for being bisexual *and* black to top it all off." She held up her palm, five fingers splayed. "I'm tired. I've been tired. Aren't you?"

"Yeah," Naomi whispered. "I'm tired. And scared. But still weirdly hopeful. My other fear..." She paused, weighing her words. "What if—what if Valerie isn't the person who can make Cavendish what we need it to be?"

Hart's head jerked back. "You're expressing doubts about Valerie?"

Naomi shifted herself closer. The comms in the room were off, but she kept her voice low anyway. "Not doubt, exactly. But she's still angling to be the leader, isn't she? No one coming to the planet without her say-so. Moulding a whole generation."

"Power corrupts absolutely, and Valerie's already had more power than most," Hart mused. "It sounds so rational, on one hand. They put women and children in the lifeboats first on a sinking ship. But, I mean, how does she plan to filter information to the children? What will she censor, omit, change?"

"You speak like she'll become fascist," Naomi said. She wasn't sure she was suggesting Valerie would stray that far.

Hart gave a shrug of a shoulder. "I always go right to the worst-case scenario. It drives Jerrie up the walls. You can't deny that history is written by the victors. Valerie will weave a narrative."

Naomi tapped a finger against her lip. "It's not like I have any better ideas for getting people to Cavendish. Do you?"

Hart made a moue with her mouth. "I mean, we've all got good leadership skills. That's why we're on the ship. But it's a hell of a lot of responsibility I'm not sure I want. It's not what I signed up for."

"The four of us will have to be her checks and balances. To call her up on it if she starts believing her own mythos. We do make a good team. She chose us for a reason."

"You think she'll agree to that? She does *not* like being told she's wrong."

"I've done it before. It's difficult, but if I make my case, she sees reason." Naomi hesitated, then barrelled on. "I'm the reason she shared the clemency deal with the ship. She wasn't going to. I found the message and confronted her."

Hart whistled. "I wish I could say I'm surprised. If she's already hiding stuff, that doesn't bode well, does it?"

Naomi hunched her shoulders. "I know. I can't stop asking myself what else she's not telling us."

Hart sucked her teeth. "You saying we should try and find out?"

Naomi hesitated, then nodded. The movement felt like a betrayal.

CHAPTER TWENTY-THREE

126 Days After Launch

5 Days to Mars

123 Days to Cavendish

"Everyone, to the rec room," Valerie sent on the comms. "We have a message from Earth."

It was an hour before they were all due to have their evening meal. Lebedeva slouched against the wall, arms loosely around her knees. Hixon and Hart leaned against each other, Hixon rubbing Hart's palm with her thumb in a soothing, circular motion. Naomi stood to Valerie's right, resisting the urge to cradle her stomach.

Valerie's skin looked stretched tight across her bones. "I haven't opened it yet," she said. "We'll all read together."

Her eyes didn't flick to Naomi, but Naomi felt the rebuke as much as Hart's silent bristling.

Valerie reached forward and the message scrolled on the wall of the rec room. They read in silence. Earth had reiterated their original stance. Cochran's fury bubbled through the officious language more than before. What the president was really saying was essentially he had been more than generous, and the *Atalanta*'s levels of disloyalty to America, to Earth as a whole, knew no bounds. They would not package up an exodus ship of children to send their minds to be warped on Cavendish. Basically: no deal. The Atalanta 5 were traitors, and there would be no mercy once the *Atalanta II* arrived on Cavendish.

He was calling their bluff.

"Well, we tried," Hixon said. "It was ballsy, but that's that. Prison beckons."

"There are still options," Naomi offered. "We can go public through Evan, can't we?"

"We could," Valerie agreed, narrowing her eyes at the message. "I'm not sure it'll do much good. Even if plenty of people want to send their children, it'd take protests on a massive scale. So many still don't believe the Earth is truly under threat, even with all the evidence in front of them. They wear the filter masks and hire private firefighters and proudly declare the sky is not falling. They're still stuck in the system that we are trying to break. Too many people in power are in the way."

"We've only been hearing from Cochran and the U.S. primarily," Hart said. "What is the rest of the world thinking?"

Naomi was glad Valerie answered, afraid of accidentally revealing information she'd only received from Evan on the private channel.

"Some deviations. A few countries are more amenable than others. There is the chance another country might start sending ships to us, agreeing to our plans. Russia has more than enough money."

"That they do," Lebedeva said, blandly.

"Smaller countries could pool their resources," Valerie continued. "Europe and its ESA. China has the capital, and India could potentially join them. Or Japan. West Africa has upped their space funding, too. The United States would be angry, because they've funnelled so much taxpayer money into the Cavendish probes, *Atalanta*, and now the *Atalanta II*. They're falling into the trap of already thinking of the planet as theirs, even though they know they technically have no legal jurisdiction there."

"Neither do we," Naomi pointed out.

"No, but our vision echoes the underlying principles of the treaty, doesn't it? *Res communis*. A planet for all of humanity, starting with its children. The United States has always liked to pretend they are the primary players here. They are not."

A silence tinged with worry rolled off the others in waves. Only Lebedeva appeared unbothered. She hadn't had a home in the same way the rest of them had, not for years. Being untethered like this was nothing new for her. Naomi almost envied her that.

Valerie took down the message and left the walls on the default grey grid.

"Deep down, you knew they wouldn't agree, didn't you?" Naomi asked. "We can't say we didn't try."

Hart pressed the base of her palms against her eyes, muttering something that sounded like a curse.

"Come on," Valerie said. "Let's go get some dinner. We can still have the chocolate. This shouldn't dampen the sense of accomplishment of what we've achieved. We already did the impossible today. This will work out. Have a little faith." Her words were breezy, but it didn't fool Naomi.

What's your plan B, Valerie?

*

Naomi brought the precious chocolate back to her room. It rested on the desk. Fifty whole grams. Naomi had run out of paint, but the walls were covered in stylised vines. Her little zinnias were doing well, their orange blooms bright next to the snow globe shuttle Valerie had given her. She touched a velvety petal with the tip of a finger as she loaded up the tablet. The women had scattered again. Naomi brought up the ship map, and sure enough, Lebedeva was in the gym, running her steady cadence on the treadmill, or lifting weights because that was easy, that was simple. Pick up the heavy thing. Put it back down again. Count to ten. Do it again. Hart and Hixon were in their quarters, turning things over in detail. Valerie was in the observation room.

Once everyone was asleep, she planned to go back to the rec room. Dig through folders and subfolders, see if she could access Valerie's personal drive.

She didn't want to find any more secrets. She wanted to discover that was it—this was Valerie's plan, which hadn't worked as she'd hoped. Perhaps other countries in the world would finally step up, edge ahead of the U.S. in the race to Cavendish. Russia or China would have little reason to imprison the five of them for crimes against another country—though if Valerie insisted on messing with the warp ring on Cavendish, all bets were off. There were too many unknowable components. Too much uncertainty. If there was one thing Valerie hated, it was unnecessary complications.

Naomi sent Evan a message. It would be the middle of his work day back on Earth, so she wasn't sure if she'd have a response.

Naomi Lovelace: *The U.S. is angry. It's no deal. Their offer has expired.*

She sent along a summary of their conversation for him to read once he was back in the bunker. Naomi picked up a piece of chocolate and broke off a corner. She placed it on her tongue and closed her eyes in bliss as the sugar shivered along her taste buds. One hundred and twenty-six days without chocolate. She'd had a cheap candy bar the morning of the launch after breakfast, a comfort and an extra burst of quick energy she didn't need. She remembered folding the wrapping into the tiniest gold square she could manage before throwing it away. Seemed so long ago.

By the time the little bit of chocolate dissolved, the taste of it still lingering, Naomi received a response. She sat up in surprise. Probably about nine minutes between messages with their current alignment with Earth.

Evan Kan: *What will Valerie do next?*

She broke off another minuscule piece of chocolate.

Naomi Lovelace: *I don't know. So much seems dependent on how the rest of the world responds. Do you know how I can access Valerie's personal drive? It'll be encrypted but with your help, maybe I can crack it. She's been keeping a log, I know that. I'm hoping I won't find anything, but.*

She tapped her fingers against her thigh, waiting impatiently for the message to send and the reply to return. Was everyone asleep yet?

Evan Kan: *But you want to check. I'll start working up some instructions during the communication lags.*

Naomi Lovelace: *Thanks. Are you at work?*

Technically he'd be able to route messages to his tablet, but that would have likely taken extra time, plus leave him vulnerable to discovery.

Evan Kan: *I'm playing hooky. Needed a day not around people.*

He wasn't dashing off then. Naomi wouldn't be interrupted by anyone. A chance for a proper conversation. She took another nibble of chocolate for strength as she tapped.

Naomi Lovelace: *I need to tell you something. There is no easy way to say it.*

Here goes. She sent the next message a minute later.

Naomi Lovelace: *I'm nearly twenty-one weeks pregnant. I'm sorry for keeping it from you. Wasn't sure it'd stick, or if I should carry on with the pregnancy. But the foetus is in good health, and Hart is monitoring everything. So I've decided to keep it. Her. I don't know how involved you want to be, or not. It's up to you. I'm not asking for anything you don't want to offer. Valerie thinks it's Cole's. I haven't corrected her.*

She'd pressed send. No way to wrangle the signal back. It was a long four and a half minutes until it arrived at the base, and an even longer ten minutes before she received a response.

Evan Kan: *Well. Whatever I was expecting you to say, it wasn't this.*

Naomi Lovelace: *I should have told you sooner. It was a lot to take in, on top of everything else. I tried to, a few times. Chickened out. I've also been too afraid to ask if you regretted what happened. Or what it meant.*

She closed her eyes as she pressed send. If she was going to open up to him, she might as well go all in. She wished she could see his face, though for so many years he'd been hard to read. Throughout her teen years, she'd been convinced Evan hated her. She'd been convinced she hated him. He could grasp things that took her hours of studying to understand. Learned how to break encryption just for fun. Yet he'd never had a clear plan. Stumbled about until Valerie made him go to a university. He was good at whatever he tried, whereas Naomi had to work at it.

Getting to know him had been a slow, gradual shift. The night under the juniper berries. Then they'd had a shared elective class, and at first she wasn't sure if they were studying together more out of tolerance or because their old competitiveness meant they worked harder, determined to beat the other's test scores (Naomi had won by three percentage points).

Though they didn't see each other much during Naomi's master's, they had kept in touch with little messages and caught up around the holidays. Then that disastrous party and years of reverting to their teenage selves.

Evan Kan: *In college, I saw you on your own terms, and you saw me on mine. Without Valerie pitting us against each other. She never missed a chance to point out that you were doing what was expected of you, and I was not. I resisted her plans for me at every turn. She gave up on me and focused on you.*

That connection we had. That was real.

Naomi stared at the screen. She'd seen that kiss as a confusing misstep, especially once she'd tried to reach out to him at his father's funeral. She'd taken the rebuff as a clear signal: there was nothing there. There couldn't be. They'd missed their chance. Or she thought they had, until he showed up at her door.

She wanted to defend Valerie and say she hadn't made them clash, but she couldn't. When Evan elected to stay away from Valerie and grow up half a world away, Valerie had shifted her attention to Naomi. Did Evan resent that interest, even as he'd pushed it away? Without the freedom and the funding to make the Cavendish biome, Naomi would never have gotten into NASA. Never been on this ship. That was what she'd always wanted, wasn't it?

She could imagine Evan's response: *Valerie is very good at making things seem like they were your idea all along. Haven't you said that to me?*

Another message came through.

Evan Kan: *It doesn't matter. We wasted time. Went our different directions. I know I messed up, after my dad died. I shut down. By the time I realised how I felt, you were already with Cole. So I stepped back. Tried to forget. Dated other people. Nothing stuck. Then you divorced, but you were in Scotland. I could have booked a flight. Or called. Something.*

Evan Kan: *Haven't you wondered why I agreed to be Valerie's point of contact on Earth? I didn't do it for her.*

Naomi didn't know what she'd been expecting. A promise that he'd send the kid some birthday messages. Maybe be around once he landed on Cavendish, whenever that would be. Not this. She had wondered why Evan had agreed to man the communications base on top of his job. It wouldn't have been out of loyalty. She thought perhaps Valerie had something over him—bailed him out of legal fees, perhaps. His hacking abilities and infernal curiosity could easily get him into just a little too much trouble.

She'd thought that last night before quarantine was simply a release of pent up physical attraction. Like a gasp after holding their breath for too long. The knowledge that it wouldn't matter, no one would find out. Instead, he was telling her he'd wanted her for fifteen years. The whole time she was in college, and when she was married, he had been hung up on her. She'd stumbled through that crumbling marriage, for what? Evan had been there. He'd been right there.

Naomi Lovelace: *We wasted so much time, letting what others would think trip us up. What do we do now?*

She stewed while she waited.

Evan Kan: *What we can. But I'll be as involved as you'll let me be and as much as I can be from here. It's still weird. I never thought kids were in the cards for me.*

Much less under these circumstances. We'd win longest distance relationship.

She laughed, and it caught in her chest.

Naomi Lovelace: *It's late. Everyone will be asleep by now. I should go hunting for more secrets now that I've told you mine.*

Evan Kan: *Good luck. And thanks for telling me. Don't know exactly where we go from here, but we'll figure it out. I'll send through your instructions after this message. Goodnight.*

Naomi scanned what he sent, making sure she understood the steps before she turned off the tablet.

"Shitting shit," she muttered in the darkness, but she was lighter than she'd been in weeks.

Before she went hunting through hard drives, Naomi tiptoed back to the observation room with the last square of chocolate. She curled up on the little window seat, pressing her body against the enforced panes that looked out in the darkness. She licked the gold wrapping for the last hints of chocolate.

It'd been a while since she'd sat there and stared into the abyss on her own. Mars wasn't visible from this angle. They were speeding back to where they'd just been to go so much further. She didn't know what it meant, for her and Evan. There were so many miles between them. Soon it would be part of a galaxy.

She stroked the rise of her belly, letting her thoughts swirl. The chocolate's sweetness faded.

Time to upturn some stones and see what lurked underneath.

CHAPTER TWENTY-FOUR

127 Days After Launch

4 Days to Mars

122 Days to Cavendish

Naomi couldn't crack the encryption.

She tried until two hours before the rest of the crew was due to wake up. Eventually, she had to give up and catch some sleep, hoping she'd covered her tracks well enough. She slept through breakfast—when Hart tried to wake her up, Naomi pleaded pregnancy exhaustion. Valerie officially gave her the morning off the lab, and Naomi had a brief flare of guilt until she fell back into a deep, dreamless sleep.

She was groggy when she woke. She fell into her work, her hands on autopilot. Harvesting algae. Setting up a new crop. Checking the others. Tending to the plants. Transforming the algae harvested yesterday into more nutriblocks. She forced herself to eat three, still vaguely warm from the machine. She wanted to gag. She had been neglecting the gym and her exercises. Gravity on the ring would mitigate the worst effects of being in space so long, but she should still be staying active. She was, if anything, at an increased risk of losing bone mass compared to the others, the foetus only too happy to leech the calcium from her bones. Little parasite.

Hours passed, her mind whirring along. She'd try again tonight, but what if she couldn't break encryption? There was only so much Evan could direct her with from here. She had a message from him she'd missed while she'd been sleeping.

> Evan Kan: *Long day today, back at work, so won't be able to check as often. There's another illness outbreak, over by where you did that internship for Argaine in undergrad—probably not crop infestation this time, perhaps tainted water. It's spreading fast, so aiming to contain it today. This sort of thing is only going to become more common. Let me know if you found anything? Stay safe.*

Flu vaccines were growing less protective every year, making each year of Evan's work harder. Illnesses spread as quick as wildfire in the crowded areas teeming with refugees. Even in the more affluent areas, young professionals were crammed in close quarters, renting overpriced bunk beds with up to thirty people in a dorm. If anyone had a cold, it'd jump from bunk to bunk, through those flimsy blackout curtains that gave the illusion of privacy, and then spread to the overworked people's offices. Sick pay was something technically available but never taken.

Earth would only grow hotter, more crowded. More dangerous.

She sent him an all-too-brief update—that she'd had no luck and asking if he had any other suggestions. Despite her exhaustion, she struggled to stay still. There had to be somewhere else she could look, something she could do while she waited for Evan's next instructions. She was doing this to make sure she could trust Valerie past the warp ring and once they were on the new planet. Naomi didn't want to doubt her. She needed to know that Valerie did plan to work with Earth once they landed, to make sure Cavendish started with peace and prosperity, like she claimed she wanted. They were on the same side, weren't they?

Hart came to check up on Naomi just before dinner, asking how she was feeling. Hart had her own circles under her eyes. Sleep hadn't been kind to her, either.

Naomi told her about her attempts to crack Valerie's files. She didn't mention Evan and that they could speak directly. She trusted Hart more than anyone else on board, but she was already risking too much.

"I'm going down in the storage bay," Naomi said. "I need another lamp anyway. Going to have a look around." Her neck was stiff.

Hart read between the words. "You haven't been down there since they were defrosted, have you?"

Naomi gave a sharp jerk of her head. She'd successfully bypassed it when they'd gone down to the bridge for the jump.

"I've been avoiding it too. Think we all have, to be honest. I need a few things for the med bay. Let's go down together?"

The muscles at the base of her neck loosened. "Sure."

Their steps on the ladder of the spoke echoed until they could rappel themselves down the last section in microgravity free fall. Naomi peered into the window of the door to the storage bay, steeling herself. No one was on the bridge, the ship set to autopilot until Hixon came down to check on it in an hour or so. Naomi pushed open the door, sliding through.

It all looked much the same, save for the lack of the blue glow of the pods. Cole's empty pod was closest to her. She still wished she could have done more, but it was on Lockwood for putting them on board in the first place. All systems were functioning smoothly since the last power surge, at least. No unexpected surprises.

Naomi took the right side of the storage bay, and Hart the left. They systematically went through every cupboard, every trunk. The chances of them finding anything was small, but at least it helped Naomi feel like she was doing something. Anything. In the spare supplies, Naomi plucked out her lamp, and Hart found the syringes she needed. Nothing looked suspicious. The area with the equipment they'd only need once they landed on Cavendish appeared untouched. No one had brought anything sentimental on board that wasn't already in their cabins. If Valerie was hiding something, it was almost certainly in her room, and there was no chance of searching that without being found out, even if Valerie was distracted elsewhere on the ship. Naomi reached out and touched the blank face of one of the humanoid construction robots. At least a small part of her mother was on this ship, too.

"Maybe I'm trying to find something that isn't here," Naomi said.

Hart's face was sympathetic. She wore her wedding ring on a gold chain around her neck, and it'd escaped from under her jumpsuit to float near her face. She tucked it back in as she put her medical supplies away. "Maybe we both are."

"I'm letting myself be distracted. What Earth does when we land is important, but there's nothing we can do. Either we'll be arrested, or we won't. We can set up infrastructure, prove our worth. Return the stolen property of the *Atalanta* and use the treaty to claim sanctuary. Live off the land. There are so many little islands on that world. Maybe they'll let us live on one undisturbed."

"All we can do is keep doing what we're doing," Hart agreed, readily enough. "We've been unconventional. We broke laws. I still don't regret taking off. If we've had this many struggles on a ship we know inside and out, that replacement crew wouldn't have stood a chance. This ship would already be dead, not just the backup crew."

"You think so?" Naomi asked. If the botanist of the crew meant to replace the Atalanta 5 couldn't have figured it out, they could have defrosted Lee. He would have been able to solve Naomi's algae problem—she was sure enough of that. The power surge would have been trickier. What would have made or broken them would have been the teamwork. The camaraderie, the ability to adapt and help each other. When she was still on Earth, she would have insisted that she and the other women would have functioned as a seamless team. Yet here they were, two already breaking away.

"How much have you told Hixon?" Naomi asked. "About your suspicions?"

"Very little," Hart admitted. "She's so focused on the Alcubierre drive, I worry about distracting her. I—" She stopped. "For all her years out of the military, Hixon's still very loyal. She follows orders, she doesn't tend to question leadership. I worry that she might not agree. Think I'm looking for something that isn't there."

"And Lebedeva basically worships the ground Valerie walks on," Naomi said, quiet.

"Sure. But a few months ago, I'd have sworn the same about you."

Naomi grimaced, but didn't correct her. She floated over to the pods, stopping in front of Cole's.

"Do you miss him?" Hart asked.

"No," Naomi answered honestly. "I wish he wasn't dead, but no."

As she moved away, her fingertips grazed the screen that had once shown Cole's readouts, the ones that Hart had scoured for evidence that whoever was in those pods was no longer there. The screen blared bright, as if it had just been in hibernation.

Hart's head snapped towards it. "Valerie said she disconnected those entirely from the system."

The screen display was different, but Naomi couldn't make out what it meant. "Hart—" she started, but Hart had already drifted to her.

Hart squinted. "This doesn't make any sense. It says it's still active."

"But it's dark, and no one's in it," Naomi said. "And we've had no other surges."

"Yesterday Jerrie said fuel efficiency was all good. What if I just—"

Hart clicked the release on the cryopod. They both jerked back. Naomi reached for a handhold to steady herself, and Hart grabbed Naomi's forearm.

Cole's pod lid hissed as it released outward. Inside was empty, dark. Naomi's skin prickled with goosebumps. At first, she put it down to nerves, an uneasiness of staring into what was essentially a coffin, but Hart's skin was the same.

The air was colder.

Naomi grasped the lip of the cryopod. The metal was frigid. If she squinted, right at the corner was the barest glimmer. She pressed her finger against the faint, blue light.

"There's something behind it," Naomi whispered. "In the walls."

A hiss as Hart opened the cryopod next to Cole's. Who had that one belonged to? Josh? She'd already forgotten.

"Don't see any light here," Hart said. "But it could be fitted better?"

Naomi ran her hands along the inside of the cryopod, trying not to think of Cole, cold and stiff and gone. Her fingers found a latch. Her fingers almost burned with the cold. With a sickening certainty, she clicked it.

The back of the cryopod shifted out of the way. Cold fog rippled through the storage bay, floating, with no gravity to hold it down. Canisters of grey metal with blue tops were in a vault behind the cryopods, built into the wall. Shallow and small enough to be easily hidden. Hart found her catch, and the pod opened. All five must have them. A few canisters behind each pod.

Hart and Naomi exchanged looks. Hart went to the backup supplies and came back with two pairs of gloves to protect against the cold. Naomi reached forward, untwisting the cap, but they both knew what they would find.

More nitrogen smoke floated from the open canister. Hart shifted to her left, reached in with medical tongs. Drew out small vials, filled with pale, frozen liquid.

Naomi's breathing grew shallow.

Embryos. Hundreds, thousands of embryos hidden behind

the cryopods that had stored the backup crew. Already fertilised. Another seed vault that neither of them had known about. Naomi would put good money down that Hixon and Lebedeva didn't, either.

Naomi screwed the top back on, slid the canister back. They watched as the false bottom of the cryopod slid back into place. The nitro fog slowly cleared, drifting into the filters in the walls.

Hart and Naomi stared at each other.

Naomi forced herself to say the words.

"I think we found Valerie's plan B."

CHAPTER TWENTY-FIVE

5 Years Before Launch

Houston, Texas

They would never let Naomi go into space.

Training had gone well, and she had technically graduated to the astronaut corps. But it didn't matter.

NASA never said so outright, and those within the organisation wanted to send women up there. To treat everyone with equality, build on the strides they'd made over the last few decades. The system was already working against them. Bigotry had a way of sliding through the cracks.

It didn't matter how hard Naomi worked. How well she placed on various tests and examinations. Her job description would always come with a desk. She was so far down on the waiting list for a mission to the moon, the ISS, or the under-construction Gateway that she might as well not be on it at all. She'd been five to ten years too late.

Naomi felt like she'd disappointed the little girl she'd once been. The quiet, nervous child who still faced her fears and went to science camp every summer and wore NASA emblazoned everything. She'd promised that girl she would go up in a rocket. Every day, she was surrounded by people who urged her patience, who assured her she still had a chance. Well qualified, hardworking men who were blissfully unaware at how so many others around them didn't have that shot, no matter how much they proclaimed otherwise. It was Mercury 7 and 13 all over again.

Naomi didn't grow depressed, exactly, but everything was a little more muted. At least once a week, she debated phoning up Valerie and asking if she could go back to Hawthorne. There, she had freedom, opportunities. Hawthorne was angling to usurp Lockwood out of its monopoly on space stations. There was still a chance she could go to low Earth orbit through the corporate sector.

She started looking at jobs, furtively. Late at night, when Cole was asleep. She'd scroll through them, peering at the job descriptions. They were either jobs she wasn't quite qualified enough for, or openings that fit but were in places she didn't want to live. Areas where the sea levels were going to rise, or the weather was increasingly violent, or there was simply nothing to do. Part of her wanted to leave the U.S.—to go further afield to countries where women had more freedom. Her father had been Scottish—she could qualify for an ancestry visa. She scrolled through the ESA website, but there wasn't anything worth applying for.

As her eyes grew tired from the blue light of the screens, she worried her lip. If she really wanted to leave Houston, would Cole follow? Especially if it was for a job?

Cole had been raising the idea of children. An offhand comment now and again. But if there was anything she'd learned from growing up under Valerie's roof, it was spotting when someone was pretending nonchalance to cover a calculated move. Naomi still hadn't told him. She'd done her research.

Even with PCOS, she could still potentially have a child. With the reduction in stress, her cycles had become more regular. There were options: metformin, or other medications. IVF. Adoption—there were more than enough orphans displaced by climate change, though she had the sense Cole wanted a child with his DNA. She wasn't being fair to him, but she was afraid. He'd married her with the unspoken expectation they'd likely have kids and settle down. She didn't want to admit to anyone, much less him, that it wouldn't happen quite how he'd imagined.

Cole's best friend at work, Shane Legge, and his wife had just had a baby. They went over for dinner one Friday night. Naomi held the small bundle, wrapped up in a blanket, warm against her chest. It felt nice. He smelled of talc and soap and that ineffable baby smell. She passed him back to his father, quickly, before the ache in her grew worse.

She didn't want to have children any longer. The world was still too grim. But she wanted to *want* to have them. It was a subtle distinction. It was strange to grieve for something she didn't know whether or not was right for her.

Every time children came up, she demurred. Weeks turned to months. Cole spent longer at work. She found more excuses to go back to California for visits. It was easier, to let Valerie distract her with her various projects at Hawthorne. To go to lectures and dinners full of interesting people.

For the First Man of Mars had become utterly boring to Naomi. When she was home, they sat at the dinner table in silence. Cole could feel his fame waning. Mars had been years ago. Everyone was fascinated by the Gateway and the moon again. Breakthroughs and cost reductions made it not quite so astronomically expensive to set up bases and grow food. Naomi had considered a transfer at her work to focus on the Artemis missions to the moon, save for the fact doing so would annoy Cole further.

Cole was itching to find a way back into the spotlight.

"I was thinking of doing a documentary," he said one morning over breakfast, before work. "A production company is interested. They'd follow me around, and it'd delve into the next Ares mission preparation. I'd be able to get NASA to put me in charge of training if I did that."

"That sounds good," Naomi said.

Cole poured another mug of coffee. "They'd want to film both of us. They're interested in your research, too."

Naomi swallowed a bite of cereal. She wasn't sure their quiet meals would make for riveting television. "You already spoke to them about this? Before asking me?"

He sensed the misstep. Hid it with another sip of orange juice to take his vitamins and pills. "I had to make sure it was viable first, Naomi. You know how that industry is. Promise you everything, blow a bunch of smoke up your ass, then disappear."

Naomi pushed her spoon through the dregs of her cereal. "I'm not sure," she said. "I've never been good in front of the camera. Can't they just focus on you?" She flashed him a smile. "You're the Man of Mars, after all. I just grow some plants."

Cole made a frustrated sound in his throat. "You always do that."

"What?"

"Diminish your own accomplishments. You're a leading expert in your field. The masses would love to see what you can do, how to make plants grow even in the harshest environments. Red and green plants. It's got a certain poetry, right?"

Naomi bit her lip. It did make a sort of sense. "I'll think about it. Okay?"

Cole beamed and knocked back his juice. He magnanimously cleaned off the table, scraping the remnants of their meal into the trash.

"I'll be back late," he said, kissing Naomi's cheek. "A meeting with the production company. Unless you want to come?"

Naomi shook her head. "No, you do your thing. But do tell them I'm only a maybe. And if I want to stay out of the spotlight, that'll be okay, right?"

Cole's teeth were white. "Of course."

"Cole, you forgot your—"

The door closed with a snap.

"—jacket." It lay on the back of his chair. She picked it up, and something clattered as it fell from his pocket. She bent down to pick it up, pinching it between thumb and forefinger.

A small white pill stamped with DMAU. His birth control pill.

The door opened again. Naomi shoved the pill back into his pocket.

"Forgot my—ah, thanks," Cole said, plucking it from her numb hands. He gave her another kiss, this time on the lips, as if he couldn't help himself.

"Have a good day," Naomi said, faintly.

She'd seen him put the pill on the table next to his vitamins, like he did every morning. He'd seemed so good at taking it every morning. She knew he'd forgotten a time or two, but he'd not known what consequences she faced. They'd stopped using condoms a few months ago. He complained they kept bunching. She wasn't fond of them either, and so she'd relented. It didn't matter, anyway.

But he didn't know that.

She went to the medical cupboard, picked up his pill pack, flipped it to the back. Days of the week. Today was Wednesday. The pill was missing. Had he forgotten to take it another day... or had he palmed the pill that morning and only pretended to take it with his orange juice?

Naomi hadn't told him about the pregnancy, but this, this was like poking holes in condoms and not telling her. Wasn't circumventing birth control revoking consent?

She sat back down at the table, staring at the whorls of the wood. A pregnancy and a baby would be a great subplot for a documentary series about the Martian astronaut and the space botanist, wouldn't it?

She downed her bitter coffee in one gulp.

CHAPTER TWENTY-SIX

127 Days After Launch

4 Days to Mars

122 Days to Cavendish

"What the hell do we do about this?" Hart asked.

They were in the greenhouse. They'd put the embryos back behind the cryopods. Naomi checked the crops, dark as charcoal in the purple light. She'd be able to harvest the latest crop of strawberries soon. Eat some fresh, dry the rest for their stores. She picked the berries, one by one. Naomi snuck one, the sweetness bursting on her tongue. Hart came over and helped. If anyone peered in through the window of the door, it'd look like they were busy at work.

"If Valerie checks the map, she'd know we were both in the storage bay for close to an hour," Naomi said. "That'll look odd. We should get ahead of this, tell her what we know. Maybe they were put there by Lockwood and she doesn't know they're there. It makes sense to add them. Insurance, like our seed vault." Even as she said the words, she realised how silly it sounded. "Why would Lockwood put embryos on an all-male space mission?"

"The technology for cloned organs still exists, even if it's illegal," Hart pointed out. "They could have applied for an exemption and gotten it." She sounded just as doubtful.

Haven hadn't been the only company investing in cloning. Companies providing hearts and kidneys and the like still flourished—it was only wombs that were banned. Dennis Lee would definitely have had the skills to grow organic wombs. He'd helped pioneer it. Her eyes flickered to the thin tendrils of growing vat meat on the far wall. Naomi would be able to make them, especially if Hart helped.

It could be difficult to synthesise the growth medium in situ on Cavendish, or create the scaffold of alginate for the cells to grow in gravity. More fun with algae. Or they could grow them in orbit in the main body of the *Atalanta*. Valerie would have blueprints for the bioreactor where everything came together—would Lebedeva or Hixon be able to create it? Could they retrofit the vat meat bioreactor? So far Naomi hadn't had any trouble so far with her vat meat experiments, but creating a hamburger was a lot easier than a womb.

Very worst-case scenario, the women on board had something the men didn't.

"Those caretakers Valerie selected, a lot of them have already looked after babies in artificial wombs," Hart said.

Naomi had a sudden, strange mental image of embryos in glowing tanks parked right next to the sofa in a living room.

"You're saying this is what she'd always planned?" Naomi's voice was weak.

Hart popped a strawberry in her mouth. "Valerie has consistently lied to us. It's far more likely she put them there than Lockwood. Maybe it was added security, an insurance policy she hoped never to cash in on. It also implies that she knew the backup crew would be on board when we took off. Either way, she still didn't tell us. And that's inexcusable." She clicked her tongue against her teeth. "What if a trigger tripped when we opened the chambers and she already knows what we found?"

"All the more reason to ask her. She came clean the other times. When she had to." Naomi's mouth tasted of iron. "We should talk to Hixon and Lebedeva first. Though, what if they know?" She realised how that sounded. Hixon was the second in command. If Valerie told the pilot it was top secret, would that military history mean Hixon would follow orders? Keep it from even her own wife? Lebedeva was fiercely loyal to Valerie. "God. What if they all already know and we're the ones left in the dark?"

"No." Hart shook her head, too hard. "Jerrie hates the idea of being pregnant. I mean *hates*. The idea of disembodied babies growing in vats would have given her nightmares. And if they failed or couldn't grow on Cavendish and there was even the slightest possibility that Valerie would ask *us* to carry the embryos—this is not something she'd keep quiet about. She wouldn't do it even if it meant saving humanity. I'd carry two to spare her it. If I had to." Her lips were stained dark with strawberry juice.

Naomi gave her a small smile, despite the tingling in her fingertips. "I suppose that's a spot of sweetness in this horror." Her smile faded. "She wouldn't make us carry them, surely." One womb on board was already occupied. Was that why Valerie had taken the news so well?

Hart made a derisive noise in her throat. "She'd frame it as a choice. Not sure it actually would be."

Naomi left Hart to the strawberries, taking down the algae tubes for that day's harvest as an excuse to gather herself. The batches were all growing as they should. No flickering lights, the algae a vibrant purple beneath the glow lights, not milky from contaminants. She hoped she never saw the tubes pulsing again.

As she loaded yesterday's algae into the nutriblock machine, a terrible thought unfurled in Naomi's mind. So awful she almost didn't mention it to Hart, but if she didn't speak it, the thought would burrow its way deeper.

"If she added the embryos, they'd have been a last-minute addition," Naomi said slowly. "She must have bribed someone to look the other way as the robots brought the embryos up and hid them as they installed Cole and the others."

Hart gave a grunt. "Wouldn't have been easy. Wonder how much she paid? And what else could have been done with that money."

"It wouldn't have gone through the same quality checks as everything else. What if—what if that addition was the reason for the power surge? It'd explain why Hixon was so frustrated by the calculations."

Hart's hands fell still. She picked a strawberry leaf, twirled it in her hands. "You're saying Valerie could have been responsible for their deaths?"

"Unintentionally, perhaps." Naomi's forehead crinkled in pain. "She came down, when I was saying goodbye to Cole. She said it was her responsibility to pull the plug, to see to the bodies. I thought it was a kindness."

Hart's eyes were filled with pity. "She did it so she could make sure no one found out what was hidden behind them.

To check the cryopods still had power and the embryos were still safe."

Naomi let out a sob but swallowed the others. The grief for Cole rose up as fresh as the day it'd happened. After so many years under her roof, Naomi knew how to work through Valerie's likely thought patterns. "What if the bodies weren't even damaged? She saw that the fuel efficiency was compromised, and rather than risk the embryos, she could have adjusted the screen readouts. What if—what if we were the ones who voted to kill them?"

Hart left the strawberry plants, coming close and resting a hand on Naomi's forearm. "I wish I could say I couldn't see her doing that, but I'm not going to lie to you, Lovelace. Valerie Black needs fealty. Hell, doing it could have been a test. What do we choose to do when faced with such a tough decision? We made the choice she wanted. We agreed to pull the plug. Maybe that means she knows that, when push comes to shove, we'd fall into line with the embryos. Or whatever else she's up to."

Naomi had no response to that. She gripped the empty algae tube so hard it'd have shattered if it wasn't reinforced.

Hart continued, relentless. "Valerie always had that loyalty from you, and she knew this. She's well aware Oksana and Jerrie also feel like they owe her everything. Valerie could give you all that NASA no longer could. A chance to come up here."

"Weren't you desperate to go to space?" Naomi asked.

Hart laughed. "Not really. I mean, it's cool and all, don't get me wrong. A monumentally important moment, arguably the defining moment of humanity. We'll go down in the history books, and that's damn satisfying, even if they might paint us as the villains. But I also would have been happy enough back on

Earth. With my friends, my family. I'm never going to see my niece grow up. She's only two. When those I love are dying, I won't be able to say goodbye in person. Of all of you, I think I left behind the most. Oksana already gave up everything when she left Russia. Jerrie's been cut off from her family since she came out, and she pulled away from her friends when she realised we had an actual shot at this. You did the same, didn't you?"

Naomi opened her mouth in denial, but snapped it shut. She had plenty of friendly acquaintances on Earth—people she'd see for coffee, or to catch a film and grab dinner. Co-workers, usually. It'd been years since she'd allowed herself a close friend. Who had she turned to when things were difficult? After the NASA rejection, and then the acceptance. When she planned on the abortion. When she needed comforting after the miscarriage. It had always been Valerie, and often only Valerie.

Hart's voice was soft. "Valerie was never as sure with me, I don't think. She respected my work, my abilities, but I always had the sense that she would have rather chosen someone else to be the flight surgeon if I wasn't a package deal with Jerrie. I'm not diffident enough." She raised her hands, then let them fall. "I'm not saying you all are, just..."

"I am, I think. Or I was." So many little things Naomi never stopped to think about. The way Valerie would fire people at Hawthorne if she didn't find them respectful enough. She'd distanced herself from her own son when Evan hadn't moulded his life the way she wanted. Naomi had long learned to stay silent, keep her head down, focus on the work. One of Naomi's most painful memories was that rift that opened between her and Valerie when she moved to Scotland. Before then, and once she'd come back to Hawthorne, she'd been desperate to prove she was worthy of the attention Valerie had given her over the years. The money Valerie spent on her education when her parents' inheritance ran out.

Had she been loyal to a fault?

Her entire understanding of who she was, the life she thought she had, was shifting to something she didn't like the look of.

"So we speak to Hixon and Lebedeva first," Naomi said. "Lay it all out, then go to Valerie."

"Agreed." Hart leaned over to Naomi's tablet, brought up the ship feed. "Valerie's in her office. Hixon and Lebedeva are down in the bridge. Should we go to them now?"

Naomi nodded. "Yes, I'll just wrap this up and be right behind you."

Hart let out a long exhale. "Right." She looked like she was trying to psych herself for whatever was to come. Naomi didn't blame her one bit.

When the lab door closed behind Hart, Naomi grabbed her tablet. Typing as quickly as her shaking fingers would allow, she sent Evan an update of what she'd learned over the past few hours, hoping for a response sooner rather than later. After her long message, she dashed out a short one before she made her way down to the bridge.

Naomi Lovelace: *I think I might have been wrong about her for all these years.*

CHAPTER TWENTY-SEVEN

127 Days After Launch

4 Days to Mars

122 Days to Cavendish

Naomi hated the sound of the lock to the bridge hissing shut.

There had been no need for locks on the common areas of *Atalanta* before.

Hixon glanced up from her navigations, frowning. Naomi made sure the comms panel by the door was switched off. Lebedeva floated closer, moving gracefully between the handrails. "What's going on?" she asked, gaze shifting between Naomi and Hart.

"We've come across information you need to know about before we jump." Naomi tethered herself to her chair, gathered her strength, and told them everything. Hart added a few comments here and there. Naomi tried to read the pilot and the engineer's expressions. If Hixon knew or had suspected anything, she was good at hiding it. Lebedeva could be a stone statue for all she reacted. Perhaps it was not all such a shock to her. If something ever went wrong with the embryo storage, for example, it'd be Lebedeva Valerie would call on to fix it.

"There has to be a rational explanation," Hixon said. "There was with the message from Cochran. It was a distraction when we needed to focus on the test jump."

"She would have told us when she was ready," Lebedeva agreed.

"She told you because I made her," Naomi said. "I found out about it on my own and confronted her. I'm not sure she would have, otherwise." The words were heavy. "Hixon, you're second in command—she should have told you at least, shouldn't she?"

Hixon's chin rose. "You're the one questioning her authority and mine in one swoop." Her gaze flicked to Hart. "Both of you are."

"So we shouldn't question anything?" Hart asked. "You think we should follow orders even if they put us all in danger?"

The silence was sharp. Charged.

"The embryos are merely a protection. Assurance," Lebedeva said. "The power surge would not have been on her. She would have checked the numbers."

Naomi's gut tightened. "You knew."

Lebedeva blew out through her nose. "No."

The smallest flicker on Hart's face, the barest meeting of gazes. Neither she nor Naomi knew whether to believe her. A few months ago, Naomi would have sworn no one on this team would lie to each other. She couldn't pretend she was any more honest than the others.

"I know she would not have jeopardised the backup crew," Lebedeva said.

Naomi wished she could be as sure. Hart raised her eyebrows at Hixon. "Well?"

"I don't know what to believe." Hixon's voice cracked.

"That's why we should all speak to her," Naomi said. "Pose

a united front. Have everything on the table and make an informed decision, like we did with Cochran's message. Maybe you're right and there is an explanation, or we're rushing to conclusions not supported by the facts. I mean, I want to be proven wrong. I don't want Valerie to have done this. I think we can all agree on that."

"We have to make decisions before the jump, or it'll take months to send word back to Earth," Hart said.

"And if you decide you do not like that Dr. Black kept things from us?" Lebedeva asked. "What, you suggest mutiny?" She gave something like a *tch*. "If we break, none of us will make it."

Hixon grimaced. "It won't come to that. We know Valerie. All of us. She wouldn't kill five people. She won't force us to do anything we don't want to do. This crew is a collective. We work together, as a team. It's not didactic, or a dictatorship. Secrets have no place here, though, I agree. We air everything."

As if on cue, Naomi's tablet in her pocket beeped with a new message. Lebedeva startled, then her eyes narrowed. They all knew that noise. Their tablets were identical, but no one else had heard that sound since Earth.

She picked it up. Read Evan's message. Blanched.

She took in a breath, lowered her voice. "I've been able to access messages from Earth." She figured it was safer to let them think she intercepted official information rather than that she was in direct conversation with Evan.

Hixon crossed her arms. "Looks like Valerie isn't the only one keeping secrets."

"Berate me later. The message says there's a potential illness outbreak." She copied the text of the message to the larger screen, hiding who had sent it.

That local outbreak is a virus. Something new. Something vicious. We're still investigating it, but so far it's like an unholy blend of Marburg spreading like a common cold. Could be airborne. Fatality is high. It's early days, but I don't know if we'll be able to slow its spread. We're locking down a perimeter, and my team and I are trying to find either a vaccine, a cure, or something to help slow the symptoms. That'll take time—months at least, years more likely—and we might not have it. They're trying to avoid making a widespread announcement on Earth, but it's only a matter of time. I don't think we'll be able to contain this.

The four women stared at the screen, reading silently.

"Who sent this?" Hixon asked.

"A contact," Naomi said, worried to admit even that much. The blood had already rushed to her face from the lack of gravity, the skin of her cheeks hot and puffy. Her arms and legs had floated up, leaving her suspended, and her fingers and toes were cold.

A virus. Evan had mentioned it after the test jump, but she'd been so distracted she'd glossed over it. She knew that area from that first summer working at Argaine. Dry and dusty, the corn fields even more choked than when she'd been there as an undergraduate student. The nearest town had thirty-five thousand people. If it was airborne and deadly, that was a big enough node to spread. How many people had already passed through that sleepy, sunburned town? A quick, hot meal while their car charged. It was a place to pass through on the way to Los Angeles.

"If this spreads, that'll be a catastrophe," Naomi said. "A pandemic."

"There've been plenty of outbreaks recently," Hixon said. "That Marburg outbreak on the East Coast a few years ago. It'd been bad, but. And remember Ebola before they found a vaccine?"

"Ebola only spread through bodily fluids like blood or semen," Hart said. "And it took them years before they had something resembling that vaccine. A sickness as lethal but airborne? It could be a modern-day plague. Wipe out a sizable percentage of the population." Her voice was hushed.

"That means that Valerie's plan, if it was hers, was good idea. Embryos were worth keeping," Lebedeva said. She gave them a look, blue eyes catching on Naomi's growing belly. "And yes, I would carry one. If I had to," she said. "It will not come to that."

"Stop," Hixon said. "Let me think." Her face tightened as she worked through the new information with the ruthless efficiency she'd learned in the military. "We are still a crew. A team. No more postulations. No more what-ifs. We speak to Valerie."

"That's the right answer, Hixon," came Valerie's voice over the comms.

CHAPTER TWENTY-EIGHT

127 Days After Launch

4 Days to Mars

122 Days to Cavendish

Naomi's body jerked in mid-air, the adrenaline firing through her nerve endings.

The women had spent hundreds of hours on the *Atalanta* simulators and grown to know every corner of the craft after living on it for months. Even in the emergency instructions, there was nothing about being able to overhear or see someone in a room if they hadn't accessed the comms, and Naomi had made sure they were switched off before she said a word.

Valerie told them to meet her in the rec room. For the barest hesitation, Naomi and the others debated staying put, barricading themselves on the bridge, but that would only last as long as their hunger and thirst did. They climbed the ladder back to the ring, rung by rung, their bodies gradually growing heavier. As second in command, Hixon took the lead, Naomi next, with Hart and Lebedeva trailing behind.

Valerie waited for them. She'd shifted the background of the rec room to the proposed landing site on Cavendish—a clearing surrounded by the same blue-green moss and ferns Naomi had grown back on Earth. The gentle waves of the freshwater lake lapped at the shore. Mountains rose in the distance, tinged orange and pink in the haze. Valerie had uploaded her blueprints to the program, as if Catherine Lovelace's robots had already erected the ghostly outlines of buildings. The sleeping pods were clustered around a main structure that would be largely 3D printed. The bridge of the *Atalanta* would remain in orbit. The ark ships out would hopefully carry hundreds, or at least dozens, rather than five. Their largest ships were designed for thousands. The VR wall showed the outline of the greenhouse where Naomi was to conduct her experiments. Valerie had even added vague animated figures coming and going. Living their idyllic, golden life on their new planet.

Valerie perched on a raised chaise that fit her body like a cupped hand. The orange of Cavendish's sun softened her features but couldn't erase the obvious anger coiled through every line of her body. Naomi fought off the urge to curl her shoulders; it was like she was fourteen again, standing in front of Valerie to be berated for some infraction.

"Take a seat," Valerie said as four more chairs rose from the ground—lower than Valerie's, Naomi noticed. She eased into her chair, her heartbeat thudding steadily in her ears.

"Well," Valerie said after they'd settled. "You've certainly been busy."

"You're spying on us," Hart said.

Valerie gave a sardonic half-smile. "Don't act sanctimonious now, Hart, when y'all have been questioning me, my leadership, and the mission." With a pained sigh, she gave each of them an uncomfortably long look. "I thought when I picked you out of the hundreds of candidates clamouring for the job it was because you knew the significance of reaching Cavendish. That it was of the utmost importance, no matter what happened back on Earth."

Naomi focused on the spiderweb of the base camp spun in delicate gossamer over the backdrop behind Valerie.

"Why are there embryos on board, Dr. Black?" Hart asked, biting back her anger. "As medic, I should have been made aware. There are experiments I could have been conducting, ensuring their health and viability."

"We all should have been informed," Naomi said. "Between this and not mentioning Cochran's message until the last possible moment, we're understandably concerned."

Valerie's gaze snapped towards Naomi like a whip.

"We're a team," Hixon said, playing peacemaker. "We need to understand. To know what's at stake."

"The mission is of utmost importance," Lebedeva said. "We realise this. I am still committed to Cavendish. As we all are."

Valerie's expression flickered. She drummed her fingers against the armrest.

"Cavendish is a marvel," she said. "An unprecedented chance to start again. Earth has thirty years at best. We don't know how long it'll take to build the exodus ships, or who they will choose to send. Trying to influence that blew up in our faces, so of course I wanted to bring a backup, just in case."

She pressed her lips together, choosing her next words. "We spent weeks coming up with the basis of a new society. Where people can't be kept down. Not everyone would be able to game the system like I did, working my way from nothing to everything. I had to make compromises to get where I was, and I'm not proud of it. I'm not going to pretend I haven't shifted my moral compass to an uncomfortable direction at times, to make sure my overall direction was true. That didn't mean I wanted to put you through that." Her face was distant.

With a wave of her hand, she changed the background from Cavendish to overpopulated, trash-strewn Earth. Rivers choked with garbage. Beaches carpeted with debris.

Naomi shifted her stance. This had all the makings of one of Valerie's grand speeches. A TED Talk or a keynote. How long had she practised this?

"You didn't agree, at first, that we should consider taking a ship of children to Cavendish and establish the new society," Valerie continued. "So people like Cochran don't copy and paste the same goddamn problems. You didn't like it, but you saw my reasoning." She rose, pacing, unfastening the top button of her coveralls. Committing to the performance. "We can't let them come. We gave them enough chances to do the right thing. They will learn nothing." She clenched her jaw, the cords standing out in her neck. "They won't change. They're incapable of it."

"What are you saying, Valerie?" Naomi asked. "What are the embryos, beyond insurance?"

Hart widened her eyes at Naomi's boldness, and Hixon's gaze flattened. As second in command, she should have been the one asking the hard questions, but she'd clammed up, too afraid to hold Valerie accountable in front of the others.

Valerie exhaled, forcing herself to release the tension. "You are scientists. When an experiment has failed, when a sample is contaminated, or when you can't figure out how to undo all the things that have gone wrong, what do you do? Do you keep conducting the same experiment, over and over, with the tainted batch? Or do you start again, fresh, with different conditions?"

Naomi couldn't breathe.

"Earth isn't an experiment," Hart said. Lebedeva ran her hands through the buzz of her hair.

"Earth is already a lost cause. Thirty years was overly optimistic. Humans will find ways around the bans, the limits, the sanctions. Cheat, take, let others worry about the mess they leave behind. That's how we got into this mess. I thought we could break the cycle, with one ship of young people. Cochran didn't give us the chance." Valerie licked her lips. "It might not have worked anyway—there's the risk that the children would already have society's influences embedded in them. Travelling so far, so young, would have psychological effects, but people like you, Hart, would be able to mitigate that." A sardonic nod of her head at the doctor. Hart's nostrils flared.

Naomi's skin tingled. "How convenient, then, that something so awful has broken out back home. With Earth so distracted, it'll be easier to jump through the ring. Hard for countries to divert resources to an exosolar planet with chaos on the ground."

Hixon's head snapped towards Naomi. "You can't mean—"

Valerie held up a hand. "Now, now, let Naomi finish her accusation."

Naomi sucked in a breath. She'd first assumed the illness was due to climate change factors. The strains of antigens change each year, and quadrivalent strains of flu shots had been losing their efficacy. Trying to increase vaccination success to former levels was Evan's entire job. But this made her question that.

God, Valerie might have even gotten the idea from her son.

He'd talked about infectious diseases at the dinner table one Thanksgiving until Naomi had thrown a bread roll at him and begged him to stop describing pustules while they were eating. The outbreak had started not far from Evan's work—which meant it also wasn't far from Hawthorne's headquarters. Naomi cursed herself for a fool.

"Valerie can't be behind this. We left months ago. Anything that contagious would have already taken effect," Hixon said. Hart lifted her chin, mouth working as if to bite back sharp words towards her wife.

Valerie hesitated just a beat too long.

"No," Naomi whispered. "Valerie."

"If your algae dies, do you keep working with the dead cells?" Valerie asked, soft. Her pupils were wide in the orange glow. She didn't blink. "I've tried every option. Run every other scenario. They'll notice, soon, that it's developed from Seventh Disease." No one on board had ever come down with the childhood disease—the oldest people who had it were probably only about nineteen or twenty. Naomi remembered seeing photos of the red splotches across children's skin, larger than chicken pox sores but just as itchy. A few years ago, they'd developed a vaccine they'd started giving children, but they hadn't bothered with adults. The illness, unlike chicken pox, was milder in adults than children.

Hart blinked fast, making the same connections. "Oh, God."

Naomi struggled to keep up. "You're killing the adults but keeping the children?"

"Some adults will survive," Valerie said. "Perhaps five per cent."

Lebedeva squeezed her eyes shut.

"Valerie, you can't do this," Naomi said, her throat tight. "You can't."

"It's a tragedy, but I'm being kinder. No drawn-out suffering. No inevitable war and violence as Earth grows hotter and they continue to compete for resources. Brazil has the largest amount of clean water in the world. Think they'll look after it as well as the Amazon? This will be quick. A few months, no more." She didn't blink as she spoke. She had the fervour of a zealot.

Hixon's head jerked back. None of them wanted to believe Valerie capable of this. Lebedeva moved towards the door of the rec room, her arms crossed, and Naomi couldn't help notice it was as if she guarded it.

Hart and Hixon's heads turned to her as the same knowledge dawned.

"How long have you known?" Hixon asked.

Lebedeva's face was smooth as slate. "Months." She said the word, heavily, not as if it had been weighing on her, but as a relief that she could finally set it down. She had lied to them, back on the bridge. She'd known about the embryos. About all of it. Was she the one who had turned the comms back on, without the others noticing?

Everything around Naomi shifted. Her vision went close, her skin clammy and cold.

"You're not killers, either of you," Naomi tried. "You can't just stand by and let this happen."

"This is what's best for humanity as a species. You'll see. We'll be free. No need to worry about Earth following us through. Whichever country has the most money, the most power, the most weapons, would be able to oust us and disrupt our vision." Valerie's expression was bright, resplendent.

It was a terrible moment, to look at the woman who had raised her and fully realise that the person Naomi had put so much faith into, so much loyalty, was unworthy of all of it. Naomi had defended Valerie so many times, made so many excuses. So many had called the CEO of Hawthorne selfish, mercenary. Naomi had always dismissed it as jealousy, or insisted that they were intimidated by Valerie's drive.

It had been that, sure, but some had also been warnings from those who had seen through her.

"How does the virus work?" Hart asked.

Valerie smirked. "So you can try and magically engineer a vaccine or a cure in your little lab? You know as well as I do that would take too long. It's aggressive."

Naomi dug her fingernails into her palms.

"How did you do this?" Hart asked. "You're an engineer, an architect, not a doctor with this level of expertise. Who did you work with?"

Valerie only smiled.

For a fleeting second, Naomi worried it was Evan. He'd have the knowledge, but not the will. No. Not him. Valerie would crow about it if she'd finally convinced her son to come fully to her side. Naomi's mind whirled. "Plenty in Hawthorne work in immunology. Dr. Bryony Goulding, she's head of health research for Project Atalanta." At the tightening of the skin around Valerie's eyes, Naomi knew she'd guessed correctly. The tall woman who had sat at the same table as Naomi at that fundraising dinner on Catalina Island. She'd already have been developing it then, if not finished. Naomi pushed down on an absurd flush of jealousy. "What did you promise her?"

Valerie gave a slow blink. "Immunity and a ticket to Cavendish on the first ship out," she said.

"You can make people immune," Hart said.

"Obviously." Valerie was just shy of rolling her eyes. "I wouldn't engineer a disease without a cure."

"Valerie," Naomi said, with a stab of hope. "You can get Bryony to leak it. No one ever needs to know. You can undo this."

Valerie's brow rippled. "Now, why would I go and do a thing like that when everything is going so well?"

"Evan is down there," Naomi said, hating how her voice thickened with tears. Valerie despised any show of weakness. "The father of your granddaughter. Please. You can't."

Valerie blinked three times, a lump moving down her throat as she swallowed. Then her features schooled into the coolness Naomi had seen countless times before.

The others suppressed their surprise. Naomi knew Hart had suspected Cole was the father, despite their divorce. Hixon and Lebedeva had never asked who the father was, but they clearly hadn't expected her to sleep with Valerie's son.

"I gave him so many chances. To do what I needed him to do to fulfil his potential. But he couldn't commit." Valerie's forehead smoothed. "There is no place on Cavendish for him."

Naomi's breath came short and fast. "Bullshit."

Valerie's head reared back, a cobra flaring its hood.

"No." Naomi pressed on. "This is murder. Genocide on a global scale. You can't use morality here. There is none."

Valerie's eyes flashed. "Don't test me, Naomi. You've already pushed me enough."

"I guess you can take comfort that your DNA will live on," she said, her voice bitter as wormwood.

"Indeed it will," Valerie said. "Hixon."

The pilot's head snapped up, almost to attention. A soldier through and through.

"Stay the course. We'll jump on schedule."

Hixon's spine was straight as the ghostly blueprints behind her. "Valerie..." she began.

"Dr. Black," Valerie corrected. "That's a direct order, Hixon. Now's the time to decide: are you staying to the mission or wavering?"

Lebedeva shifted subtly by the door.

Hixon's shoulders fell, her head dipping. She slid past Lebedeva, who watched with narrowed eyes.

"Jerrie!" Hart called after her. Hixon paused, but didn't turn back. Hart's face creased in betrayal.

"Now," Valerie said. "Hart, you are to be confined to your quarters. Naomi, you'll be in the lab. Lebedeva will bring through your mattress. You're to keep tending to the crops and processing nutriblocks. You'll both stay there at least until we jump. After that. Well. It depends on you."

Lebedeva took cable ties from the pocket of her coveralls. She clamped Naomi's hands behind her back first. Naomi debated fighting back, but between Lebedeva's strength and her growing belly, she didn't have the bravery. Lebedeva's brows drew down, as if she guessed Naomi's thoughts.

Hart's nostrils flared, and she made a run for the door.

Lebedeva caught her by the ankle with a hooked foot, and Hart went down, hard. She struggled, and Lebedeva wrenched her arms back, securing the cable. Naomi clenched her jaw. What was the point in running? Where could they go on a locked ship?

"Earth is gone," Valerie said. She looked at Naomi, and Naomi alone, as if pleading for her to understand. The plastic of the cable ties dug into Naomi's skin. "It is a fossil. A past civilisation we'll study on Cavendish, no different than the ancient Romans or Egyptians. All empires fall. But we can build something that lasts."

Valerie drifted closer, rested a hand on Naomi's cheek. "I suggest you start thinking about what you want your place in this new world to be. What sort of life on Cavendish you want my grandbaby to have. We can make it a blank slate for the both of us. It's up to you." Lebedeva tugged Naomi, dragging both her and Hart from the room.

Valerie turned back to her vision of Cavendish.

CHAPTER TWENTY-NINE

4 Years Before Launch

Pasadena, California

When Naomi discovered Cole had found another woman, her first emotion hadn't been anger, but relief.

She'd found out four months after the pill had fallen from his pocket. She'd watched him, palming the medicine each morning while taking a sip of orange juice. He'd have made a half-decent magician, with that sleight of hand. She'd missed her last few cycles, but pregnancy tests still showed negatives. The cysts on her ovaries might have gotten larger, blocking ovulation entirely.

Those last few months, she and Cole lived separate lives. Breakfast was the only real time they spent together, along with sleeping on opposite sides of the bed. Gone were Cole's absent-minded, lingering touches he gave early in their relationship, as if he couldn't bear not to touch her for too long. He came back later and later, but instead of being stressed from the supposed overtime, his muscles were lax. It didn't take her long to put it together.

She packed up a suitcase of what she wanted to keep and donated the rest to goodwill, a few bags at a time. She had no need for the furniture, and most of it wasn't to her taste, anyway. She'd bought it so that when people came over, they saw an apartment befitting the Man of Mars. Futuristic, swish, too expensive. Who the hell was she trying to impress?

Naomi debated leaving a note, simply disappearing, but she was someone who craved closure. She didn't want the end niggling at her, late at night—something she poked at like a sore tooth.

She stayed calm, rational. She laid out the evidence. The pills, the affair. She'd suspected and followed him from work one day, certain she'd been wrong right up until she'd seen him walk up to a woman with dark hair, his face lit up with the smile he no longer gave Naomi. He'd kissed her, right on the sidewalk, and Naomi had asked the car to take her home.

Naomi had found out the woman's name, hating herself for looking her up online. It hadn't been hard. Mel Simmons. One quick search found photos or witty statuses on her social feeds, her bylines on news sites. Mel was a sharp writer, her articles punchy and persuading.

Naomi finally, finally told Cole that she couldn't give him what he wanted, and that he'd be better off with Mel. She would be used to the sharp teeth of the public world. Mel would shine in the documentary, whereas Naomi was someone who would happily sidestep the spotlight.

Cole had spat insults, called her a cold bitch for lying, even as he knew he had no leg to stand on. She'd taken it, waiting until he sputtered out and her silence made him sheepish. She'd pulled up the handle on her luggage and rolled out of that godawful apartment and made her way to the airport.

She'd thought she'd cry in the car, where no one could see her except for the automated driving system. Everyone had grown used to giving orders to the pleasant-voiced feminine robots. Alexa, Siri, Sophia, Sage, do this for me. A perky "okay," and your wish was her command. They'd all been doing it for years before women started realising the men in their lives had been conditioned to do the same to them. And by then it was too late.

Even Cole had done it to Naomi. He'd asked for a glass of water, except it hadn't been an ask, exactly, and there was no thank you when she clinked the glass against the ceramic coaster. She'd done it without thinking. She'd been conditioned, too.

Her eyes remained dry in the car. In the airport, another automated robot with a female voice checked her in and sent the boarding pass to her phone.

"Have a pleasant flight," the robot voice intoned.

"Thank you," she said, and the man behind her in line gave her a strange look.

Another robot scanned the pass before she walked up the temporary stairs to the craft. A robot would fly the plane, though they still had a bored pilot in the cockpit just in case they needed to override the controls. Still another robot would serve her drinks and snacks. She bought a double gin. The robot scanned Naomi's public health profile, determined the alcohol units and calories were within her allowance, and poured it for her. She scowled at its back as it continued down the aisle.

Valerie waited for her at the airport. Naomi was surprised at that; she'd expected her to simply send a car. She'd offered to send a plane when Naomi phoned to tell her she'd left Cole, but Naomi had demurred at that extravagance. Especially knowing Valerie wouldn't like what Naomi had to tell her once they were alone.

Valerie nodded at her. No hug. "How are you doing?"

Naomi gave an empty smile. "Fine."

Valerie snorted.

"No, actually. I'm fine. Whatever we had broke a while ago. I was just the one to rip off the band-aid. And get the hell out of Texas."

"Like adopted mother, like adopted daughter," Valerie said with a laugh, taking one of her suitcases for her.

When they reached Valerie's mansion, Naomi tucked herself on Valerie's green velvet sofa. This was the sofa she should have bought for her apartment (well, a budget version). The softness enveloped her. She arranged the cushions and pulled the throw blanket around her. Valerie had to work, and so Naomi watched television on the screen that took up nearly the whole wall, and she was seventeen again, back at home the summer before college.

Naomi waited to tell Valerie her news until after dinner.

"I'm not staying," she said, without preamble.

Valerie paused in slicing the cheesecake she'd bought. She dropped a slice on the plate.

"It's what spurred me to leave," Naomi continued. "I was offered a job I couldn't refuse."

"Leaving NASA," Valerie murmured, sticking the spoon in the cheesecake, where it stood at attention like a flag. She passed the plate to Naomi. "Not transferring?"

"I thought about it. I could do good work at the AMES centre. Or go corporate again."

"You know there's always a job for you at Hawthorne."

"Of course, and I'm grateful for that. I am. But I feel like... I need to stand on my own two feet. Somewhere where I'm not under Cole's shadow. Or yours."

Valerie speared her slice with a spoon. "What's the job?"

"Life sciences botany research for the ESA and Lockwood. At the Sutherland Space Centre in Scotland." Naomi pressed her spoon deeper into the cheesecake.

"You're taking a job with my main rival?" Valerie asked, her voice flat.

Naomi took the smallest spoonful of cheesecake. Vanilla and the comforting fat of cream cheese. "I know, I'm sorry, but the job was too good—"

Valerie rose, clutching the plate. "No."

Naomi blinked. "Come again?"

"I said no. You are not working for Lockwood. You are not moving halfway across the world to work in some tiny, backwards spaceport surrounded by sheep."

"I've already accepted the offer."

"You'll stay here, at Hawthorne."

"Valerie," Naomi said, struggling to keep her voice firm. "I'm not."

Valerie's back was straight, her nostrils flaring.

"Valerie, I have to live my life," Naomi said, standing. "Cole already tried to get me to do things I didn't want to do with my career. I love you, but I'm not letting you do the same."

Valerie's face worked, her hands clenching the marble countertop of the kitchen island.

"I'm sorry," Naomi said. "But I need to do something on my own."

"On your own," Valerie bit out. She put her plate on the

counter. "You realise that with one call, one whisper, I could make that job disappear?" Her eyes were dark pools, features shadowed by the light above her.

They stared at each other in an impasse.

Naomi's mouth was dry. "I do, but I didn't think you'd do that to me." The hurt in her voice made her plaintive. The worst part was that she knew she was being ungrateful. Throwing Valerie's help back in her face. But she couldn't stay here, fold herself back into Hawthorne, surrounded by people who knew Cole, or at least knew of him. How long before that documentary aired with Mel instead of Naomi?

Valerie leaned back, took another bite of cheesecake for time to compose herself.

"Fine," she said, as if unconcerned. "Leave. You'll see. When Lockwood lets you down, when the ESA keeps you strapped to a desk as surely as NASA did, you'll come back to me." She narrowed her eyes in satisfaction. "You always come back."

Naomi took a step forward, but Valerie strode from the room.

The next morning, Valerie was gone on a business trip.

By the time she returned, Naomi was in Scotland. There she remained, until Valerie came calling, and proved her words right.

CHAPTER THIRTY

128 Days After Launch

3 Days to Mars

121 Days to Cavendish

Naomi's lab was twenty-three steps long and twenty steps across.

She'd paced it exactly one hundred and seven times that day. She was determined to keep moving, to let the rhythm of the steps help her think. To find some way through this.

Valerie would likely be watching her pace, listening to her low mutterings. Waiting for her to come to her senses and be the obedient little girl she'd always been. Almost always been. She'd had her one rebellion, when she went to Scotland.

Earlier that day, Naomi had spent one and a half futile hours trying to open the door. Valerie had changed the code. She wouldn't be able to lever the doors open with anything, and in any case, Lebedeva had been through the lab and taken out anything that could be used as a weapon. No trowels—Naomi would have to dig up her crops with her bare hands. Lebedeva would take her to the toilet twice a day, and she had a glorious bucket in the corner as a backup. Naomi was instructed to keep up the algae crops, and Lebedeva would come at the end of each day to collect the nutriblocks, leaving aside a portion for Naomi.

Naomi still had her tablet, but she'd been afraid to check it too often. Valerie would know that Naomi was in contact with someone on Earth, and she'd have to assume it was Evan. Hopefully she'd think it was only through the console in the rec room, not on the tablet. More likely, Valerie knew about the tablet but let Naomi keep it so she could monitor their conversations. There were no new messages. Naomi had tapped out a terse update. It wasn't easy telling him that his mother had destroyed the world and sentenced her own son to die.

Naomi wouldn't be able to force her way out of the lab—she'd have to use charm. Machines were harder to break than people.

When Lebedeva came to collect the nutriblocks, Naomi stood in the corner as instructed, hands on her head, the purple tubes of the algae pressed against her back.

"I need to see Hart, so she can check on the baby," Naomi said.

"No, you do not. You just had scan after we jumped. You are up to something," Lebedeva said.

"I'm under a lot of stress. I want reassurance."

Lebedeva grunted. "I will mention it to Dr. Black."

"Thank you. Oksana—" Naomi tried. She hadn't dared use Lebedeva's given name before this.

"Do not bother, Naomi," Lebedeva said, packing the nutriblocks in a bag. She'd returned the favour at least. That was something. A little chink in her armour. "You are not changing my mind. I know where I stand."

"*Eight billion people*," Naomi said, switching to Russian.

Valerie was undoubtedly listening, but she didn't speak the language. "*They are dying as we speak. How many yesterday? How many tomorrow? How many right now?*" She stumbled, a little, and her accent was atrocious.

Lebedeva paused, pinching a nutriblock hard enough to warp the shape. "It does not matter." She spoke English.

"*It does,*" Naomi said, stubbornly continuing in Russian. "*It has almost certainly spread beyond California now. It will be out of the U.S. by next week. You still have family in Russia. They are at risk.*" She didn't know how to express in Russian that she suspected Valerie hadn't even dosed Bryony, and the woman had killed the planet for a broken promise of inoculation. "*Valerie...she uses people, Oksana. She has done it to me my whole life, and I was too stupid to see it.*"

She was pushing hard. A week ago, she wouldn't have. It was freeing, in a way, to know with such clarity what was important and what was immaterial.

Lebedeva didn't respond. The grow lights turned her blond hair violet, and her eyelashes cast shadows on her cheeks. The muscles of her jaw clenched.

"Oksana—"

"*Nyet.*" The word cut, but Lebedeva had switched to Russian. "*This is happening, Naomi. It is horrible, terrible. I am not going to pretend it is not. They had their chances to fix things, and they did not. They knew what was at stake, but they still bought plastic, ate beef, took flights. I did, too. If I had been left behind, I would have died with them. But that is not my fate. It does not have to be yours. Think, Naomi. Valerie is making the hard decision, the impossible choice, so we do not have to.*"

"*I do not believe that*," Naomi said.

"*It does not matter what you believe*," Lebedeva said. "*This is what is happening*." She tied the neck of the bag of nutriblocks and made for the door.

"*If your*—" a pause for the word—"*conscience wakes up, Oksana, you know where to find me. It is not too late*," Naomi said.

Lebedeva halted for the barest breath, and then she was gone.

Naomi dropped her hands, her palms tingling. She worked feeling back into them, grimacing. She sat at her lab table, poked at her evening meal of four nutriblocks. Finally, she stuffed them in her mouth, forcing the stuff down as quickly as possible, before she went over every inch of her lab again, determined to find something she could use as a weapon when Lebedeva came back the next day. Naomi needed to distract or disable Lebedeva as soon as the door opened.

Naomi's hand strayed to her stomach. Horribly, this bump was what might save Naomi's life. Valerie wouldn't risk harming her granddaughter. She'd want her blood to survive on Cavendish. Though Naomi would put good money on the odds that some of the embryos in cryo were Valerie's own, frozen when she was younger, perhaps. If growing artificial wombs proved difficult, would Valerie be able to carry a child easily? Or would she make the others carry them instead?

Naomi paced. Twenty-three steps. Twenty. Twenty-three. Twenty. It would be easy to let the grief settle in the crevices of her mind. For Evan. For everyone she knew back on Earth.

Her friends, like Lynn, and her family. Her NASA and ESA and Lockwood co-workers. Her Hawthorne colleagues had given everything to Project Atalanta, not realising they were engineering their own destruction.

How long had the Valerie Naomi thought she knew been a lie? The woman who had hugged her in the storage bay had seemed warm, and kind, but in the next breath she'd pulled the plug on five people who would have survived if she hadn't tampered with the cryo in the first place. The woman who had risked everything to grant Naomi the abortion. If the doctor had sold her out, Valerie would have been ruined. Lost her company, been even more vilified by the media. They would have crucified her. Yet she'd still risked it. Had that been a lie?

Valerie had bandaged her cuts and bruises over the years. She hadn't pushed her when she couldn't speak after the fire from the trauma. How could that woman bring about the end of the world?

Naomi needed a weapon that could incapacitate but not cause permanent damage. Lebedeva had taken away the bleach. Come on, come on. There had to be something here. Something simple.

She paused, staring at the crops. The newest tomato plants were flowering nicely, but her eyes snagged on the plants to the left of them. Chillies. She'd harvested and dried plenty of them already, to add spice to their meals. Most were in the kitchen, but—

She forced herself to walk to her desk calmly, as if her heart wasn't racing. She opened the middle drawer. It was low enough Valerie wouldn't be able to have a clear view from the comms panel. There was a little container of relatively fresh chillies.

She put them in the back of the dehydrator for the algae when she prepped the next crop. She lay down and waited until the middle of the night, when she was reasonably sure Valerie would be asleep, before she crept back to check the chillies were dry enough. She stayed low, finding a good angle behind the glowing, purple algae tubes. She ground the chillies in a mortar and pestle she'd mostly used for cracking seeds or grinding their precious store of spices so far.

Soon, she had a few tablespoons of chilli powder. She submerged it in some rubbing alcohol usually used for cleaning beakers and algae equipment and stirred it vigorously. She resisted the urge to look furtively over her shoulder at the comms panel. She had no way of knowing if it was on or not. Either Valerie would see and suspect something and send Lebedeva to be her muscle, or she wouldn't.

She worked slowly, making as little noise as possible. Next, she added a tablespoon of oil—cheap, vegetable stuff used to lubricate certain parts of the nutriblock machine. She put the solution in an opaque container to let it settle, hiding it behind other supplies. She'd still have to figure out how to filter it without anyone noticing and hope she could rig it into one of her aerosols she used for spot-spraying fertilisers. For a relatively easy solution, there were still things that could go wrong.

Naomi stood, coming back into view of the comms and harvesting the last of the algae and leaving it to dry, and prepped the new crop. If Valerie fast-forwarded through the feed of the night, she'd see her about her usual business, even if it was at unusual hours. Naomi had always been an insomniac, doing most of her best studying in the late hours of the night or early hours of the morning. Evan had been, too. They'd pulled plenty of all-nighters in undergrad.

Don't think about Evan.

Naomi hefted one of the reinforced empty glass vials thoughtfully, squeezing it tight. With enough force, it could hurt, especially with the metal cap at the end. She had over a hundred clubs in the lab that Lebedeva and Valerie couldn't confiscate. She took a spare one and slid it underneath her mattress, which was close to the door.

Finally, she crawled into bed, lying on her back, bone tired but wide awake. She ran over the options in her mind, running her fingertips over her stomach. A headache pulsed at her temples.

By the time she eventually drifted off into a fitful sleep, she had a plan.

CHAPTER THIRTY-ONE

129 Days After Launch

2 Days to Mars

120 Days to Cavendish

Someone woke her up, grabbing her by the upper arm and hauling her upright.

Naomi blinked at Hixon, bleary from fractured sleep. By the time she remembered the glass vial under her mattress, she'd already been dragged out into the hallway.

"I'm taking you to see Hart," Hixon said, voice tight. "Lebedeva is bringing her to the lab for your scan."

So Lebedeva had mentioned it to Valerie, or she had been listening through the comms. Naomi hadn't had time to slyly filter her pepper solution or enact any of the rest of her plan. What if she didn't get a chance to complete it? At least this was a chance to speak to Hart and Hixon. Valerie was keeping her distance.

"This better not be some ill-thought-out ploy," Hixon said.

"I want to make sure the baby is healthy," Naomi said. She eased from foot to foot—her ankles were swollen. "Hart is going to be so very happy to see you as her jailer."

Hixon's grip tightened. "Watch it, Lovelace."

Hixon had chosen her side, but she'd be an easier mark than Lebedeva.

"How do you actually see this working out?" Naomi asked, keeping her voice low. "Valerie doesn't give a single goddamn about anyone who won't always worship the ground she walks on. Even Cavendish isn't going to be her perfect vision. Nothing in reality ever matches up to the dream in your head."

If Naomi had more faith that it could be, would she have crossed the line to support Valerie? Would she be more tempted to let the old way of life disappear to make way for the new? Like Lebedeva and Hixon, standing by, letting it happen.

Hixon's fingernails were digging into Naomi's skin.

"You prepared to kiss her ass for the rest of your life, Hixon? Power is going to corrupt her as surely as it did Cochran. It already has."

"Valerie isn't anything like that soft-boiled asshole," Hixon hissed as she marked Naomi to the med bay. "Shut. Up."

"Ah, yes. She's always listening," Naomi said, almost singsong.

The doors slid open. Hart was by the autodoc, and at the sight of her wife, she stiffened. Lebedeva stood, arms loose, legs hip-width apart, ready for any trouble they might cause. Naomi sensed this was a test. Valerie watching as the rest of her crew conferred. Making sure Hixon and Lebedeva were as loyal as they claimed, or seeing if Hart and Naomi could be convinced to fall back into line.

Hart came forward, helping Naomi into the autodoc. Her hands were gentle. "Are you all right?" she asked.

"As well as can be expected. You?"

Hart wordlessly shook her head.

Naomi put her hand on the glass of the autodoc before it could close.

Hixon ignored her wife, expression as cold and empty as the surface of Mars.

"Look," Naomi said to both of them, keeping her voice as low as she could. The comms speakers weren't oversensitive, and the humming medical equipment helped provide white noise. "Hixon, would we be able to loop Mars and use our remaining fuel to head back to Earth instead of Cavendish?"

"Doesn't matter," Hixon said. "That's not the mission."

"Jesus, Hixon, turn off that robotic urge to follow orders and answer the fucking question," Hart said, making a show of hooking Naomi up to the autodoc for the benefit of the camera.

Hixon shook her head. "I'm not answering." Her lips thinned. "Please. This is awful. Beyond awful. I want to save Earth, but Valerie isn't going to change her mind. Our best hope is to make it to Cavendish. Make things as best we can for the next wave of humanity. We can't help any of them if Valerie kills us, too."

"You think she'd do that?" Hart whispered.

"If she felt we were no longer required, if we were getting in her way and she could make it without us? Yes." Hixon's voice was a soft murmur. "I'm trying to make sure we all survive."

"That's still cowardice," Hart said, turning from her wife in disgust.

"The cure will be on board," Naomi said, her voice barely a whisper. Hixon caught it, but Hart was over at the autodoc. "Or at least the formula will be. She wouldn't risk anyone infected following us to Cavendish without it. You're good with computers. See if you can get through Valerie's personal encrypted files. Evan tried to help me with them, but I couldn't figure it out. We have to try. But please—please run the calculations to see if we can go back. Just in case."

Naomi lay back in the autodoc, watching emotions play over Hixon's face as Hart started the scan.

"Irene—" Hixon began.

"No," Hart cut her off. "You don't say a goddamn word to me until you come to your senses."

Hixon blinked quickly, but the tears didn't fall. Hart was dry-eyed.

"Have you had any symptoms that worried you?" Hart asked Naomi, all business, even as they both knew Naomi had only claimed she needed a scan as an excuse to talk.

"Some headaches," she said, which was true. "Swollen ankles." Also true.

Naomi kept her body still, focusing inwards. But she sensed the baby was still there, clinging on.

The scan completed and Naomi stood up, the blood rushing to her head. She clutched at the foam of the autodoc to steady herself.

"All looks fine so far, but here—" Hart passed Naomi another cup—"take a piss. Better safe than sorry."

Naomi did as she was told. If Hart and Hixon spoke while she went about her business, she couldn't hear.

Their body language was stiff when she returned. Hixon's head tilted up at the scan. Was she thinking about what would happen if they arrived in Cavendish and for whatever reason couldn't grow viable artificial wombs?

Hart was quiet, head bowed. Hixon took a few steps towards her, hesitant. Hart raised her head, weary. She didn't pull away as Hixon rested a hand on her upper arm. Their anger had sparked out. Hixon drew her close, and Naomi saw her whisper something in her ear.

Hart pulled away, searching her wife's face. Hixon had let the tears fall, finally, unashamed. Hart wiped them away. "I understand," Hart said, aloud. "You're doing what you think is best. But don't think that makes it right between us."

Hixon sniffed, once. "Let's get you back to your lab, Lovelace. We need the next crop of nutriblocks."

Hart's gaze caught Naomi's, trying to signal what had passed between her and her wife. Naomi nodded. Learning how to read lips as a child had proved useful. Hixon had whispered: "I'll search for the cure. You're right. We can't do this."

Naomi didn't know if Hixon had truly wavered and been lured by their captain's plan. As Hixon marched Naomi back to her lab, she had no idea how to ask. All the same, as the door to her lab swung shut, out of sight of the comms, Naomi mouthed a thank you to Hixon. The pilot gave the barest tilt of her head before the metal snapped shut.

For the first time since she'd been confined to her lab, Naomi felt maybe there was a chance. Hope blared right next to the anger.

She checked her tablet, subtly. No message.

CHAPTER THIRTY-TWO

129 Days After Launch

2 Days to Mars

120 Days to Cavendish

Naomi had finished filtering the pepper solution and gently decanted it into a refillable aerosol can. After an hour of prepping algae, startling at every sound, her tablet finally made a soft, silent flash.

Naomi hid behind the purple algae vials to read Evan's message, dread dripping through her.

> Evan Kan: *Sickness is spreading. They're calling it the Sev. Death toll of those infected is roughly eighty per cent, with the possibility to rise. Eight per cent of the U.S. population is showing symptoms, and that will certainly increase. Breakouts are being reported elsewhere in North and South America, Europe, China, Africa—we won't be able to stop the spread in time. Japan, Australia, New Zealand, and Iceland have completely closed their borders, though I doubt that will slow it down for long. We still don't know exactly how the virus behaves. Half of my team is already dead.*

An ache travelled from her chest to her fingertips. Eight per cent was already affected and it'd only been a few days.

Evan Kan: *I haven't publicly spread that Valerie started the virus. No one knows it was her. Hopefully you can use that as leverage, to try and get her to tell us where the formula or existing doses of the vaccine she developed concurrently are stored. I don't think we can afford to wait on her whims. Can you?*

Evan Kan: *If she's hidden it anywhere on Earth, I think it might be in one of her off-book warehouses. The one nearest the outbreak is the one I'll check first. Yes, I know, it means going into the most heavily infected area. There are guards on the perimeter, but they're stopping people leaving, not entering. I'll try to sneak through. Hopefully, I'll find something. Anything. I have to try. By the time you read this, I'll already be heading there. Messages will reroute to my phone, but I don't know if there will be service. Plenty of cell towers are already down. If I don't make it back, I'm sorry. And, not to get too mushy, but I love you. I'm sorry we didn't figure it out fifteen years ago, but we got there in the end. Hopefully I'll see you on the other side.*

Naomi bowed her head over the tablet, squeezing her eyes shut. She wanted to scream at him. To tell him to come back. But if he said he was leaving right after he sent the message, he would have. She simply wrote back the three words he'd told her and hoped that he'd survive to be able to see them.

She tried not to think of guards, in top-grade filter masks

that still weren't enough to slow the spread, machine guns heavy in their arms, eyes scanning the horizon for any movement. Even if he got the cure, dropped it into the hand of one of the guards, and spread the information to those far and wide, they wouldn't let him back out in case he was infected. He'd take precautions—gloves and a filter mask of his own—but that was no guarantee. He was being all heroic and she hated it.

Naomi harvested a small crop of potatoes, scrubbing them too hard, their brown skin peeling back to reveal the white flesh. In frustration, she threw one against the wall. It bounced, skittering across the ground, dented but still intact. With a sigh, she picked it up and added it to the others. Calories were calories.

As the hours dripped past, Naomi ground her teeth until her jaw ached. She had to hope that either Hixon had made good on her promise already, or that Lebedeva would come to collect the next dose of nutriblocks. Hixon hadn't promised to do anything to deliberately take Lebedeva or Valerie down, and Naomi wasn't convinced Hixon's bravery extended that far. For all her military accolades, Hixon had never seen combat.

If the pilot did find the cure, that would spur her to action, but if she didn't, would that convince her to renew her loyalty to Valerie? If humanity couldn't be saved anyway, make the best of it for the children left behind or the new children they'd grow on Cavendish?

Naomi renewed her pacing, the pepper spray gripped in one hand. Lebedeva had seen Naomi use aerosols plenty of times. She gave it a last shake for good luck and slid it into her coverall pocket.

When Lebedeva arrived, Naomi didn't know if she'd be

brave enough to use her makeshift weapon. It felt so silly, so paltry, just some chilli oil and water. Lebedeva could have an actual weapon, for all Naomi knew. Another secret Valerie could have smuggled into the ship without the rest of them any the wiser. Even if she didn't, Lebedeva was taller, corded with muscle from her endless hours at the gym. She'd run half marathons in the rec room until Naomi told her she had to knock it off because she was burning energy that they couldn't afford to replenish. She'd overpower Naomi without even trying.

Lebedeva finally arrived just before dinner. Naomi shuffled to the corner of the room. Her mouth went dry, breath shallow.

The door swung open in a swish. "Naomi—" Lebedeva started, her hand at the comms control, but Naomi didn't give her a chance to finish. Naomi grabbed the aerosol from her pocket and dived forward, spraying Lebedeva in the eyes. In the same motion, Naomi grabbed the empty algae vial beneath her mattress and used it to wedge the door open.

Lebedeva charged at her, even as she couldn't see. Naomi made a run for a second vial but Lebedeva in her half-blinded state still managed to snatch Naomi's wrist. Naomi twisted, afraid of falling. Lebedeva's grip was a vice.

Lebedeva opened her mouth in a pained cry with a stream of colourful Russian swearing. She let go of Naomi's wrist. "*I was coming to break you out*," she cried, tears streaming down reddened eyes.

Naomi had bent down to wedge the door open further, but stopped cold.

Lebedeva heaved great gasps, trying not to scream, hands balled against her eyes.

Naomi didn't know whether to trust her, but her gaze stuck

on the comms panel. Lebedeva had switched it off when she entered. Valerie had insisted it was kept on at all times. Valerie couldn't see them right now unless she realised it was off and turned it back on remotely.

"Fuck," Naomi whispered. "Don't touch it!" She dragged Lebedeva to the sink. She sprayed some soap into a bowl, diluting it with three parts water. She held it steady as Lebedeva doused her face in it, the soap helping break down the oils in the spray. Lebedeva came up for breath, gasping, and did it a couple more times. She was vulnerable. Naomi could tie Lebedeva up and leave her in the lab.

Yet Naomi passed her a wipe soaked in the soapy water, and Lebedeva gently rubbed her face until the worst of the burning had passed. She blinked rapidly, tears helping clear the sting further. She'd be in pain for a while yet, but at least she could speak again.

"Pepper spray," Lebedeva muttered. "Really?"

Naomi held another empty algae vial like a baseball bat. "Hurry up and explain," she said. "The comms might not stay off for long."

Lebedeva held up her hands, eyes bloodshot, the skin of her pale cheeks splotched pink. Her chest heaved, fighting down whimpers. It was strange to see Lebedeva's shoulders hunched. She tilted her head back, gave something like a laugh. "*Like I said, coming to get you out.*" She kept to Russian.

"Why?"

Her laugh trailed off, her eyes still watering. "*I have not slept in two days*," she said.

Naomi tightened her grip on the glass, more confused than ever.

"*I thought I would be fine. That the first night was only stress. I thought I understood. I thought Dr. Black's plan was right.*" She gave another hiss of pain. "*Then I did not sleep again. Maybe I am now so tired I no longer care. Or care too much. It was why you could surprise me. Reflexes are slow.*" Her head lolled, lips pulling back from her canine teeth. "*I see my family every time I close my eyes. Even if they hate me, I cannot let them die. They might have already.*"

Naomi's fingers loosened on the vial. Slowly, she lowered it.

"*Dr. Black caught Hixon trying to break into her files,*" Lebedeva said.

Naomi's skin tightened, fear thrumming through her. "Shit. What happened?"

"*Dr. Black is locked in her room with Hart. So they are together at least, though I think they still want to kill each other. Only Dr. Black has the code to their quarters. You are easier to break out. And you know Dr. Black better than any of us. You know what will change her mind.*"

Naomi swallowed. "I thought I did. Not sure I do anymore." She gave a weak laugh. "God, I maced you for nothing." She spoke in English; she could understand Lebedeva well enough, but the adrenaline had chased away her Russian.

Lebedeva blinked again, gave a cracked smile. "*I commend your ingenuity. Come, we've wasted too much time. Hixon said she ran the calculations, and we can return to Earth with our existing fuel supply, but it is not easy. We'd have to loop around Mars to help us turn and to give us enough velocity, and we'd need to change our trajectory soon. Today. Within two hours.*"

Naomi sucked in a breath at that. Two hours. She held out

her hand, and Lebedeva took it with a sigh. Naomi kept the vial in her right hand.

Naomi went to the comms panel, her body half-turned to Lebedeva. The Russian held her hands splayed wide and empty as she kept shaking her head and wincing from the burning. Sure enough, Hart and Hixon were both in their quarters. Valerie was in the bridge.

A crackle through the comms. Perhaps Valerie had still watched while it was off, and they'd never had any privacy at all. "Come on down, Naomi," Valerie said. "Let's talk. Leave Lebedeva in the lab; I have changed the code on the door." The words were languid with her slow drawl.

Naomi's heart rate hammered.

Lebedeva's shoulders fell. She shuffled back to the sink, ready to rinse her eyes again.

"It is all right," she said. "I will stay. You will get through to her."

Naomi nodded, hoping she exuded a confidence she didn't feel. She left the door wedged open and kept her grip on her vial. There was a chance the camera angles had hidden it and that Valerie wasn't checking schematics that closely. Worth a try.

"*Break open their lock*," she called out to Lebedeva behind her. Lebedeva grunted her assent.

Naomi stuck the vial in a beltloop of her coveralls, slid the pepper spray into her pocket, and made her way to the nearest spoke. She took a deep breath and climbed into the dark.

CHAPTER THIRTY-THREE

129 Days After Launch

2 Days to Mars

120 Days to Cavendish

As Naomi climbed along the spoke towards the main body of the ship, she wished she could speak to Hart and Hixon. Questions pummelled her. Was the two hours a hard deadline? What if it was two and a half hours before Naomi could get her hands on the controls? And if they changed trajectory without the cure...If about a third of the world was under twenty-one, plus five per cent of the adults proved immune, it would still mean returning to a world that was over half dead.

There was also the chance that Lebedeva's change of heart was only temporary and fear could drive her back to Valerie. Or that her engineering skills weren't enough to break open Hart and Hixon's door in time.

What if their plan all hinged on a cure that wasn't on the ship? That this was the one thing Valerie didn't make a backup for because she knew she'd be light years away?

What scared Naomi most was not knowing which version of Valerie was waiting for her in the bridge. The one she thought she knew, or the woman Naomi suspected she'd never known.

The door opened.

Valerie perched on the captain's chair, a leg through one armrest and a hand on the other to keep her tethered. The screens dotted about the bridge showed feeds from around the ship. There was Lebedeva outside Hart and Hixon's room, unscrewing the metal cover of the comms panel. Valerie must have already known Naomi had left the door wedged open. Valerie's back was to Naomi as she stared out the window at the scattering of stars. Her brown curls rose around her head like a flame.

Naomi floated closer, using the handrails. She held the pepper spray in one hand.

"Give me your pepper spray," Valerie said, twisting her face towards her. "Should have known Lebedeva was as cowardly as the others, but well done on rigging that up, I suppose." Valerie's eyes flicked briefly towards the screen.

"I'm not handing you my weapons," Naomi said.

Valerie made a sound in her throat. "Put it under a chair or something, I don't care. You're not going to attack me, anyway, and I'm not about to mace a pregnant woman. What kind of monster do you take me for?" She grinned.

The smooth assurance made Naomi only want to clutch her weapons closer. She slid the vial out of her beltloop and put it in the pocket on the back of Hixon's chair along with the aerosol.

"There," Valerie said. Her body language was relaxed. "So, you got a plan, Nomi?"

Naomi gathered her breath. "I've come to make a deal."

Valerie laughed. "I'm not sure you're exactly in a negotiating position."

"Neither are you. Even if you managed to keep us locked up for four more months, you're outnumbered. Eventually we'll find a way to take you down, unless you kill all of us, but it'd be damn hard to make it on your own on Cavendish. So you have to keep up the vigilance. It's already tiring, I'm sure. None of us are with you, not when it counts. But we could be."

Valerie's face went still.

"You don't want to land on Cavendish with four prisoners you have to force to do your bidding," Naomi continued, emboldened. "You need us until you can grow or deliver enough children, and hope they grow up to be loyal in the ways we currently are not. It'll be years of threats and watching your back. There's an easier way to get us on your side. To make us a crew again."

Did the three other women have any way of hearing what was happening down on the bridge? When they were all free, would they come for her?

Valerie gave Naomi a long, cool look.

"You've already killed close to ten per cent of the population. So you've done it. The fabric of society has broken. They can't come after us, Valerie. All their energy and focus will be on solving what's happening to them. So let them. Establish Cavendish, see if they'll still send a lifeboat or two. You have the upper hand. If you give Earth the cure, the four of us will follow you. Without hesitation, without reservations. We will help you in your vision of utopia."

Valerie was listening. Naomi pressed on. "Evan hasn't told them you were the one who spread the virus."

A flicker, difficult to read. Had she read all of Naomi and Evan's messages?

"You'd be the hero, Valerie," Naomi pressed. "Ferrying survivors, starting with the children and your chosen caretakers. The adults won't stop you now. They'll want to keep the next generation safe. You woke them up. So don't you see? You've already won."

"You're asking me to give them a slow death instead of a quick one," Valerie said. "That's all. It'll take time to establish Cavendish. By the time we're sending for the adults, they'll have boiled to death on their compromised rock."

"Humans are tenacious. Give them a chance to show you they're capable of change."

Valerie scoffed. "They won't." Her gaze went distant. "What's to stop you from turning on me again, if I bowed to your demand?"

"Because you're trying to kill billions of people, Valerie!" Naomi's attempted calm fractured. "I've had my moments where I look at humanity and think it'd be better if we just burned it down and started again. Haven't we all? Doesn't mean I actually do it. Even if we understand your reasoning, it is murder on an impossible scale. Earth is in the past for us, yes, but that doesn't mean it has to be gone. We can't start our legacy on genocide. What example does that set for a future generation?"

Valerie unhooked her leg, letting herself rise. She drifted forward, her body angled towards Naomi.

"If you do this," Naomi said, "then my child will grow up knowing the good part of you. The part of you that would be horrified at what you're doing, even if logic says it's a viable plan. But if you drag us through and let everyone back on Earth die, I'll do whatever I can to keep her from you. Or to make sure she knows from the beginning just what her grandmother is capable of."

"You still think you can threaten me," Valerie said.

"Like I said, it's an offer. A clear laying out of terms. If you do this, I know it's because you respect me, you want me at your side. In return, I won't be going anywhere."

Valerie's chin jerked up. She reached out to touch Naomi's cheek. Naomi didn't let herself flinch.

"Give them the cure," Naomi said, her throat growing tight. "And then let's go home."

"To Earth or Cavendish?" Valerie whispered.

"Whichever you want." Thirty years on, Naomi couldn't remember if she thought those words a lie or not.

Valerie's expression was softer than Naomi had seen in weeks. Her eyes were wet. "How can I trust that you won't betray me again, Naomi?" she asked again, voice pained. "I took you in after your mother died, even though I wasn't in her will. You were meant to be packed off to some distant relatives in Scotland you'd never met. Grow up somewhere rural, with no money. You'd have had to grow up like I did. Grasping for every goddamn scrap. Would you have had the same drive? Achieved all you have? I don't know."

Naomi's mouth went dry.

She'd always assumed that Valerie was listed in Catherine's will as Naomi's legal guardian after her death. She'd almost not grown up underneath Valerie's shadow. Who would she have been? Not here. Definitely not here.

"My mother had money," Naomi said. "That would have gone to my legal guardian. How did I end up with you?"

She forced herself to keep her tone mildly curious, even as her heart thudded. They were wasting time.

Valerie shrugged a shoulder. "It was an old will—she hadn't updated it in years. When we first created Hawthorne, all our capital was in the company, so it didn't seem as pressing. But I knew she would have wanted me to keep you close. We'd been such a partnership." Her gaze went distant.

Naomi had muffled memories of Valerie and Catherine together before the fire. She'd always thought they'd had a deep bond, like sisters more than business partners. Laughter, wine, fine food. Naomi's father rarely came to their gatherings, citing work as an excuse. He had no scientific inclinations, but he'd liked making things with his hands. He was a carpenter, and even though his work had been beautiful, Valerie had given enough subtle digs that Naomi knew Valerie considered Alan Lovelace beneath Catherine and all she had achieved.

"What did you do?" Naomi asked, softly.

"Offered them enough money they didn't mind not taking in a girl they'd never met, who never spoke and rarely slept without waking up from nightmares." She gave a smile. "But I wanted you. I gave you everything. I want to trust you, Naomi, I do."

Naomi swallowed. "Then give me the cure, Valerie, and I'm yours. I always have been." Her voice was thick.

"Prove it. Prove you believe I know best." Before Naomi could blink, Valerie's hand was under her chin, gripping tight.

"I promise, Valerie," Naomi said, trying to pull away but unable to gain leverage in microgravity.

Valerie's fingers clenched against Naomi's skin. "No. I need to know, before we jump. That you'll do what it takes. That you won't shy away from the hard decisions."

"I let my ex-husband die because I believed in this mission," Naomi said. "And my friends, my co-workers. Dennis Lee was my mentor. Doesn't that prove it?" Naomi's breath came shallow.

Valerie shook her head. "No. It might have once, but there were all your little schemes since." Her eyes were wide, showing the whites. "How can I be sure you won't turn on me again when it suits you? You're trying to usurp me."

Warning lights flashed throughout the bridge in pulsing purple. Valerie and Naomi's eyes snagged on the screens. Lebedeva had tripped something trying to open Hart and Hixon's door.

"Better hope it's just the alarm due to the breach and not anything actually damaged. I mean, do you trust Lockwood's workmanship?" Valerie asked mildly, as if a defective ship wouldn't kill her just the same.

Naomi's hand snaked down to her stomach, as if she could protect it.

Flash. Flash. Flash.

The lights hurt her eyes. She just needed to convince Valerie to give her the cure. So she could tell Evan not to risk himself. To save him and so many others. *Tell her what she wants. Anything she wants.*

"How can I prove it to you?" Naomi asked. They'd already wasted more than half an hour.

Valerie's mouth curled. "Do it again. Prove that you'll kill one person to save billions."

Naomi counted five blinks of violet light before she responded. "What?"

"Lebedeva. Even now, she's trying to release the others, even though I ordered you to leave her in the lab. So kill her. Do that and leave Hart and Hixon where they are. Then I will give you the cure."

A ringing sounded in Naomi's ears. "You can't be serious. We need her. Her skills." *And I can't kill someone*, she screamed in her mind. *Not even for you.*

"We still need Hixon for flight and Hart's medical expertise, but Lebedeva's engineering skills can be picked up by the rest of us. It will be a loss, but I'll gain something that's worth it to me. Assurance that if I ask, you will follow through. You can be my new second in command, like you wanted." Valerie's hair was backlit by the alarm lights, tinging the brown purple. Naomi stared at an errant curl, furiously trying to think of the right response that wouldn't anger Valerie further.

"Give me the cure first," Naomi said. "So I have assurance too. What if you don't even have it on the ship?"

"After. You'll just have to trust me." Valerie's smile grew. "How you do it is up to you. But you better hurry. Every minute means another few deaths, doesn't it? Earth's waiting."

CHAPTER THIRTY-FOUR

129 Days After Launch

2 Days to Mars

1.5 Hours to Change Trajectory

120 Days to Cavendish

Naomi climbed the spoke. Valerie followed. Her captain had plucked the pepper spray and put it in her coverall pocket.

Naomi desperately hoped this was some sort of bluff. That if she seemed willing enough to do it, Valerie would consider the test passed. When she glanced behind her, Valerie's upturned face was pale against the dark blue of her stolen uniform, the commander of a stolen ship.

Work the problem. Find the solution.

Even if she managed to somehow surprise Valerie and subdue her, Valerie wouldn't give up the formula unless she damn well wanted to. She would probably even hold up under torture, though no one on the ship would have the guts for that.

Valerie was willing to turn on a woman who had served her loyally until she realised billions of lives was too high a price to pay. Even if Naomi did this, she had to hope that

Valerie's past as a woman who kept her promises continued. That Naomi wasn't simply being used, yet again a tool for her mentor's whims.

Gravity took hold, making Naomi's limbs heavier. Their footsteps echoed down the spoke. Naomi's ankles were swollen from the pregnancy, her chest tight with stress. Every step was bringing them nearer to Lebedeva and Naomi still didn't know what she'd do.

Valerie stayed close. In the hallway that pulsed with warning lights, she loaded the map on the nearest comms panel. "Lebedeva's outside Hart and Hixon's door still. She won't be getting through any time soon. Time's ticking, Nomi."

"Valerie—I will do this, if you ask. But it's a waste of good intellect and skill. She'll come back to our side."

Lebedeva was not replaceable, whatever Valerie said. The others' engineering skills weren't nearly as sophisticated, and on a ship that had already faltered twice, they'd need her, notably if Lockwood's cut corners continued to jeopardise the craft's systems. And what about once they landed on Cavendish?

"I've laid it out, Naomi. It's up to you whether you're brave enough to follow through. If you do this, I know you'll do anything. And Hart and Hixon will know that, too."

There were so many things Naomi wanted to say. That loyalty through force was not loyalty at all. That by forcing Naomi to do this, Valerie was breaking any chance at true allegiance for any of them. Perhaps Valerie knew that, and simply wanted to hurt Naomi, break her down into a tractable mould. Her mentor's eyes were blazing with fervour.

Valerie Black was a zealot to her own cause. To her, everything she was doing was rational. She would never be persuaded to another path. She'd take loyalty bought with blood as long as people followed her.

This whole scenario was a rigged, exaggerated version of the trolley problem, Naomi realised.

In Valerie's mind, what she was doing to Earth was simply the same thing—destroy some to save the species as a whole. In her mind, killing those on Earth meant protecting the lives that could one day flourish on Cavendish, free from humans making the same mistakes as before.

Naomi went to the med bay, Valerie following, peering as Naomi arranged the medicine. Sodium chloride—saline. Sodium thiopental to knock Lebedeva out. Potassium chloride for cardiac arrest. Quick. Painless. A mercy.

Valerie said nothing, letting Naomi choose her methods. She remembered what Hart had taught her not long after they'd taken off. Back when they all believed in the mission, in Valerie. It had been only a few months ago, but she already thought of her past self as heartbreakingly naive.

"Let's finish this," Naomi said, her voice heavy.

Valerie's face broke into a horribly sweet smile. "Call her here," Valerie said, drifting back into a corner. "No Russian, no warnings."

Naomi stepped closer, sending her comms to the hallway outside Hart and Hixon's quarters. "I'm back up in the med lab. How are things with the door?"

A silence and then the crackle of the channel opening. "Still unsuccessful. The lock is difficult to crack. What has happened with Dr. Black? Has she agreed to share the cure?"

"Yes. With a caveat. Can you come to the med bay for a second?"

"Are you injured?" Lebedeva asked, concern colouring her voice.

Naomi closed her eyes, feeling her face crumple as she lied. "Yes. Need help with a bandage."

"Coming."

Valerie crouched, spider-like. Did she truly think that this death would bond them, along with all that happened on Earth? People always said that astronauts were so brave. To ride a controlled bomb up to such an inhospitable place. To risk death on so many occasions. At that moment, Naomi felt cowardly.

She could refuse Valerie, try and find another way to get the cure. She could hope that Evan had found it, negating her need to do any of this. Or she could fall into line, sacrifice Lebedeva for the cause. Sacrifice her own morality at the same time. Flip the switch.

Lebedeva came in. Naomi wasted no time, wrenching her hands behind her back. Lebedeva struggled when she saw Valerie in the corner and rammed Naomi into a wall, hitting her shoulder hard. Panicked about the baby, Naomi whispered "trust me" in Lebedeva's ear, out of sight of Valerie.

Lebedeva kept struggling, but more for show than a concerted effort to escape. Naomi could feel the tension in every line of Lebedeva's body as she took the engineer to the autodoc and strapped her in.

"What are you doing?" she asked. "Dr. Black? Naomi?" Her voice went up at the end in restrained panic.

Naomi wished she could explain, apologise, cajole—anything. Her throat was as stiff and closed as just after the fire. She couldn't make a sound even if she wanted to.

Valerie crept forward as Naomi prepped the IV line.

Lebedeva began to struggle again, and between that and Naomi's shaking hands, she made a mess of the insert.

Stop, she wanted to say. *Don't struggle. Don't make this worse than it has to be.*

Naomi lined up the medicines.

Her breath caught on a swallowed sob. She sent the saline through.

Don't make me do this, she wanted to cry. But Valerie would simply say she wasn't making her do anything.

Lebedeva went limp on the autodoc. Valerie took a few steps closer.

"Ah. I am caveat," Lebedeva said. She knew how Valerie's mind worked almost as well as Naomi did. Naomi gave a terse nod.

Naomi felt Valerie looming behind her.

Lebedeva's face worked as she took it all in. "Do it."

Naomi's head jerked back.

"It is all right, Naomi." Her hand moved beneath the constraints to rest on Naomi's. "I am only one person. It is all right."

Naomi scrunched her eyes closed, then opened them. Valerie was watching Lebedeva with something like avarice. Naomi steadied herself, and prepped three syringes, drawing the liquid from ampoules. They went straight into Lebedeva's IV. Naomi bit the inside of her cheek, hard, and plunged.

Lebedeva went still, waiting to die.

Naomi bowed her head, resting her forehead against Lebedeva's. Whispered in her ear.

Naomi wondered what floating away would feel like. Would Lebedeva have felt her heart rate slow, the blood stop in her veins? Would she have seen anything, just before she left this plane? And where would she go?

Lebedeva was limp, her face tilted away from Valerie.

Naomi raised her head. "The cure," she croaked, barely able to force the words through her throat. She undid Lebedeva's bonds.

Valerie gave a sigh, letting the silence stretch. "I'm surprised you haven't already guessed how I'd shuttle off the cure." Naomi frowned at the odd word choice. Valerie came closer, to check Lebedeva's corpse. Naomi's heart thudded.

Valerie held her hand out to press against Lebedeva's neck.

"Oh!" Naomi exclaimed, as if Valerie's words had made sense, and Valerie stopped and twisted, a smile unfurling on her face. Naomi still had no idea, but it was a chance to play for time to come up with something better. Naomi held her hands out as if for comfort. Valerie exhaled, her arms coming around Naomi, her head resting near her neck. "I'm proud of you, Naomi."

Naomi's mind kept whirring, and then it clicked into place. Ah. In her mind's eye she saw her snow globe, resting on her desk. The glitter held down by gravity. One of the few personal items she'd brought on board. It was like Valerie, to hide it right under Naomi's nose. Could it really have been there all along, even when Naomi had unwrapped it that Christmas morning?

Before she could pull away, Naomi glanced over Valerie's shoulder, watching as Lebedeva rose from the autodoc like Lazarus. Naomi stepped back just as Lebedeva grabbed Valerie. Valerie yowled, reaching for Naomi, frantic, her fingernails scratching across Naomi's right cheek hard enough to bleed.

Naomi hunched her shoulders, wrapping one arm across her stomach and cradling her face with the other.

Valerie twisted, clawed, but she was weak compared to Lebedeva. The Russian wrestled her into the autodoc, snapping the restraints around her arms and legs.

Valerie spat, screamed.

"Hold still, or this will hurt," Naomi said, prepping a new syringe. Her cheek burned. Valerie reluctantly stopped thrashing as Naomi slid the IV needle into her vein, ready to inject it. Naomi's hands still shook, but she did better than she had with Lebedeva.

Valerie's breathing was short and fast, sweat beading at her brow. "What—?" she asked.

"Injected Lebedeva with saline," Naomi said. She indicated the syringe she held. "This one is sodium thiopental anaesthetic. Never even prepped the potassium chloride. You didn't watch closely enough." And she'd let herself be distracted by Naomi's act as the submissive daughter before she could check if Lebedeva was actually dead.

Valerie had always seen Naomi as someone who needed to be led. Even though Naomi had just been working behind Valerie's back with Hart and Evan, Valerie thought her adopted daughter would always be fundamentally truthful to someone's face. Incapable of a little, simple sleight of hand.

Naomi gave her captain, her boss, her mentor, her almost-mother a smile before she pushed the syringe into the IV line.

"Nomi..." Valerie began, before her words slurred and her eyes flickered shut.

CHAPTER THIRTY-FIVE

129 Days After Launch

2 Days to Mars

43 Minutes to Change Trajectory

120 Days to Cavendish

Lebedeva sagged against the wall. "You did it." She was clearly shaken. She'd made her peace, accepted what Naomi was about to do, and then…not died.

Naomi stared down at Valerie's prone frame. Her head was turned to the side, her mouth open. Features softened and slack. There was grey at her temples where her dye had grown out.

"I am glad my fake death was convincing," Lebedeva said, wryly. "You should have used the potassium chloride. Saved us all a lot of trouble."

Naomi shook her head. She found a clean cloth to press against her cheek to help staunch the bleeding. "I won't let her make me a killer."

Lebedeva grunted. "What will we do with her?"

Naomi considered. "Can you carry her to the rec room? We can set that up as a cell easily enough."

Lebedeva nodded. "Sure."

"Okay," Naomi said. "Valerie will be out for a few hours with that dose, so we'll leave her tied up here for now. First priority is to finish breaking Hart and Hixon out." She thought for a moment. "To do that, I'll get Hixon to see if she can crack encryption on Valerie's files from her tablet—I'll share the information Evan gave me on that. I wasn't successful, but she's better with computers." If they couldn't unlock the rooms, they wouldn't be able to change trajectory and Naomi wouldn't be able to get to her snow globe.

Naomi picked up her tablet, elation sinking as she saw no new messages. *Focus on the current problem. Don't think about Earth. Don't think about Evan sneaking into a warehouse surrounded by guns and germs.*

Lebedeva wasted no more time, leaving the med bay. Naomi gave Valerie one last look and then followed.

Hart and Hixon asked what was going on, but there wasn't time to say more than that Valerie had been captured. Naomi read the instructions for breaking the encryption through the wall, having to almost yell them in order to be heard.

Hixon blessedly made quick work of the encryption, and she found the new lock code, as well as plenty of other notes on the modifications Valerie had made to the *Atalanta*. Nothing on the cure or the virus, though, at least not at first glance. When the locks finally clicked open, they had less than half an hour to make the trajectory shift.

Hixon's black eye was darkening to a lurid purple. She sprinted down to the bridge to begin prepping coordinates, trajectories, and velocities. Hart gave Naomi a brief, hard hug before following her wife, limping from when Lebedeva had tripped her. Naomi wondered what had happened between the couple behind closed doors. Whether they were still at odds or had found a truce. Lebedeva went to shift Valerie from the med bay to the rec room before she woke up.

Naomi entered her quarters and picked up her snow globe. The glitter shimmered. She tried untwisting the top. Tapped the bottom. It sounded hollow, but there was no catch. She clawed at it, wriggling the cheap plastic back and forth until she finally managed to pop it out.

Her fingers snaked around inside. Nothing. Empty. She stared at it in horror. She'd been so sure she was right.

Naomi threw the snow globe on the floor and it cracked, the liquid leaking out. Glitter-studded water pooled on the floor of her room. She picked it up again, managed to unscrew the top of the globe. She was careful, but she still nicked her fingers on the broken glass. She prised the shuttle off its little stand, but her hopes sunk. It was solid plastic. Not a hidden drive.

"Fuck!" She hit the wall of her cabin.

Time was ticking down, minute by minute, second by second. Valerie was knocked out. She should have made sure.

Naomi had treasured this cheap bit of tat. She'd been touched when she'd unwrapped it, to realise Valerie had gone to the effort of hunting down a matching one to remind them of that day—

She stopped.

She scrabbled up, almost slipping in the puddle left behind. She darted through the hallway, the alarm lights still pulsing, as if the ship was reminding them of how little time Earth had left.

Naomi entered Valerie's quarters. Hixon had opened all the locks on the ring. The room was as spartan as the day they'd left Earth's orbit, save for one thing.

Naomi picked the snow globe up from the desk, praying she wasn't wrong again. She turned it upside down, the globe turning murky and sparkling. Valerie's had a little clasp at the base, unlike Naomi's. Holding her breath, she unfastened it and the bottom popped out. Inside was a sleek and silver data pod, the same size and shape as her thumbnail. She clutched it, breathing a shaky sigh. She still held the snow globe. She threw it to the bed in disgust.

She flitted to the observation room, loading the pod on the screens. "Please, please, please..." she muttered, searching. She rubbed her shoulder—it was sore from where Lebedeva had rammed her into the wall of the med bay.

She worried Valerie would have encrypted it and that would waste still more time as she had to drag Hixon away from her trajectory shift prep to break it. Guessing Valerie's passwords would have been useless—she always chose randomised ones for maximum security. But it opened just fine. Maybe Valerie thought the snow globe was protection enough. Maybe, deep down, she wanted to be stopped.

Yes. There. The information began to load, transferring annoyingly slowly from the data pod to the ship's drive.

Valerie had looked through Naomi's microscope at the cyanophage like she'd known nothing about viruses, fully knowing what she'd helped create and was about to unleash.

She clicked open the files. The first was the formula for the virus. And then the formula for the vaccine. The notes from Bryony's experiments, photos of magnifications of the virus under a microscope. Detailed write-ups of the virus's morphology. Medication types and doses or other methods for treating existing cases. Everything they needed.

She sent it to Evan first. There were no notes, but her last message was marked as read. That was something, at least.

Immediately after, she fired the information off to the location of the missives the U.S. government had sent Valerie from Earth. She slid the data pod and the tablet into her pocket and climbed back down to the bridge to Hart and Hixon.

"Did she have it?" Hart asked. Lebedeva arrived, her expression questioning.

Naomi nodded, showing her the formula on the shared drives. Hart scanned it, eyes narrowed, and visibly relaxed. "Thank God." Lebedeva let out her breath in a long, slow whistle.

"I've sent it to Evan and the return location of the U.S. missives. There has to be a way to relay it to everyone, though, right?" She didn't trust the government not to weaponise or capitalise on it.

"I can do that," Hixon said. She loaded the information and sent it as widely and broadly as she could in Earth's direction. A satellite at Mars or near Earth should pick it up. If there were enough systems still online for them to receive it. Naomi tried not to think of Evan's face. Of everyone she'd worked with back on Earth. Her friends, her schoolmates. The barista with a tattoo of dragon scales on her forearm who had taken Naomi's coffee order every morning as she walked in to work. Naomi didn't know her name, or anything about her, but she hoped she was all right. Naomi let out a breath. They'd done all they could.

"All right," Hixon said. "Before next steps, I need to ask you something. All of you."

They stared at her wordlessly.

Hixon's face twisted towards the window, leaving her half

in shadow. Mars was visible from their angle, a disk of rust. The tips of her right fingers were inked solid blue. "We have a choice. We can turn the ship around, loop Mars, and arrive at Earth in roughly another one hundred and thirty days. Or—" she paused—"we can continue on to Cavendish."

"We don't know if what we sent them is a viable cure," Hart said. She checked the records again. "No confirmation yet."

"We need to make a decision soon. As in, pretty much now," Hixon said. "So it's a leap of faith. We could end up pointing our way towards a nearly empty Earth."

"The children and some teenagers will still be there no matter what," Hart said. "The ones who were vaccinated, who didn't succumb to some other disease or starvation. And five per cent of the adults."

It was a grim picture. They took this in, all of them staring at Mars and its small moons, at the just-visible warp ring. Two paths.

"If we go, they will have trouble following us, whether the cure works or not," Naomi said. "That's what I argued with Valerie. Earth will be too distracted, too focused on survival. We could still establish a base, give growing embryos a try. Help those back on Earth build more crafts to follow." She felt the tightness of the scabs forming on her cheek.

"You mean we basically continue Valerie's goal, and hope we do a better job?" Hart asked.

"What's waiting for us back on Earth, if the adults and something resembling existing society survives?" Hixon asked. "Prison, a trial?"

"I don't know," Naomi said, thinking of the child curled up within her.

"Saving most of the adult population should hopefully get us a pardon," Hart pointed out. "Hell, they might even let Lebedeva back into Russia."

"Hmph," said Lebedeva, which could've meant anything.

Naomi went to the window, traced the shape of Mars with a fingertip. "What needs us more? Earth, or Cavendish?"

"Earth," Hart said, without hesitation.

After a beat, Lebedeva echoed her.

Hixon's lips were thin. "A large part of me wants to go to Cavendish, I have to admit. It's painful, to get this close only to turn around."

"The cure will work," Naomi said, more confidently than she felt. "If it doesn't, it's all the more reason to go back. We will return to Cavendish, I have to believe that; we just might no longer be the first. If we jumped there, what would we do with Valerie? I don't want to be her jailer for years, until people arrive again, whenever that could be. She doesn't deserve to set foot on that planet, even if it's behind bars."

On that, they all agreed.

"We could send her out of the airlock," Lebedeva pointed out. "No longer a problem."

"That's tempting," Hart said, crossing her arms.

"I told Lebedeva back in the lab—I don't want her to turn me into a killer. Or any of us. She's already tried."

That silenced them.

Hixon heaved a sigh. "We go back, then. Help clean up the mess we unintentionally made."

"Is that a unanimous decision?" Naomi asked. "It has to be all of us."

A pause as they all worked through their thoughts. They gave longing looks at the warp ring.

One by one, they nodded.

"Let's go home," Naomi said.

Hixon nodded, prepping the coordinates. With a flash of clarity, Naomi realised that the pilot had remained second in command. The others were looking to Naomi for guidance. She had made the final call. Valerie had accused Naomi of trying to usurp her position as captain. Looked like she had.

Hixon walked them through what she was doing—something about gravity-assist slingshots, staging, rotation velocity, and synodic periods, which Naomi only understood about half of despite her scientific background. She had to trust that Hixon knew the numbers and would get them home in one piece.

"And we are successfully on course for Earth," Hixon finished. "Arrival in one hundred and thirty-two days."

It was a tiny shift, rather anticlimactic, so subtle they didn't even feel it in the craft. But that was it. The job was done. There were no cheers. Hart let out a juddering breath, her hands in a prayer position against her lips.

Lebedeva's eyes were still red, but Naomi suspected tears as well as pepper burns. Hixon's eye had nearly swollen shut, but her other one was bright. She lifted her face in sad satisfaction. Naomi gripped the handrail, her feet kicking uselessly as she floated in front of the window, resting her palm over the warp ring. So close, so far.

"Goodbye, Cavendish," she whispered.

CHAPTER THIRTY-SIX

130 Days After Launch

1 Day to Mars

~~121 Days to Cavendish~~

131 Days to Earth

Hart shook Naomi out of an uneasy sleep. She kept waking up, more faces of the possible dead flashing in her mind's eye. What if no one could receive their message and the key to saving themselves?

"Come on," Hart said, urgent. "We've got news from Earth."

Naomi let Hart drag her from her bed and they made their way to the observation room. Naomi patted the bandage on her cheek to make sure it was still in place. It was only when they were most of the way there that she realised she'd left her tablet behind, and hadn't checked if there was a new message.

The others were already in the observation room, and when she entered, Hixon's wide smile, made garish by her swollen eye, caused Naomi's legs to falter. Hart caught her, helping her to the nearest chair.

"It worked?" Naomi asked.

"The vaccine is holding," Hixon confirmed. "New cases are slowing down. And they have better methods of supporting those who are already sick now they know how the virus behaves."

Naomi crumpled in relief. It'd worked. It'd worked. They hadn't changed their trajectory and bypassed the warp drive to arrive back home to a planet one-third dead.

"Extra bit of good news: Cochran died. The VP too. Both contracted the virus. Even if they hadn't, they'd have been deposed by now, I reckon." Hixon smirked in satisfaction. "Lots of people are blaming them for what happened. His policies loosened a lot of safety regulations for companies, so people currently think the virus was a result of that."

"Feels a little wrong to be so happy to hear about someone's death," Hart said. "But eh. I'll live."

"So no one knows it was Valerie?" Naomi asked. The information hadn't had anything in it to hint at Hawthorne's involvement.

"The government, or what remains of it, does," Hixon said. "But it doesn't seem to have gone wide yet. So far, the public seems to think the leak was an inside job. Matter of time, though."

"Things back home look...messy," Lebedeva said. "Hard to know what we'll be arriving at in a few months."

"We'll just have to wait and see." Naomi paused and asked the question she feared. "Anything from Evan?"

Hixon chose her words. "Not through official channels. Have you checked your tablet?"

"No." Naomi stood, flexing her fingers in agitation. "Excuse me."

She turned her back on their sympathetic expressions.

The walk back to her room felt long. The ship was still

pristine, clean. No more flashing lights or alarms. The same as it'd always been. Hixon and Lebedeva had been over all the systems, and everything was still working fine. If Lockwood had cut any more corners, it wasn't obvious; nothing had broken yet. Hopefully it'd be solid enough to get them home.

Naomi entered her room and picked up the tablet. She sat on the bed cross-legged. Centred herself, fingertips tracing the shapes of the vines beside her bed. Her desk was empty. She'd put the snow globe in a cupboard, unable to look at it. Maybe she'd chuck it out of the airlock.

She gathered the courage to press the tablet screen and wake it up. She ran through the scenarios in her head. Evan could be dead, either from infection or the resulting chaos. Shot down trying to enter the dead zone. He could be desperately ill. If the virus had caused too much damage, the cure would only do so much. She tried not to imagine him too thin, his skin sallow beneath his tan, sheened with sweat, eyes glassy.

She tapped it.

New messages.

Her heart thudded, but she clamped down tight on any hope. It could be someone using his account to tell her bad news privately.

She pressed her lips together and opened the first message.

Evan Kan: *Hello from Earth,* Atalanta. *I'm all right, Naomi. Well, mostly.*

Naomi sagged, relief flooding through her like a drug. She'd been convinced he'd be just another casualty out of many. That they'd return to a planet where the person she wanted most to see was gone.

The first message had arrived only an hour ago. What had delayed him? She kept reading.

Evan Kan: *I got into the warehouse, but there was nothing there, so that was a complete bust. I was trying to find a way back out when the news broke. I turned myself in to the authorities to try and get out—they checked me and I showed no symptoms.*

Evan Kan: *In fact, I was immune.*

Evan Kan: *She must have inoculated me before she went. If I'd known, I could have tried to research the beginnings of a vaccine from the antibodies in my blood. It still likely would have taken too long.*

Evan Kan: *When they first told me, I worried Valerie would have given me the dubious honour of starting her plague and then leaving me alive to watch everyone around me die. But I wasn't the index patient. Don't know if she made me immune out of some sick sense of love, or if she wanted to punish me. Knowing her, maybe both.*

Naomi dragged her fingernails across her scalp and the short bristle of her hair. Evan would always feel guilt that he was never truly at risk.

In Valerie's mind, she would have thought giving him immunity was a sick sort of kindness. Letting Evan survive, so that if she came back for the children, she could gather up her son and welcome him into the fold of her new world. Ever the hero. Would Valerie even have considered the trauma he'd have had to endure?

Evan Kan: *I'm still being detained by the authorities, or what's left of them, but they agreed to let me send these messages. They'll be reading what we write, but we don't have anything to hide.*

He was alive. He was safe. Imprisoned, sure, but safe. She laughed softly, despite everything. She closed her eyes, imagining the way his eyes narrowed, crinkling at the corners when he concentrated. How many looks had she stolen at him as they studied in undergrad, hoping he wouldn't catch her?

He'd run his fingertips along her scars that last night. His skin was so smooth, but she remembered discovering the tiny scar in the corner of his left eyebrow that she could feel more than see. She'd asked him about it, after, tangled in the bedsheets. He'd bashed his head on a counter when he was young. She remembered the feel of the square of his jaw beneath her fingers. There were so many miles between them, but she desperately wanted to be held, to fall asleep next to him, breath in his scent, forget all of what had happened to them the last five months, at least for a moment.

The morning she'd left for quarantine, she'd woken up to the bed alone, only the spicy scent of his shampoo and the gentle bruise of a love bite on her shoulder to remember him by. And, though she didn't know it then, a little more.

She sent her response, not knowing how long it'd take for whoever was monitoring their communications to let it through.

Naomi Lovelace: *I'm glad you're all right. That we both are, considering. We're coming back. Decided not to jump through. I know you're feeling survivor's guilt, but remember: this is not your fault. It's not mine. We couldn't have known what she planned. It's Valerie's sin, and Valerie's alone. See you soon, but not soon enough.*

She turned the tablet off and fell back on to the bed. Four months back to Earth.

CHAPTER THIRTY-SEVEN

131 Days After Launch

0 Days to Mars

~~122 Days to Cavendish~~

130 Days to Earth

They flew directly past the warp ring. Hixon gave it a reluctant wave as they passed.

Unsurprisingly, none of the crew wanted to deal with their former captain.

Lebedeva had stocked up the rec room with enough food and water to last a couple of days. Gave Valerie the bucket she'd made Naomi use as a crude chamber pot.

Two days after they changed direction, the day they were supposed to stretch and condense space-time again, Naomi decided she should visit Valerie.

Lebedeva came with her. She'd been keeping an eye on Valerie more than the others.

"How has it been, seeing her?" Naomi asked as they walked slower than they needed to down the ring corridor.

"You mean since she tried to have you kill me?" Lebedeva shrugged. "It has been satisfying to see her powerless. I have not throttled her, if that is what you are asking. I might have imagined doing so. No promises."

"Fair," Naomi said.

Naomi's stomach fluttered with nerves as they approached the door. They'd kept watch on Valerie through the comms panel, spying on her the way she'd spied on them. She spent some time hitting the walls, at first, then did a lot of pacing. For the last few hours, it'd been a lot of sitting and staring at nothing. She was eating her food, drinking her water. No hunger strike. Conserving her strength.

Lebedeva had put her engineering skills to work creating a small handheld stunner that she held at the ready. Little more than a glorified cattle prod, really. Naomi fervently hoped they wouldn't have to use it. Naomi held a water allotment and some toiletries, so Valerie could brush her teeth and give herself a sponge bath after they'd left. In Naomi's pocket was a wrapped bundle of nutriblocks.

"What about you?" Lebedeva asked. "You could have asked Hart or Hixon to do this with me. No one would blame you for evading her."

"Avoiding," Naomi corrected, absently. She squared her shoulders. She didn't need the others to protect her. She'd locked Valerie up—Naomi should face her prisoner. Still, she hesitated, staring at the seam of the white and silver doors. In that room, they'd all eaten their evening meals when they'd tired of the canteen, or on special occasions like the Fourth of July. They'd been surrounded by echoes of Earth or visions of Cavendish. They had laughed, teased. Been a crew.

The last time they'd gathered behind those doors, Valerie had told them what she'd truly done. Tried to make them see that her course was the correct action to take. She'd failed, but if Naomi knew anything, it was that Valerie would still be at her mind games.

She pressed the button, letting the doors whoosh open.

Valerie's head rose. She had her hair over her face, and some stuck to the sweat of her forehead. The eyes were the same—bright and dark and furious. The muscles of her jaw jumped beneath her skin.

Lebedeva pointed her makeshift weapon at Valerie. "Don't think about it. Get in the chair," Lebedeva instructed.

Valerie did so, deliberately slowly, the restraints curling from the malleable material to trap her hands and feet.

Naomi set down the basin of water, toiletries, and nutriblocks, then backed away.

Valerie's eyes raked over Naomi's face, lingering on the healing scratches on her cheek. Naomi hadn't expected to see some broken, battered woman, but she'd still hoped for something—a whisper of regret, acknowledgement of her sins.

"I can take it from here, Lebedeva, thank you," Naomi said.

Lebedeva gave an incline of her head, passed her the weapon. "I will stay outside if you need me."

When the door swung shut, Naomi faced Valerie. She thought the fear would still be there. Anger. Betrayal. Instead she was left numb. A headache bloomed at her temples and her eyes blurred with exhaustion.

Valerie's hair was greasy, her pale skin dry and flaky. She was no longer the polished CEO of Hawthorne.

"Have we jumped?" Valerie asked. She wouldn't have been able to feel it.

"No."

"So we're going back."

Naomi saw no need to respond.

Valerie rolled her neck. "I'm right about Earth. It'll be people fighting over scraps. Still trying to keep the bones for themselves. You should have gone to Cavendish. You'll see."

"Perhaps," Naomi said, easily enough. "We decided to see if we can help make things better."

Valerie gave an incredulous grunt.

"You used to think more of humanity," Naomi mused. "My mom always said Hawthorne was created to help make life easier for people." Automated robot labour to free up leisure time. To help pave the way for governments to roll out a universal basic income. Not that the governments cooperated, but it did morph into the birth bonus, which was not what her mother had in mind. Naomi sat, resting her back against the door. "After she was gone, I believed you when you said you were carrying on that vision. You promised we'd do great things together. But I was just one more person to fall for your lies."

"I was carrying it on," Valerie said. "Cavendish would have been all Catherine wanted. A place with a gentler pace, shared resources, her creations helping to build a new, better society."

"She wouldn't have agreed with the cost of it." Naomi clenched her teeth together. "God, if she could see you now."

Valerie's bravado flickered, her expression something Naomi couldn't read.

Naomi pounced on it. "You never explained why my mother didn't name you my legal guardian. Why she'd rather send me thousands of miles away instead of letting me grow up under your roof. I don't buy that she didn't update her will."

Valerie pulled at her arms, testing the restraints. Naomi's grip tightened on Lebedeva's weapon. "Valerie," she said. "Tell me."

Valerie's mask went back in place. "I expect because she was planning on moving back to Scotland, so those relatives would have been closer if anything happened."

"What?" Valerie's words loosened a few fragments of memories. Catherine mentioning the village where Naomi's father had grown up. Far in the Highlands, not far from Sutherland, really. They'd been planning to visit that Christmas, but Naomi found the body in the garden three months beforehand. Now, years too late, as an adult rather than a child, it gave her pause. Naomi knew depressive episodes could come on like a flick of a switch, but if Catherine Lovelace was going to end her life, why was she planning a trip?

Naomi had buried that image of her mother's sprawled body as much as possible, along with the months surrounding it. Her hair and clothes had been wet with morning dew. Her neck bent at that horrible, unnatural angle. Naomi had been young, but she'd still heard the whispers about the cocktail of drugs in her mother's system. Enough to kill her even if she hadn't fallen.

Naomi and Valerie had only ever had that one, blazing fight, just before Naomi moved to Scotland. She had thought Valerie was overreacting when she was so furious at Naomi's plan. How she hadn't understood that Naomi needed to remake herself somewhere where the reach of both Valerie and Cole was weaker.

Naomi had left Valerie, just like Catherine had threatened to do. Unintentionally poked hard at a tender spot.

"My mother's fall wasn't an accident," Naomi said slowly, the weapon forgotten at her side.

Valerie's bravado fell. She was stripped bare, guilt that she'd never shown even while she risked the fate of Earth rising to the surface. Valerie's head tilted forward.

"God," Naomi whispered. "Did you start the fire, too?"

She should have known by now—Valerie would do anything to get what she wanted. Catherine and Valerie had made Hawthorne from nothing.

Valerie gave a sharp shake of her head. "That was a wildfire. If that'd never happened, we'd all be on a different path."

"But my mother didn't fall," Naomi repeated.

"She wanted to break up the company," Valerie said, almost pleading with Naomi to understand. "Hawthorne wasn't doing well—all risk, no growth. I couldn't afford to start over. And she'd be taking you with her."

Naomi stopped breathing.

"Evan hated me by that point, but you? You hung on to me, clung like glue. If I gave you a problem, you trotted off to solve it. Came back so proud when you'd cracked it. You loved me. At that point in my life, you were the only one who did."

Naomi's breath hitched as it restarted. Her vision wobbled. She took a step back, then another, until she was pressed against the wall of the rec room.

"When you left for Scotland, I thought I'd lost you. Catherine's promise kept years later. Then you came back. It was us against the world again. But I overestimated you. You don't have what it takes for truly radical change."

"That's one way to describe it," Naomi said. Even after

everything, the sting of disappointing Valerie bit deep. She edged closer to the door. "I'm not a toy soldier to wind up and march in whatever direction you choose. I never was. Destroying what's in your way doesn't leave you anything." She gestured at the constraints. "You'll never get what you want."

Valerie let her hair fall over her face, the fight leaving the line of her shoulders. "It was a critical error. Pushing too far. If I had simply given you the cure, we would be on our way to Cavendish now, wouldn't we?"

"We might," Naomi admitted. "You still lost any chance of keeping me by your side as soon as you released the virus." Naomi strode forward, bent down to Valerie's eye level. Pressed the weapon underneath Valerie's chin, forcing it up so she couldn't look away. "You killed my mother. My ex-husband. You tried to kill everyone I've ever known. You may have inoculated your own son but you still left him there."

Valerie hesitated. "Is Evan...?"

Naomi laughed, the sound harsh. Her finger was still on the trigger, but she hadn't pressed it. She wanted to give Valerie a blast of electricity, let it ripple through her nervous system like lightning. "*Now* you ask? Did you think he'd skip along merrily to your version of Cavendish after you let him watch the world die?"

Valerie raised her head, shaking her curls back, unable to meet Naomi's eyes. "I have nothing left. I've made all my plays." She lapsed into silence.

When she spoke again, her voice was hesitant. "I don't want to live my life behind bars. I don't deserve it, but I'd like to ask one last thing of you." She swallowed, the whites of her eyes showing as she leaned closer to the weapon against her skin, glancing at the hull as if she could see through it. "Leave me out there."

Naomi stayed crouched in front of the woman she'd loved, worshipped, been so damn desperate to please.

She was tempted. Naomi allowed herself to imagine Valerie wrapped in the same black rubber sheeting as Cole after she'd killed him. Pressing the button. There, then gone. An eternity out in the cold.

Valerie saw Naomi waver. "Please."

"You're afraid to face what you did," Naomi said. She pulled the weapon from Valerie's skin. The tip had made a small indent against her neck. "You'd have to live with them cursing your name. Easier, isn't it, to blink out now?"

Naomi stood, her knees protesting, and went to the door.

"Why take the easy option?"

CHAPTER THIRTY-EIGHT

177 Days After Launch

84 Days to Earth

Over the next few weeks, the *Atalanta*'s reduced crew had settled into some semblance of order. The four of them did the work of five people, with the added bonus of looking after a prisoner. Naomi had officially bowed out of that duty after her last conversation with Valerie. No one pushed her on it.

Naomi's belly filled out her coveralls. Twenty-seven weeks along. The baby was big enough its lungs breathed amniotic fluid. She felt it kicking, the inside of her stomach tender.

On the forty-sixth day since they bypassed the warp ring, Naomi's swollen ankles puffed up so much it was painful to walk. There was a ringing in her ears, a dappling of her vision. She'd tried to get out of her bed and fallen right back down. She felt a dampness and brushed between her legs with shaking fingers. Blood. Hardly any, but still red.

She called for Hart on the comms, who came and helped her limp to the med bay.

Naomi tried to quiet her panic, but she couldn't. This all pointed to worryingly serious symptoms. Hart had gone silent, with a tightness around her eyes that was never a good sign.

Hart led her to the autodoc and instructed Naomi to remove her coveralls. Blood stained Naomi's underwear and the skin of her ankles was distended and tight with water. "Bleeding. Oedema," Hart said, clearly alarmed but trying not to show it. She brought up Naomi's last scans, including her urine samples. All had been normal.

"The spotting might not be anything to worry about," Hart soothed as she passed Naomi a cup. Naomi didn't know whether or not to believe her. Embarrassingly, the doctor had to help steady Naomi so she could give the sample. Hart took a small vial of Naomi's blood, still outwardly infuriatingly calm. Naomi looked away from the needle, pushing away memories of IV lines.

While they scanned, Hart barraged Naomi with questions about symptoms.

"Headaches?"

Naomi nodded. She'd had them constantly the last few weeks, but migraines had followed her even before pregnancy, usually triggered by stress. There'd been no shortage of that.

"Nausea?"

"No more than usual. No vomiting."

"Any abdominal pain or tenderness? Or anywhere else?"

"My right shoulder hurts," she said. "But Lebedeva did knock it. Might have sprained it."

Hart pressed Naomi's shoulder, and Naomi grimaced.

"Fatigue?"

"Yeah, but I'm sleeping badly, pregnant, and overworked."

"Stop with the qualifiers. Any visual disturbances?"

"Bit of wobbling, like a migraine aura."

A line appeared between Hart's eyebrows. She took

Naomi's blood pressure—high. The samples finished scanning, and Hart studied them.

"Well, fuck." Her calm façade had cracked.

Naomi's heart rate ratcheted up. "What?"

"There's protein in your urine. Your blood pressure's high. Your body is breaking down red blood cells, elevating your liver enzymes, and your platelets are low, so your blood's going to have trouble clotting. You have HELLP syndrome, a variation of pre-eclampsia." She hissed a breath through her teeth. "This is something the literature warned could be a side effect of pregnancy in space, but gravity should have mitigated a lot of the issues. I have been screening for it specially, but you haven't shown symptoms before this. HELLP rarely develops before twenty-four weeks' pregnancy, but the odds are better after thirty."

Naomi was smack dab in the middle. Guilt bled into the fear. In her years of training and in trying to break into a field that wanted to keep her out, it had become second nature to push aside minor discomforts. Don't show any weakness that meant they'd send a man up to orbit instead. And nothing had seemed worrying until this morning. She should have documented every niggle.

"What do we do?" Naomi asked. She'd heard of pre-eclampsia before, but not HELLP.

Hart grimaced. "I'll watch you closely for expectant management, but there's a high chance we're going to have to deliver your baby sooner rather than later. If we delay and you worsen, the baby can be in distress and you're at a high risk for seizures, strokes, or organ failure."

Over the last few months, Naomi had learned Hart was

never someone to gloss over the realities of what they faced out here. No sugar-coating or delicate bedside manner. She was gentle, but unflinchingly honest.

Naomi settled into the med bay, a room she'd soon grow distressingly used to. She lay there for four hours, hands rubbing her stomach in soothing circles. She focused inwards. Some deep, primordial part of her knew that the foetus still lived. When she eventually felt the turning and quickening beneath her hands, Naomi went soft with relief. She'd stopped spotting.

Hart monitored her blood pressure every half hour. It held steady, then rose, quickly—too quickly. Naomi felt worse, and she broke out in a nosebleed barely staunched by spare rags.

Hart wasted no time. She checked between Naomi's legs. Naomi was too afraid to ask if the bleeding had started again. She tried to stay calm but it was impossible. She didn't need Hart to tell her that this was more dangerous than her miscarriage had been. They were on a ship cleaner than most hospitals, true, but it was just them, alone, with no one who could help if something went truly wrong.

Hart gave Naomi just enough drugs to keep her calm and blur the world about the edges. Hixon left the bridge to help, acting as Hart's assistant, and Naomi felt the prick of the needle against the crook of her arm. It was as if Naomi had taken a step back from it all, watched it from a distance. As she was put on the autodoc, Naomi tried not to wonder if her liver would rupture or if, even now, her brain was filling with water.

Hart never told Naomi the details of what happened during those reddened hours, and Naomi was grateful for it. She'd filled in the blanks. The epidural pain relief shot right into her lumbar spine. She'd needed blood transfusions, and thankfully she was type AB. Everyone on board ended up donating a little, so as not to overload anyone.

Even Valerie.

Naomi never asked if Valerie had given it willingly or not. She wasn't sure which answer she would have preferred.

The autodoc had scanned her, pinned her in place, and Hart oversaw the program that performed the surgery. With the embedded AI and steady machinery, it was lower risk than Hart doing it herself. Naomi found it oddly comforting that her mother's programming would help save her life. She was cut open like a plum to free the stone, then sealed back up. As soon as it was possible to move her, Naomi was shifted to the antiseptic table next to the autodoc, so the glass chamber could function as a neonatal intensive care unit.

Naomi suspected there were complications—a few horrible moments where those around her wondered if she or the babe would make it through.

There had been fractures of pain, of beeps, low, urgent voices muffled by the glass of the autodoc. Strange snippets of jagged visions, overlaid with memories of the miscarriage. At one point, she thought Valerie had come through, to grip her hand tight like she had in the hospital room, but she'd looked down at her palm to find it empty.

Naomi remembered blinking up at the ceiling of the med bay as she came to, one of the little cleaning robots skittering across the white to suck up any errant dust. It moved like a spider, and Naomi watched it make its methodical way towards the vent in the corner.

Her gaze travelled downwards and snagged on the autodoc.

The glass was fogged slightly; the autodoc's temperature had been raised to make sure the baby within didn't get hypothermia. Naomi could just make out a little wrapped bundle in the centre, impossibly tiny, and a blur of a pink face among the white. She let herself cry for the first time in she didn't know how long. She'd often pressed tears down, unwilling to show weakness. For a time, she'd wondered if she'd forgotten how.

The sounds of her subdued sniffles brought Hart to Naomi's side.

"Hey there," Hart said, softly.

"Is she all right?" Naomi croaked.

"She's very premature. Weighs in at just over two and a half pounds. So far her vitals are as good as can be expected." She listed the details dispassionately. "She needs help breathing, and we're feeding her intravenously with dextrose and general nutrition, though we'll start transitioning her to milk feeds over the next few days. Her blood pressure isn't too low. No signs of infection. No indication of any brain damage. So far, so good."

Naomi's eyes grew wetter, weaving tracks down her temples.

"This is where we dubiously have to thank Valerie, because she made sure the autodoc was programmed to be compatible with babies, knowing that we might be growing newborns once we landed."

Naomi released her breath in a sigh.

"You're doing pretty well too, all things considered," Hart said, answering Naomi's next unspoken question. "It'll take you a while to recover, but you shouldn't have any lasting effects. Just a few more scars than you had before."

Naomi remembered her mother's C-section scar, like a little

zipper just above her bikini line. The autodoc would give her a scar so thin it'd heal almost invisible, but she'd be able to feel it.

"Want to see her?" Hart asked.

"God, yes."

Naomi managed to get up and shuffle to the cot right next to the autodoc Hart had set up so Naomi would be able to rest near the makeshift incubator. She was pumped full of painkillers, so nothing hurt, exactly, but her body still knew it'd been through the wringer. She resisted the urge to lift her medical gown and see the wound and her partially deflated stomach.

Naomi placed her hands against the glass of the autodoc. She could see in better from this angle.

Her first thought was that she didn't realise babies could be so small. Her daughter was such a fragile little thing, covered in a fine layer of down. She hadn't plumped up yet and was too thin, arms spindly. Her skin was red, tiny hands reminiscent of a salamander, her veins still visible through her skin. Her eyes were still shut, but there was a whisper of hair on her head—dark black, like Evan's, rather than Naomi's own lighter brown. She had a serious, small face, but was that pointed chin a mirror to Naomi's own? She stared through the glass in wonder for minutes, hours. Her breasts were sore and heavy. She wanted to hold her child, cradle her close, feel the first painful latch and then the rush of endorphins. To run her hands along the softness of the skull, delicate as a bird's. Her whole body cried out with a fierce possessiveness.

Mine. That's mine.

"Have you thought of any names?" Hart asked.

Naomi had been turning names over in her mind. She and Evan had come up with a shortlist, but it was up to her to make the final decision once they met.

"Yes, but I'll sit with it for a day, make sure it feels right." She paused. "Does Evan know? Did anyone tell him?"

Hart shook her head. "There hasn't been time, and we weren't sure if you wanted to tell him yourself."

"He would have worried," Naomi said, still staring down through the glass.

Eventually, Hart placed her hand on Naomi's back, rubbing between her shoulder blades. "You should lie back and rest," she said. "And express your milk."

She did, finding it awkward and painful, and Hart dumped the container—Naomi still had too much medicine in her system for it to be usable. Hart left her alone and Naomi finally lay back, woozy. The baby moved her head, side to side, a hand rising, almost in a wave.

"Hello, Grace," Naomi whispered. "Grace Lovelace Kan."

She fell asleep with one hand on the glass.

CHAPTER THIRTY-NINE

275 Days After Launch

14 Days in Lower Earth Orbit

By the time they arrived back in orbit, the shape of the new version of the Earth began to emerge.

Grace and Naomi had eased their way back to health. Grace was no longer a salamander child. She had plumped up, pale and soft as peach skin. Her hair was still black, and she had Evan's eye shape and dark brown eyes. She had a serious little expression much of the time, always listening intently, taking everything in.

Naomi had pointed Grace's little face down at Earth. When Naomi had left, she'd thought she'd never see this view again. She'd been entirely prepared to spend the rest of her life on Cavendish.

From above, Earth didn't look so different. Blue and white swirls, still too much brown and too little green. Despite the vaccine, many of those who had already been infected had still died. They'd had better treatment plans, but fifteen per cent of the population still perished, all told. More than a billion lives snuffed out since she last had this view. All because of the woman the four others on board had vowed to follow to the ends of the universe.

Naomi had to admit she was nervous about what awaited them down there.

By the time Evan was released from custody, the world had turned on Valerie Black with unsurprising viciousness. The house in the hills where Naomi had grown up under Valerie's watchful eye had been ripped apart, beam by beam and stone by stone. They'd been smart enough not to burn it at least, with the summer grass dry as kindling. It would have been too full circle. With the president and vice president dead, the former Speaker of the House, a man named Nicolas Flores, was the new president. He'd been in a mass shooting at his school when he was twelve and didn't have full use of his left hand from a stray bullet. He had another scar on his neck from a graze that nearly killed him, just visible above the collar of his suit in a silent reminder.

He was firmly centrist—not radical enough to offend, but not full of enough conviction to inspire, either. He claimed he stood for equality and forward change, but Naomi had little faith left in anyone willing to do what it takes to get into power. She'd wait to see if his actions spoke, rather than his pretty speeches at the beginning of his presidency.

His immediate problem was figuring out what to do with the bodies of the dead—the morgues and funeral homes were overloaded. They'd also worked up a rudimentary universal healthcare system to ensure the Sev was fully eradicated. It was a start. Naomi didn't know how long it would last, but it was a start.

Flores had decided to paint the Atalanta 4 as heroes. The first baby in space helped the PR spin. They received a pardon for stealing the ship on the assurance that the court would have their full cooperation in the upcoming trial.

Valerie was the one charged with the relatively minor crimes of theft as well as kidnapping and murder of the backup crew. Of course, they paled compared to the charges of terrorism, war crimes and genocide.

The backup crew had received a lavish state funeral, empty coffins lowered into the ground. Naomi had watched the stream from orbit. Dennis's wife hid her face in her hands the entire ceremony. Dave Webb's and Josh Hines's parents were bowed and grey beneath their grief. Devraj Chand's partner looked lost, as if it still hadn't hit him that Chand was never coming back. Mel Palmer stood at the front, tear-streaked but strong, holding the hand of her toddler. Naomi's body had churned with guilt and she'd had to turn the broadcast in the rec room's wall screens off.

Lebedeva and Valerie had already headed down to the surface two weeks ago. Lebedeva had handed Valerie to the authorities then overseen reloading the shuttle with an unmanned supply payload. Naomi remembered Lebedeva leading Valerie through the ship, her hands tied in front of her. Confinement had not been kind to their former commander. Flat hair, grey skin. She'd been thinner, but that was the same for all of them—nutri-blocks had put everyone off their appetite, especially when the machine broke and they couldn't even taste the echo of vanilla or cinnamon any longer.

Valerie had slowed, meeting Naomi's eyes almost hungrily. They hadn't spoken since their last conversation. Valerie had hunched her shoulders when she realised that Naomi had left

Grace in another room deliberately. Valerie had not seen her granddaughter, and Naomi would do everything in her power to make sure she never did.

Valerie had said nothing as she shuffled the last few steps to the airlock, and Naomi had offered no words of her own. Valerie's head disappeared into the capsule. The crew had already said their goodbyes to Lebedeva, and the Russian had gone beyond simply tolerating their embraces—she'd clutched each of them tight, thumping their backs. Naomi would miss her.

The next time Naomi would see Valerie, they'd be on opposite sides of a courtroom.

As they waited for the go-ahead for the rest of them to head back down, Naomi spent hours in the observation room, nursing Grace, drinking it all in.

As she, Hart, and Hixon prepared to take the shuttle back down, her reserve grew. She'd shied away from the chance to be on Cole's documentary, but now everyone knew her and her daughter's name. A photo Naomi had reluctantly taken of Grace floating in the bridge, backlit by stars, had been the cover of countless articles.

Grace was still a baby, not a symbol. There was little Naomi could do to protect her from the burning spotlight of fame, but she would try.

The day came. It was time to go home.

"Grace is going to hate this," Hart said as they tied up the last of their possessions into the shuttle and then finished suiting up. "When we were last in this thing, I did not expect to be heading back down with a crying baby."

"Me neither," Naomi said.

"God, I can't wait to eat crunchy, crumbly toast," Hixon said. "And fresh, melted butter. Well, margarine."

"Stop it," Hart said. "I'm hungry enough."

They'd had a more varied diet since Lebedeva had sent up a shuttle of supplies. They'd hopefully never have to eat another nutriblock again. Still, it wasn't the same.

Naomi had taken a last walk through the *Atalanta* that morning, and it had been so strange to see the lights low, the crops of her lab all harvested. The ship had already had the air of being uninhabited. It wouldn't be for long. Mechanics would arrive imminently, to check it all over. The ship might still very well go to Cavendish, but the women wouldn't be on it.

Earth still likely had an expiration date. That exploratory nature that humans had had since they'd first sailed off towards a distant horizon, not knowing if they'd fall off the end of the Earth, was still within them. They'd spread out across the galaxy, if they didn't self-destruct first. It was only a matter of when.

They finished suiting up. Grace was mercifully still asleep. The poor thing had no idea what was to come.

People on the ground had argued about the best way to transport a tiny baby to the surface—not something any of them had expected to have to consider for decades yet. Water could help cushion against G-force. NASA engineers had at one point considered submerging her entirely in a tank of water, a mini scuba baby. Naomi had been grateful when they vetoed that plan and instead rigged a pressurised pod cushioned with water beds—an evolution of the original chambers they'd sent chimpanzees up in during the 1960s.

They put Grace into the capsule, and she mewled in protest.

Naomi hated the click as the door of it shut. They strapped themselves in and Hixon prepped the undocking procedures. The robotic voice started the countdown. Most systems were still automated, but this time they were in full contact with NASA. There were additional steps to go through.

When they finally disengaged, Naomi and the others watched the *Atalanta* grow smaller on the screens. Its no longer new and pristine white hull was peppered with small scratches and dings from space debris. That craft had taken them to another planet, and almost another solar system. Even though they had not gone through a wormhole, it had undone them and put them all back together again.

The shuttle's engine brought them to their expected path. They planned to land in the ocean not far from Cape Canaveral and the Kennedy Space Center. It decelerated, preparing to re-enter the atmosphere. Naomi could hear Grace crying through the mic. Naomi patted the outside of the capsule, singing a nonsense song at her daughter, as much to calm herself as the baby.

The descent module separated from the shuttle, thermal protection protecting against the heat friction as they raced towards the ground.

Grace started screaming. They were all pushed into their seats by the force of five times their weight. Naomi's hands flexed, wishing she could offer comfort.

At the right moment, the parachutes deployed, slowing their descent. The rockets fired before touch down and landing boosters ensured they hit the water at no more than five kilometres per hour.

They hit just where they expected. The boats already on site out in the harbour sped towards them as the capsule bobbed in the water. Naomi's stomach lurched. She'd turned down the volume on Grace's screams, but it still grated against her eardrums.

"I know," she said. "It was not fun."

The hatch popped, and Naomi looked up through her helmet to see a patch of blue sky—sky!—just before it was darkened by the silhouette of someone from the rescue team. They'd pulled the boat close and secured it to the craft.

Naomi and Hart opened the capsule and Naomi pressed her child against her chest.

"Her life signals seem good," Hart said, eyeing the readouts from the baby's monitors. "They'll double-check her blood pressure when we're out."

Naomi stuck her head out first, squinting at the brightness. She flipped down the gold-lined shade of her helmet, then Grace's, whose screams had only grown louder at the light. Baby's first sunlight.

Naomi moved unsteadily. Two men's hands under her shoulders helped haul her out of the shuttle. Grace was still caterwauling, and the men stared at the baby, a little open-mouthed. Naomi pulled off her gloves, passing them to one of the men. The other helped Hixon out, but Naomi focused on Grace, pressing her tight against the chest of the suit. Grace's cries quieted slightly, turning into hiccoughs. The man with her gloves helped Naomi with her helmet.

The first thing to hit Naomi was the smell. Salt, brine, wet metal, a hint of human sweat. She staggered across to the boat, unsteady on her legs and the bob of the waves. She sat down in the shaded area on the deck, the suit feeling too heavy, waiting for Hixon and Hart to follow. She took Grace's helmet off, pressing her bare palms against the softness of her child's head, kissing away her tears.

The medical officer came to give Grace a check-up and Naomi reluctantly handed her over. The wind was warm against her skin. How alien something as simple as weather was after so long in a perfectly calibrated and unchanging temperature.

When Hart and Hixon were on board, they went inside long enough to shed their suits. Naomi changed into the spare clothes the rescue team had brought her. It was strange to wear jeans, a T-shirt and sneakers after so long in her uniform. The doctor came back with a freshly changed Grace and assurance that her health was sound. They'd put her in a onesie patterned with stars and planets and rockets. Naomi smiled at that.

They all smeared on the provided sunscreen, put on shades and hats. Reluctantly picked up filter masks. They hadn't missed those, and it gave Naomi a pain to put one around Grace's nose and mouth. Her daughter kept picking at it, her brow scrunched up in displeasure.

"I know," Naomi told Grace. "They're itchy. Sorry."

She went back out on to the deck. She shook the hand of everyone in the rescue team, feeling awkward at how openly they stared at her. At least the filter mask hid some of the red and ugly scars on her face. She knew she was too pale. Between stress and nursing, she'd lost her pregnancy weight fast, and from unexpected areas. The reflection in the mirror looked drawn.

She found a quieter part of the deck as the ship made its way back to shore. The sun was warm on her skin. She clutched

Grace close. Soon, she smelled the tang of seaweed, similar yet different to the algae that had kept them alive up above. As the ship pulled into the port of the Cape, Naomi remembered when she'd last been here. The climate change conference, red graffiti stark against the smooth dome of her Cavendish biome. Evan's profile as he'd scrubbed the glass with too much force.

Five women had left the Earth in secret, but three and a newborn returned to fanfare. Hart and Hixon joined Naomi, resting their elbows on the railing. Crowds clustered on the public beaches, the far-off music reaching their ears. The private dock was thick with NASA and government personnel, but right at the centre, they caught the blonde bristle of Lebedeva, who raised her arm in greeting. Hart and Hixon waved back enthusiastically, and Naomi inclined her head, her eyes already searching behind her before landing on Evan. A thrum went through her, settling deep in her chest.

Evan's face was freshly shaven, and he looked both just as she remembered and completely changed by what he'd been through. He smiled nervously, hair a little tousled, hands in the pockets of his jeans. His favourite faded NASA T-shirt, soft from hundreds of washes. A man she'd known since he was eleven, watched grow up in six-month intervals until college. As a boy, he'd been the one she competed with for Valerie's affection, letting her come between them and keeping Naomi from getting to know the truth of him. She didn't know what would happen between them now.

She was ready to find out.

Naomi kept her feet strong on the deck, her body swaying with the motion of the ship. She cradled Grace against her breastbone. She squared her shoulders, pulling down her filter mask long enough to give her best version of Cole's megawatt smile he'd always used for the cameras.

Earth was still too hot and too fragile, and soon she'd see the evidence of what people had just been through. How close they'd all come to disappearing. But she was struck by how *alive* it all felt. Greens, blues and browns. The whispers of white-topped waves. The cries of gulls. The pops of colours on people's clothes as they held up their palms, their shouts and cries just reaching the deck.

As the waves carried them to shore, Naomi gave a last look up at the sky.

30 Years After

My mother says she won't read this book.

Naomi Lovelace maintains that she simply needed to get it out of her head so it could stop haunting her. It took her weeks to tell me her story, in fits and starts, always in the middle of the night. Naomi didn't have to go to work the next day, but she seemed to forget I did.

By night, I listened to the jumbled events of her time on the *Atalanta*. She'd skip the chronology as things occurred to her. By day, I'd go to work and program my AI machines. Yes, a psychologist would likely say I'd chosen that line of work to remain close, in some way, to the women who founded the long-defunct company of Hawthorne.

In the evenings, my tired brain would try to figure out how to unpick my mother's story, to make sense of events and discover the best way to arrange it all before her voice started again, hushed in the darkness.

"Iris—" she'd whisper, startling me from slumber. "I've remembered something else."

My father and I switched places, funnily enough. I'd gotten a long-distance transfer to an office not far from Naomi's quarters, so I could stay for a few more months. He had been asked back out to Los Angeles two years ago when Valerie's health started failing. He'd stayed there, sorting out her affairs and consulting at a few companies. He sent missives regularly, but it wasn't the same. He and our mother have remained together despite the rags printing stories about them now and again, salaciously reminding the world that Grace Lovelace Kan's parents were step-siblings raised by none other than Valerie Black herself. My sister loved to read any article with her in it, running her fingertip over the shape of the letters of her name. They never bothered printing mine.

Naomi woke me up the first night just after she'd found out Valerie Black had died in prison after thirty years in custody.

She had always been this nebulous, frightening figure, our grandmother. We'd grown up hearing about her. Other children teased us, pretended we had the Sev and ran away, giggling.

Valerie Black was the woman who had nearly killed the world. The woman who thought she'd be able to make a better one. Long before that, Valerie had proved she had been willing to stop anyone who got in her way, even those she loved.

We were never allowed to meet her, not even a video message. When Grace asked, over and over, our mother grew more irate.

At fifteen, Grace found some more recent clips—unlike Naomi, now and again Valerie consented to be interviewed. Grace would load them late at night, with me tucked up tight next to her.

I remembered Valerie Black as thin and brittle, with a sharp tongue, eyes piercing as a hawk's and just as unblinking. Grace watched her grandmother avidly, and I'd realised then that if we ever did meet her, Valerie would be far more interested in Grace than she would be in me. Not surprising—I'm not related by blood—but the thought stung, just the same.

I was five when my parents adopted me. One more Sev orphan out of many. I was born the same day Naomi and Grace touched back down to Earth. Sometimes, I wonder if that's why they adopted me out of all the others out there.

My parents never made me feel inferior, but I was always diminished next to their and Grace's fame. Grace became an astronaut. Naomi always tried to shield her elder daughter from the fame that was stamped on her since birth, but Grace was always hungry for it. Her life has been star-touched in more ways than one. She floated above the rest of us. Above me. For a time, I hated her, but she was also impossible to hate.

The fight between my mother and Grace brewed for years before it finally came to a head. Grace wanted to go visit her grandmother in person. Naomi had said no, even though she couldn't actually stop her since Grace was a fully grown woman by that point. They'd had a fight to end all fights, from what I heard from my father. He, like me, is often stuck playing peacemaker between them. He, like me, often fails.

When Grace decided to visit Valerie anyway, Naomi cut off communication. They haven't spoken since.

Naomi stopped her story that morning she touched down in Cape Canaveral, but as I've been writing this book, I've investigated what happened after. She saw so much change in the world that we now take for granted. She testified against Valerie only a few days after landing, calmly reporting events on the *Atalanta* as if they'd all happened to someone else. She hadn't bothered hiding Valerie's scratches with make-up. During the breaks, she snuck off to breastfeed Grace.

My mother had watched the world change around her, knowing that she had been a catalyst for it all. Earth took what steps it could to mitigate the damage done. These days, we take wind and solar and leaving fossil fuels in the ground for granted. It never became the Atalanta 5's rosy idea of a perfect world, though. Change is slow. Utopias are lies.

Naomi and I had such different childhoods. She'd tagged along with Valerie to countless conferences and holidays on Valerie's planes; I zipped across the high-speed rails and bridges. Growing up, my mother could go into a grocery store at close to midnight and still have the full selection of fruit and vegetables on display, wrapped in shining plastic, most of it destined to rot in a landfill. It seems so shockingly wasteful with the benefit of hindsight. Then again, so much is.

And so we arrive at the question people who read this book will want to know: what has my mother been doing the last thirty years? Naomi had no shortage of work, overseeing projects of carbon-trapping algae, or assisting with reforestation, or continuing the work she began in her biomes and on the *Atalanta*. She lived her life out of the spotlight as much as she could. No great scandals.

From afar, we watched the later tragedies. The *Atalanta II*. The *Clymene*. How Earth's future dimmed, brightened, dimmed again. The struggle for Mars.

Month by month, year by year, Cavendish must have seemed even further away for her.

A very few people would say that Valerie's plan did work, after a fashion. Killing so many had sparked those who were left into action, in a way that all the facts and figures didn't do beforehand. Part of me wants to think that they're wrong, that humanity would have pulled it together before Earth broke so badly. Another part of me fears they were right.

I called Grace when I found out that Valerie died. My sister already knew, naturally. Her face was on my screen, my own in miniature in the corner. We look nothing alike. Grace looked like Dad, her skin tanned like his when she's planetside, pale when she's not. I'm tall, with flaxen hair that is straight and flat. I'm broader compared to Grace's bird bones. My skin is always red—my mom calls it ruddy-cheeked. I think she thinks that sounds better, but it makes me feel like a wind-whipped fisherman. When Grace and I introduce ourselves as sisters, there is always the split second of confusion strangers can't quite hide.

When I told Grace what I was doing, her expression had closed.

"Do you think she'll actually tell you the truth, Iris?" my sister had asked. "Valerie and Mom are more alike than you think."

I'd chewed the inside of my cheek at that. And now, after I have the story, my sister is only partially right. Naomi and Valerie were similar, but their differences were starker. I didn't mention my suspicions to Grace: that my mother had video visits with Valerie once every few months, for years. Long after what happened two years after they returned to Earth.

I could ask her, but I think she would lie. I suppose I can allow her a few secrets. Because I do think, overall, she has told me the truth.

I stiffen with anxiety each time I wonder how the book will be received once it's out there and I can't take it back. Do I want my mother to read these words? Do I wish my sister would? Yes and yes, but I'm not going to make them. Knowing they might terrifies me. But I'm not sure I wrote it for them, not exactly. I wrote it to set the record straight.

Naomi has said she doesn't care what lies people believe about her. But I do. No story is a total truth, but I have tried to stay as close as I can.

I also, selfishly, wrote it for me. To add my voice and step out from the shadows, in some small way.

I'm finally home after a long, long day, and I'm struggling to gather my thoughts. This is where the story of Naomi Lovelace and Valerie Black ends.

My father got in this morning. My mother couldn't sit still, clattering cups in the kitchen. She was desperate to see him, but also knew that he had called in a favour and was bringing Valerie's ashes with him, condensed into a little cube about the same size as that snow globe. My father was tired after the trip, but we all wanted it finished. At least the journey is much faster than it used to be.

We went up to orbit. It's smoother than it was in Naomi's day, little different than going up in a plane. I watched the lights play across my parents' faces as we accelerated towards orbital velocity. Their hands were clasped together. I could imagine them, younger, pretending to dislike each other but not doing a terribly good job.

We reached Godwin station. And there was our surprise.

Grace, wearing civilian clothes, shifting her weight to her right foot, something she did when she was uncomfortable. I hadn't seen her in person for almost three years. Naomi hadn't seen her daughter except on newscast screens for closer to five.

Our mother stopped, her mouth opening. After watching and listening to her speak for so many hours, I know her better. Naomi wanted to say something but feared uttering the wrong thing. Her mouth snapped shut and she offered a wan smile.

Grace walked towards us. Naomi held the cube in her hands. It was enamelled, lacquered in all black and studded with silver stars. No one looking at it would know what it was. Who it'd been.

Grace held her hand out, and Naomi passed it over. Grace turned the cube in her palms, investigating it from every angle with that same intensity she gave everything. With a sense of finality, she handed it back.

"We doing this?" Grace asked, meeting our eyes. I gave her a nod.

"I'm glad you came," my father said.

I should have known he'd ask her. They'd been near each other, since Grace had stopped there on the way back from her last mission. While I'd been with my mother, my sister had been with my father. He'd watched his own mother slowly die of cancer but be too stubborn to go. Grace must have visited Valerie, too, at the end. I wonder if she'll tell me what happened between them.

We made our way to the airlock. Naomi placed the black cube in the centre. The four of us stared through the window at the small remnant of Valerie Black. My sister's shoulder brushed against mine. Our mother's left hand hovered over the button to release the airlock exterior door.

A few months ago, I'd have said she was doing this out of revenge. Sending Valerie out into the void alone as a punishment. Instead, thirty years too late, she is honouring Valerie's wishes.

Leave me out there.

My father's hand came over my mother's, and together, they both pressed the button. The interior doors closed. One last pause. An opening of the exterior doors, a whoosh of air, and the airlock was empty. In an instant, she was gone.

We said no words. My mother bowed her head, and my father put his arm around her. The four of us were in the same place for the first time in half a decade. We walked to the observation deck. The few who were there recognised Grace, then Naomi. After a bit of gawping, they left us alone.

"Thanks," I whispered to Grace, folding myself into one of the seats.

She gave me a half-smile. Our parents sat across from us. Their eyes were dry as they stared at the planet below. I wondered if they still mourned Valerie, despite everything.

I exhaled and looked out the window.

I've only been up there a couple times before, but I'll never grow tired of that view. The blue-green of the oceans, the shifting textures of clouds, the orange of the sun making them look golden. The patchwork of green islands and small continents, all criss-crossed and connected with rail bridges visible even from up here. No hurricanes. No melting ice caps. No wildfires.

We came across when I was fifteen, one of the middle wave of exodus ships. I've spent half my life on one planet, and half of my life on another, never sure which one to call home.

Our pasts, our histories all faded as the four of us stood together, and watched the sun set over Cavendish.

Acknowledgements

Note: the below has some spoilers for plot points of *Goldilocks*.

These will be my longest acknowledgements to date—there are so many people to thank for *Goldilocks*. Buckle in!

First, thank you to James Oswald for having his book launch (read his books!) at the Edinburgh Bookshop (a most excellent indie), where I chatted with Alex Clarke of Wildfire and semi-jokingly asked him to let me know if he needed any thrillers. Turns out he did! Thank you for telling me to not be afraid to give *Goldilocks* the quiet moments and sense of scope of the universe.

As ever, a round of applause for my powerhouse of an agent, Juliet Mushens, whose belief in me has not wavered, despite how low my own confidence in my writing has become at certain points over the last six years.

My gratitude especially to my editor Ella Gordon for her constant championship along the way—looking at my plot spreadsheets, my messy partial drafts, my slightly less messy later drafts, and eventually the draft which was as shiny as I could make it. You have been a joy to work with, along with everyone else on the Wildfire and Orbit U.S. team: my U.S. editor, Bradley Englert, my publicists Rosie Margesson and Ellen Wright, and everyone else in marketing, sales, rights, as well as my publishers in translation.

To my usual most ardent cheerleaders: my mom, Sally Baxter, and my husband, Craig Lam. I love you taller than outer space. To extraordinary beta readers or people who let me witter on about plot problems: Erica Bretall, Amy Plum, Lorna McKay, Emily Still, Mike Kalar, Anne Lyle, Hannah Kaner, Kim Curran, and the Ladies of Literary License, Peta Freestone & Amber Lough. Thank you to my colleagues/work family David Bishop and Daniel Shand at Edinburgh Napier for dealing with my frazzled deadline state with good grace, and to my students on the Creative Writing MA, past and present. I learn as much from you as you learn from me.

Thank you to the cafes in Edinburgh where I'd haunt tables for hours, but especially to Artisan Roast Coffee in Bruntsfield and Hideout Café in Leith.

As someone with no scientific background, I am eternally grateful to those who offered their expertise and answered my many, many questions with kindness and patience. Any science mistakes within the text are my own. I'll arrange by topic...

Social Dimensions of Outer Space

I never would have had the confidence to write such a science-heavy book without the experience and network I had working on the *Scotland in Space*, organised through the Social Dimensions of Outer Space research group and a joint project between Edinburgh Napier University, the University of Edinburgh, and the Edinburgh Futures institute. I wrote a short story as part of the interdisciplinary anthology (which you should check out!). Special thanks to the literature/human geography people: Dr. Deborah Scott, Dr. Simon Malpas, Dr. Elsa Bouet, Dr. Russell

Jones. Also to publisher Noel Chidwick and PhD candidate on innovation in the space sector, Matjas Vidmar.

Astrophysics, Exosolar Planets, and the Headache of Special Relativity

Dr. Beth Biller. I loved having you in our SiS "Fringe in Space" subgroup. Thanks for letting me take you out to dinner and quiz you about which star would be best to set Cavendish around. She was the one who calculated how long the year would be and what the sun would look like on Cavendish from the surface.

Dr. James Lough. Thank you for answering all of my questions on getting to the speed of light and breaking my brain with special relativity until I realised perhaps using the Alcubierre Drive would be simpler than laser kites in space (which is the current best postulation of how to get to those kinds of speeds!).

Cyanophages, Cavendish and Climate Change

Dr. Sinéad Collins, my friend and evolutionary biologist and algae expert—she's basically Naomi except not an astronaut. She read over the algae and cyanophage sections and also came up with a better way to solve Naomi's problem on the ship with spontaneous resistance. Additionally, she helped me figure out what Cavendish would actually look like, and what it's like to go to Antarctica. Thank you to her Evolution, Ecology & Climate Change undergraduate class at the University of Edinburgh who helped me brainstorm what Earth would look like from orbit under the worst case projections in 2033 (which is mentally when I set it as that's when NASA is potentially planning to send a mission to Mars).

Dr. Maté Ravasz, molecular biologist. Thank you for your talk at the Scotland in Space seminar at the Royal Observatory and answering my email questions and letting me know about cyanophages in the first place.

In general, researching climate change for this book was incredibly distressing, as I knew it would be. We need to do our part to make sure Earth has many years left, and that includes holding those at the top responsible for making policy decisions than have much greater effects. Shout out to the teen climate activists, Autumn Peltier, Mari Copeny, Atemisa Xakriabá, Alexandria Villaseñor, Vic Barrett, Ridhima Pandey, Xiye Bastida, Greta Thunberg, and many more, whose determined faces and words I saw and heard on the news as I was writing this book. I think you'll be about Naomi's age by the time we reach when the book is set. Thanks for fighting for the future.

Babies... in Space!

Thank you to Juliet's assistant, Liza DeBlock, for letting me know that her mother, the inimitable Dr. Heidi DeBlock, looks after astronaut health. Thank you, Heidi, for giving me details about HELLP syndrome and for introducing me to your friend and human spaceflight expert, Dr. John Charles, former Head of Life Sciences at the Houston Space Center. John, thank you so much for saving my space baby. It must have seemed a very odd question when you first read it, but I hope you enjoy seeing the full draft in context.

Space Law & Policy

Dr. Pippa Goldschmidt read the first half of the draft and gave me both astronomy help and space policy assistance. She's also a fantastic author—check out *The Need for Better Regulation of Outer Space*, and her story in the *Scotland in Space* anthology. Danke (I feel like I've said thank you so many times I'm now cycling through languages). Merci to Professor Michael Dodge at the University of South Dakota for so thoroughly answering an email out of the blue from a stranger in Scotland asking whether or not you could legally steal an exosolar planet.

Viruses, Vaccines & Medicine

Thank you to Gabriel D Vidrine, Adam Christopher, Mary de Longis, and Peta Freestone for helping me develop the virus. I learned some particularly gruesome facts about infectious diseases in the process! Also, everyone get your flu vaccine. Thank you to Andrew Reid, author of *The Hunter*, science teacher, and friend, for helping me figure out the fight scene in the lab.

Other Research & Female Astronauts

If I were to list every book or article I read for this book we'd be here all day, and this is already getting quite long. For more detail, see my website under "works consulted." I do want to give a quick shout out to NASA's Houston We Have a Podcast, as I ended up listening to pretty much every episode.

A quick thank you to Jeanette Epps and Norah Patten, a NASA astronaut and an Irish aeronautical engineer, who were warm and friendly when I fangirled at them at Worldcon Dublin in the summer of 2019. Researching this book really came into focus when I started researching the Mercury 13, the women who should have gone to space around the time of the Mercury 7 but never had the chance. Wally Funk, you are one of my heroes. That's why I dedicated the book to all female astronauts, past and future.

I tried to keep a list of people I sent the book to or asked questions, so hopefully that's everyone! If not, I am so sorry and I will buy you a drink or a meal to make up for it, promise.

As ever, thank you, dear reader, for letting me imagine going into space and sharing that vision with you.

And…lift off!